FORBIDDEN MAGIC

Book One in The Lanatus Chronicles

Genia Avers

1

eBook ISBN: 9781943601806
First eBook Edition May 2012
Production by MuseItUp Publishing

Second eBook Edition October 2015
Produced by Sugenia R. Weaver
Published by Windtree Press

Acknowledgements

A special thanks to my critique partner Linda Lovely and to my original editor, Julie . I'd also like to recognize my daughter Cami; the little things you do make writing, and life, so much easier.

Don't Miss
Forbidden Flame

Available Now

Intent on saving the álfar, Jalakin travels to the new home of his sister to assist with research aimed at keeping the elves alive. When he arrives in the land of the Dökkálfar, he meets his first human, Lecala.

And bites her.

Jalakin overcomes his bloodlust enough to work with the human, but his yearning for Lecala evolves into something stronger. Problematic since any carnal relationship between elf and human is punishable by death.

Chapter One

"Hurry. We may already be too late."

Subena's brother grabbed her arm and propelled her into the cobbled street. The length of his gait barely allowed her feet to touch the ground as she struggled to keep up with him. In all her twenty-three years, she'd never seen Jalakin so discomposed.

"Slow down, Jal."

He stared straight ahead, his mouth hardened into a grim line that sent chills along Subena's skin. The sparkle had vanished from his violet eyes, the irises completely black. "No time. Another boy's dying."

"No!" Gasping for air, she managed to pull her arm free before Jalakin's breakneck pace caused her to fall on her face. "If what you say is true, he needs a healer. I'm only the technology minister."

Jalakin shook his head. "The healer doesn't know what to do. You need to use your…skills."

Her brother wanted her to break the law? Bockle help them.

She didn't resist when Jalakin yanked on her arm again. They ran together, being careful to avoid crumbling rock where the bluestone path needed repair. As they neared the town square, the dull throbbing in her head intensified. Her vision blurred, the pristine whiteness of the Mydrian Assembly Hall fading to gray. Her empathy ability sent agony rushing through her body like a thousand acid needles—each shard corkscrewed into her being, inflicting torture and increasing her fear. She felt the boy's pain.

She stopped in her tracks, cradling her head in her hands. "I can't go on."

"Fight it," Jalakin whispered. "I can't do this without you."

She blinked rapidly, struggling against the abyss that threatened to swallow her. To counter the pain, she focused on the crimson beauty of the Sun-Star. For the first time, she cursed the gentle, harmless rays, feeling rage because the star didn't possess the same spectrum of the fabled Earth Sun.

She detached herself from her dark thoughts and staggered after her brother. She couldn't let another child die.

She followed Jalakin into the central courtyard outside the Assembly Hall. A crowd had gathered around the healer, but the hushed mass parted to let them through. The healer Phillius knelt on the granite, his hands above his head, his fingers intertwined in the symbol of Bockle, the ancient álfar goddess. She'd seen Phillius chant only once before—when her father'd perished.

"Here." Jalakin pointed to a pile of blankets on the ground.

She dropped to her knees and lifted one corner of the fuzzy cloth so she could see the twitching mass beneath. "How'd the boy get here?" she asked.

"He was playing in the square," Phillius replied. The other boys came to fetch me when he fell."

She nodded and stroked back a tuft of red hair.

Alton. The quivering body belonged to the librarian's son. The once shiny crystal that hung around the boy's neck had turned a dull mustard color. The quartz-like gem could no longer sustain life.

She dared not touch the crystal—the glass would shatter, taking the boy's essence with it.

She focused her concentration, attempting to ease the lad's suffering. In the lonely days after her own father's death she'd found solace with books. And with the librarian and her little boy.

Jalakin positioned his back to her, his muscular frame effectively blocking the crowd's view. His attempts to shield her actions were unnecessary because her forbidden magic couldn't save Alton.

There was only one chance for him. Science.

She took the small flask from her cloak pocket and poured a few drops onto her finger. The odor of her medicine invaded her nostrils. The scent clung to the air, acrid and horrible.

"What's that stench?" Jalakin whispered.

Without looking at her brother, she shook her head and flashed a telepathic message: *You don't want to know.*

She carefully rubbed the foul substance over the boy's lips. Alton gagged, but he swallowed the coral-colored liquid.

Please let this work. She held her breath and waited.

A flash of color illuminated Alton's small face. A pearly glow spread over his white skin, elevating Subena's hopes. Her new concoction might actually be able to save her people.

The boy's sparkle dimmed almost as quickly as it flared. After a few seconds, she knew her effort was useless. The boy would die.

She pulled young Alton into her embrace and stroked his face, hoping to calm his mind. She could do nothing for his frail body.

He stopped shaking. The furrows in his brow smoothed and his lips curved into a hint of a smile. Then, Alton died in her arms.

It took several seconds before Subena realized the sobs she heard originated in her own throat. The warmth of her brother's hand seeped into her shoulder, but it brought no comfort. She glanced at him, before she followed his gaze and looked at the crowd.

Faces, bleak despite the soft glow from the Sun-Star, looked to her for answers she didn't have. Alton's death fueled the fear that had been steadily growing since the announcement of the crystal shortage. With no quartz to mimic the spectrum of the Earth Sun essential for sustaining álfar life, Mydrias faced imminent doom.

"Go home." Jalakin spoke to the crowd, once again regal and in control. "The Council will address this."

Moans gave way to whispers as people quickly backed away. Within seconds, the last of the observers vanished into the maze of pastel buildings surrounding the Assembly Hall.

"You too, Phillius," Jalakin said.

After the healer bowed and departed, Jalakin knelt beside her. He took Alton from her arms and placed the boy on the ground, covering the lad's face with the blanket.

"He's the third boy to die, Bena. What happened to his crystal?"

"I have a theory. A rather frightening one."

Jalakin waved his hand toward Alton's body. "How can it be worse than this?"

If her hypothesis was correct, much worse. "As you know, our survival depends on two things: sustenance for our bodies and nourishment of our life essence. Our ancestors received both from Earth's sun. The Lanatus Sun-Star provides neither."

"I know, but the crystals mimic earth's sunlight." Jalakin kicked at the moss-colored dust, his control once again in jeopardy. "So what's the problem?"

Subena didn't react to her brother's tone. More than anyone, she understood his frustration. "The crystals work well for sustaining our bodies." She hesitated. "But I think the glass actually damages our life essence."

"Damages our..." Jalakin's pale skin turned grayish. He stood and crossed his arms. "You're saying the very thing that keeps us alive is killing us?"

Without glancing at her brother, she nodded. She didn't want to see the horror reflected in his eyes.

"How can that be right?" he asked. "In the thousand years we've been on planet Lanatus, we've never had children die before."

Subena hesitated before standing to face her brother. "The crystals did affect the ancestors, but the álfar who colonized Lanatus had residual magic in their bodies. Earth magic, not artificial essence created by crystals. With each generation, parents have passed on less and less of this ancient magic."

"I'm not a genius like you, sister. What difference does that make?"

"Our ancestors had so much magic in their bodies, they didn't need the crystals as desperately, thus less destruction to their life essence. The children of our generation have little magic at birth and need more sustenance. The young draw upon the crystals more, so their life essence is destroyed faster."

"It's a vicious cycle, then?"

"Yes."

Jalakin paced. "Would it have helped if our ancestors hadn't forbidden the use of magic?"

"Probably." Subena could find no other explanation for her own excellent health. She secretly practiced magic and rarely needed her crystal.

"Damn this damn planet."

Subena stifled her anger. Jalakin had no cause to vilify Lanatus. Their world might not have the magical sun of the fabled Earth, but Mydrias, the country they'd carved out on the planet's barren surface, was a beautiful place. And the only home she'd ever known. After her family, she loved Mydrias above all else.

Fighting with her brother would help nothing. "We'd better examine all the children. The younger ones have even less of the ancient magic in their DNA. Maybe replacing the crystals more frequently will keep them alive longer."

"At that rate, our crystal supply won't last a year." Jalakin kicked at the dirt.

Their gazes met in shared pain. "No. Until we can find a better solution, we need Gatsle's crystals. Sign the treaty, Jal."

They were out of options. The treaty would give them a new source of the quartz needed to create the crystals.

She'd been so sure her experiments would yield results that she hadn't monitored the remaining crystal inventory. Now she would pay for her failure.

Strange that the blood she'd experimented with had only a fleeting effect on Alton. She'd been secretly using the elixir and felt invigorated. There'd been no need to draw upon her crystal.

"No, Bena." Jalakin curled his fingers into fists. "The price attached to the treaty is too high. You can't sacrifice yourself to that monster."

9

She shook her head, feeling darkness invade her mind where hope had once lived. She would lose her beloved home. "If we don't align with Gatsle and obtain more crystals, our kind will perish. Sign the treaty, Jal. I *will* marry Prince Kamber."

* * * *

Subena smoothed the fabric on her gown, wishing she had the courage to ignore Annika's summons. She was in no mood to endure her mother's hysterics. Alton's death had drained her energy.

After a deep breath, she entered the antechamber, but neither the empress nor Jalakin looked at her. She sent her brother a silent message. *Can't this wait?*

No.

"Stop thinking behind my back." Empress Annika sneered at her. "I will not have the two of you acting like I'm not here."

Subena flashed her brother another telepathic message. *Busted.*

Not funny. "Mother, we're not sending mind messages." Jalakin's voice resonated with syrupy appeasement. "We would not disrespect you."

Liar.

Her brother didn't acknowledge the insult. Subena wished he possessed more of the ancient magic, but telepathy appeared to be his only illicit talent.

She immediately chided herself for the foolish wish—Mydrian laws strictly forbade ancient magic. As much as they needed her, the people of Mydrias would banish her if they knew half of what she could—and did—do. "Why did you summon me, Mother?"

Empress Annika rubbed her fingertips lightly over the bridge of her nose, a sure sign one of her fainting spells would follow. "You cannot marry that barbarian, Subena. If we form any association with those dreadful creatures, we'll never be allowed to return to Earth."

Gads, but Subena was sick of hearing about Earth. The ancients had foolishly assumed not practicing magic would allow them to return. The how and why of that belief had been lost with the demise of the ancients.

"If everyone dies, there won't be anyone to return anywhere, Mother."

The empress lifted her chin, glaring at Subena with flared nostrils. "If you were a true Mydrian, you wouldn't fear death."

She didn't fear death, but álfar beings returned to nature when life ended. Since Lanatus had nothing that resembled the woodlands and valleys of ancient earth, Subena feared their kind might cease to exist. There was no point trying to explain that to her mother, though.

"Jalakin." The empress raised her voice. "Tell your sister she can't do this. The heathen has pointed ears, for Bockle's sake."

"He's also heir to the throne of a country rich in quartz ore." Jalakin sighed and slumped into his chair. "We need crystals. mum. Besides, didn't your brother have pointy ears?"

"How cruel you are to remind me." The empress shuddered. "At least he had the decency to have them rounded. These...these Gatslians are... Oh, I can't even talk about it."

"Most historians believe we have the same ancestors." Subena lifted a strand of her waist-length hair and studied it while she mentally braced for her mother's reaction.

"Do not voice such traitorous thoughts. Our ancestors were human. Those Gatslians are Drow. Beasts. Their evil antics are why all álfar were banished from Earth. They are the reason we must exist on this horrible planet."

Don't argue with her.

Subena's temper flared at the tone of Jalakin's telepathic reprimand. The entire race was on the verge of destruction and she couldn't even state her opinion?

Please, Bena. Don't give her an excuse to nullify our efforts. The Council won't approve the treaty unless Mother concurs.

"Subena must marry Prince Kamber," Jalakin said aloud, ever the diplomat.

The empress rubbed her fingers against her temples in a circular motion. "I thought she would marry Taslin."

Subena sighed, for once agreeing with her parent. She'd envisioned the same future.

Jalakin approached the empress, putting his arm around her shoulders. "We must have quartz to form our crystals, Mother, or everyone in Mydrias will die. Once we get the Council's approval to ratify the treaty, Gatsle will permit the mining." Her brother attempted to console the empress as though she were a petulant child. "The king of Gatsle has already signed the contract."

"Well, Rothart can unsign it."

Subena wondered how her mother knew the king's name. Before she could ask, Annika said, "He's a cretin, and I won't have my daughter associated with his evil."

"Fine." Subena possessed little of her brother's patience for dealing with the empress's dramatics. "Don't convince the Council. Forget the contract. Let everyone die."

The empress covered her mouth and collapsed. Jalakin caught her before she hit the floor. He carefully positioned the empress onto the settee.

"Blast you, Subena. This is difficult for her. Whether you agree or not, Mother sees your fate as worse than our extinction."

"Difficult for her? I'm the one who must sacrifice a life of my own and marry the rutting swine-head. All she has to do is sign her name. In ink incidentally, not blood."

"Don't overplay the sacrifice card." The softness in her brother's voice dealt a more effective blow than a physical strike. One lousy year older and Jalakin acted like he was her father. So what if he was right?

She sighed and perched on the settee next to her mother. "I'm sorry. I didn't mean to upset you, but another boy's died. I know you don't want that. Without crystals..." With her anger expended, Subena didn't add that the quartz was only a temporary solution.

Annika shivered, but Subena pressed her case, desperate to convince her mother. "We have to form a pact with Gatsle."

Her mother put her fist to her mouth. Her arm shook. "There has to be a better way. You can't sell yourself to that ignorant barbarian."

Subena stroked her mother's arm. "Please..."

Before her father died, the empress had been a brilliant leader. Only Annika's love of family surpassed her love for the Mydrian people. That Annika had perished with the emperor but her right to rule hadn't. The Council had appointed her empress, looking to her for leadership, even as Annika sank deeper and deeper into a state of constant agitation. Subena had to convince her mother the treaty was the right thing to do.

"There's another problem," Jalakin said. "Maybe a bigger problem. Lord Creshin's hatred for our people grows stronger. Our spies say he has declared war on all aliens. He may decide to attack."

Subena's temper flared. "We aren't aliens."

Annika blinked. "Yes we are. This isn't our home."

"Let's not have this argument again." Jalakin's face bore a strained expression. "Aliens or not, we need the Gatslian army to deter Creshin. The crystals are a bonus."

"Oh, right." Subena sniffed. "We only need crystals to survive."

"Our people can survive for a year before our crystals deteriorate." The empress drew her stature into a regal pose. "You said so yourself."

"I was wrong." Subena pressed her fingers against her temples. She hadn't expected the crystal use to accelerate exponentially.

Jalakin frowned. *Mother will never agree to a treaty with Gatsle until our supply is completely exhausted. You have to tell her about your vision.*

No.

"You're doing it again," Annika hissed. "Bockle help me. How did I raise such rude children?"

Annika hadn't raised them. She and Jalakin had raised themselves, but Subena was smart enough not to mention that.

"Bena's had another vision."

She glared at her brother.

The empress's pale face turned transparent. "I thought you'd outgrown that nonsense."

Subena fought the bile rising in her throat. Her mother supported the bizarre notion that álfar could return to Earth if they didn't practice magic. Some foolish ancestor had convinced the council that Mydrians would be accepted on the ancient planet again if they were more like humans. And humans had no magic. Visions were the worst sort of magic.

Bad enough Subena had to endure her visions. Did she also have to be treated like a freak, too? By her own mother?

"Tell her what you saw," Jalakin prompted.

"No." She and Jal were close but Subena couldn't make him understand. Enduring a vision meant more than dealing with the pain the future event would bring. In the throes of a prophecy, her body absorbed both the physical and emotional trauma of everyone involved in the event. Even talking about her latest vision brought splintered fragments of the nightmare into her present reality.

"Daughter." The empress paused to intertwine and release her fingers. "Until now, you've not had one of those incidents in…what, ten years?"

Subena's stomach knotted. Her mother had never acknowledged her visions before.

"Despite your last...vision," the empress continued, "we could not save your father. I will agree to this treaty for the sake of our people, but I will hear no more talk of false visions."

The room threatened to smother Subena. She'd tried to tell her mother that her father was dying, but Annika hadn't listened. Maybe she should've tried harder, should've told someone else. If she'd believed in her vision, her father could've been saved. She'd lived with guilt for ten long years.

After a decade of pain and grief, her mother had just tossed that guilt back into her face like soiled laundry. Subena rose, her body rigid and unresponsive. She began to walk, goaded by a need to get away—away from problems, away from visions, away from her mother.

"Bena, come back. Mother's agreed to the treaty."

She ignored her brother's plea and kept moving, one destination in mind. Away.

Her pace didn't falter until stone granules crunched under her feet and she stared into shimmering water. She surfaced from her daze, understanding why her subconscious had led her to the rocks. The hidden nook in the cliffs would make her feel better. It always did.

14

Dropping to the ground, she put her head between her hands and refused to think. An act she'd repeated often since her father's death. To console her conscience, she recalled the only vision that didn't foretell gloom and destruction, the same vision she replayed whenever she grew overwhelmed by her Council responsibilities.

In that vision, a male soothed her hurt and banished her loneliness. She hadn't seen his face, but he spoke in a voice laced with kindness and something more. *It will be all right.*

She could still see wayward the locks of dark hair that danced in the breeze and beckoned her fingers to skip through the thick mane. In the vision, her hero pulled her head to his chest—a magnificent chest. A tattoo in the shape of a diamond embellished the wide expanse of sculpted perfection. He stood so tall her ear rested against his heart; the beat calmed her weary soul.

Thump, thump, thump. Lilting, lyrical music swirled around her, massaging tense muscles. Hands that knew no boundaries touched her in secret places. His fingers stroked her breasts, bringing fire and passion to her stoic, responsible life.

She opened her eyes, for once finding no relief in the recollection. Taslin, the one she believed she'd marry, bore no such tattoo. Nor did any Gatslian. She'd scrutinized every male chest during the Festival of Bockle, hoping to find her dream lover among the tunic-less elves as they paraded down the Mydrian main street.

The impending treaty had stolen her one escape, had proved her vision false. She'd never possess her fantasy lover now that fate had intervened and exiled her to the backward lands of Gatsle with its wayward prince—a creature most unlike her imaginary lover. Maybe her mother had a point. Maybe death was better.

Genia Avers

16

Chapter Two

"Keep your damn mistress, but you *will* marry Empress Annika's daughter."

Kamber, the eldest son and heir of King Rothart, stormed from the palace, his father's command ringing in his ears like echoes from a never-ending nightmare. He picked up a stick and hurled it toward a tree. The wood splintered into fragments, along with all hope for his future. He'd done everything possible to convince his father to sell the quartz to Mydrias and forget the treaty. It wasn't as if Gatslians would ever use the damn glassy rock.

Of course, the king refused. "I don't need their money," Rothart growled.

Why Gatsle needed a treaty with the Mydrians puzzled Kamber. His country didn't need anything from the arrogant foreigners, but his father did nothing unless he directly profited.

Despite Kamber's counterarguments and his mother's pleas, or maybe because of them, the king insisted on a treaty and dispatched a special envoy to Mydrias. The Mydrians balked at the terms, but they needed crystals. They would eventually sign the treaty. No matter what the price.

"I should just leave," he grumbled and headed toward the stables.

"Kam, wait."

He kept walking, wishing his younger brother hadn't come running after him. "Go back inside, Ronan," he yelled over his shoulder. He'd never leave the purple hills of Gatsle, but his sibling spoiled his temporary fantasy. The country might not need him—his father had heirs to spare—but his brothers did. Without his intervention, Barkley, the next in line, would crumble under the king's tutelage and lord only knew what would happen to Ronan.

"Let me go with you." Ronan reached the stall just as Kamber put a halter over his equestor. He reached for the saddle but decided he didn't need it.

He ruffled his brother's hair, knowing it would annoy Ronan. If the lad wanted to acquire a taste for ale, he didn't intend to support the cause. "I need you to look after Mother. You know how Dad gets when he's angry at me. I'll see you in the morning."

"I reached the age of adulthood more than two years ago, Kam. Stop treating me like a lad in school britches and tell me where you're going." Ronan's tone held both censure and envy.

"Would you prefer I hang around and punch dear old Dad in the face?"

"Might be fun." Ronan grinned impishly. "Come on, let me go with you."

"No." Kamber frowned to hide his smile.

Ronan's grin faded. "Fine, then." His tone made it clear it was anything but fine.

Kamber wished he could stay and quell Ronan's worries, but given his own foul mood, he wasn't fit company for an impressionable youth. "I'll be late. Keep out of Rothart's way."

Kamber threw his leg over Pollo's back and pressed his knee against the creature's side. Pollo bolted. They raced until the bluestone walls of the village pub came into view, the ride-for-death pace in perfect unison with the anger surging through his body.

He jumped off Pollo and landed lightly on the ground. Tomorrow could be dealt with when it came. Tonight, he intended to get rip-roaring drunk.

"Greetings." The owner knew him but didn't use his title, thus maintaining the illusion that Kamber was an ordinary patron.

Two mugs of his favorite ale arrived at the rough-hewn table before he settled on a reed stool. He kicked at the straw covering the dirt floor to make sure nothing crawled beneath it. He downed the contents of the first mug and reached for the second.

Placing his hands behind his head, Kamber peered into the darkened corners, hoping none of the locals recognized him. The strength of the ale would render the heartiest of customers too drunk to recognize their own shadows. He intended to join them.

Chugging the contents of the second mug, he made eye contact with the pub owner. "Another," he demanded.

Kamber savored the dark, dank atmosphere. Inside the shoddy alehouse, he could mingle with commoners and forget his responsibilities as heir to the throne of a country with the most powerful army on Lanatus. In the pub, his definition of self did not include being the son of the world's biggest ass.

Despite his intentions, he succumbed to self-pity. *Why not?* Years spent observing his parents' marriage made him vow he would never become trapped in a loveless union, yet the same noose now tightened around his neck. Tomorrow, he'd leave for a land he'd never seen and wed a bride he could never love. Reports on his future wife painted her as the ice princess from Hell who considered him to be an inferior animal. It didn't matter—he would be faithful anyway. His father might sacrifice his honor and sate his lust outside the bonds of matrimony, but Kamber would never become the cheating oaf that Rothart was.

The pub owner arrived with more ale. Kamber poured the drink down his throat, finishing half of the contents before he met the owner's stare over the rim of the mug.

"Perhaps the prince would like something to eat?" the owner asked.

The proprietor had used his title. The faux pas emphasized the foolishness of getting drunk without any of his cronies around to cover his back. "Just another drink."

The owner nodded and hurried away. Kamber ran his fingers through his thick hair before he finished off the ale. So what if he fell into a drunken stupor? Being murdered by ruffians seemed infinitely preferable to the fate awaiting him. He spotted a couple kissing in a dark corner and his mood sank lower.

He wiped the foam from his mouth with the back of his hand. He should leave.

Before he could stand, he felt the blade of a knife pressed against his back. His body froze. He remained immobile, trying to clear the ale-induced fuzz from his head so he could react.

He dropped to his knees with a speed that belied his size and flung the stool at the assailant. At the same time, his left hand reached for his dagger. The move should have worked, but the attacker anticipated his response and stepped aside. Kamber found himself in a chokehold.

He steeled for another maneuver, but the arm around his throat held firm and cold metal pressed against his throat. Kamber braced for the worst.

"What do you want?" he demanded.

A deep chuckle, one that had mocked him for most of his years, resounded softly in his ear. "You're getting slow, Princey."

The arm shoved him aside and Kamber fell to the littered floor. He glared up at a giant, nearly seven feet tall.

"Damn you, Remmy. You only bested me because I'm drunk."

"Precisely my point, laddie." Remington settled his bulk on the bench, signaling to the pub owner to bring more ale. "What the hell are you doing, alone and intoxicated in a joint known for its shady clientele?"

Kamber shrugged. Holding onto the edge of the table, he pulled his unsteady body erect, standing just long enough to right his stool, and then he slouched onto it.

"Ah, let me guess," the big guy scoffed. "Our prince is feeling sorry for himself. After all, he has to marry a beautiful, intelligent creature who's rumored to have the body of a goddess. Poor you."

"Beautiful?" He snorted. "Wherever did you hear that?"

"I have my sources. They say the lady's hair shimmers like the Sun-Star and her eyes are as blue as the Lanatus Sea. And her body…" Remington waggled his brows. "I wouldn't be surprised if the God of the Mountain came down to steal her from your marriage bed."

"You're full of it." His old pal exaggerated to make him feel better. Remington had been cheering him up and getting him out of jams for as long as Kamber could remember. First as his mentor. Then, once he reached adulthood, as his friend.

Only Remington couldn't help this time. However much Kamber might wish it, there was nothing his friend could do. Kamber felt well and truly trapped.

"'Tis true," Remington murmured between sips. "Her lips are said to be so perfect, men get tongue-tied in her presence. My cousin's a spy in Mydrias and swears Subena's the most beautiful female on the entire planet."

"That explains it," Kamber moaned. "Your family thinks pollywogs are beautiful. I'll bet she has round ears."

Remington chuckled. "Her hair will cover her ears."

Kamber snorted. "If Subena's anything like her brother, she's both ugly and arrogant."

His friend laughed. "Mayhap you would not think Jalakin so ugly were you a female."

"Acquiring a taste for men, are we, Remmy?"

Remington slammed his mug down with enough force to shake the sturdy wooden table. "Prince or no, I can easily crack your skull, so watch your mouth."

Kamber ignored the idle threat. Remington understood how he felt about the sanctity of marriage. "It's the cold fish image that bothers me most, Remmy. I hear she'll freeze my wanger off if I try to bed her. I'm not keen to think the only female I'll have in my bed from now on doesn't want to be there."

Remington shrugged, but his eyes gave him away. His friend couldn't deny that Subena's most flattering descriptions conveyed the coldness of her personality.

"Perhaps she only needs the right male to thaw her, lad."

"Thaw her?" Kamber exhaled loudly. "She's a virgin in a land of sexual liberation. If she isn't thawed by now, I'll need an ice pick to part her legs."

"Ah, come on now, lad. I'm sure your wanger's a tad bigger than an ice pick."

Kamber ignored Remmy's chuckles and pulled the wedding ring that had once belonged to his grandmother from his pocket. He tried to focus his eyes as he twisted it between his thumb and forefinger. As a young prince, he'd expected to give the heirloom to the bride of *his* choice. Not only must he give up any hope of finding love, it seemed he would have to give up sex as well.

"I'll wager it will take more than a mere mortal to melt her ice." Kamber snarled. "No matter how big the pick." He flicked his grandmother's ring again. Instead of spinning, the band of emeralds flew from the table. Kamber chugged his ale, making no effort to retrieve the heirloom. He'd find the ring later.

Remington widened his eyes before he howled with laughter. "If she needs a big pick, then perhaps I'd better marry her."

When the chortling stopped, his long-time friend frowned. "I really thought we'd found a way out of the marriage when I convinced your father to insist that your future bride be a virgin. The álfar are not known for their restraint. Who'd have believed a twenty-three year old virgin existed in Mydrias?"

"It wouldn't have mattered, Remmy. If Subena hadn't been a virgin, my father would have waived the clause. I don't know why, but he's wanted an alliance with Mydrias for as long as I can remember. I doubt he expected a virgin."

In his heart, Kamber believed Mydrians to be no more promiscuous than Gatslians. The snooty people of Mydrias would never dream of anything as insidious as a virginity clause for royalty. Come to think on it, their empress had been elected so the country probably didn't even believe in royalty. That might be their one redeeming quality.

Remington clapped him on the back. "Look at the bright side, laddie. At least you'll finally be rid of Rekita."

Kamber groaned. His paramour wouldn't take kindly to his impending nuptials. Correction. Former paramour.

Remington's scowl returned. "Lord help us, lad. You haven't told her yet, have ye?" Remington banged his tankard on the table and shook his head. "You won't have to worry about a frozen wanger. Rekita will fillet it."

Kamber pulled at the roots of his hair, remembering Rekita's reaction when she'd found him with the farm girl. Rekita had screamed and cursed like a possessed banshee. If Remmy hadn't yelled, "Duck!" the knife she'd hurled would've sliced through his shoulder blade. Kamber had lunged for her, ready to strangle her beautiful neck, but her tears stopped him. The damn female used tears more effectively than his best archers used arrows. To calm her hysteria, he'd whispered endearments—that'd been a mistake. Resuming the relationship had proved to be an even bigger mistake.

He felt no regrets about using his pending marriage as an excuse to be free of Rekita. None. He deserved something for sacrificing his freedom, even if he should have kiboshed the liaison with the wild thing months ago.

Kamber glanced at the barmaid leaning over him; she bowed lower than necessary to pour Remmy's drink. Her smile left little doubt she'd be a willing participant in anything Kamber desired. He wished that just once he could inspire respect as easily as he could lust. Tonight, however, lust would do.

His normally strong libido rose half-heartedly to arousal. The server possessed some appeal, but there was a lot of her and her ample body jiggled more than the foam on his ale. He chugged the rest of his drink and her pale plainness looked a bit more luscious. When the maid put her arm around him and pulled his face against her bosom, he didn't resist.

"Have your last fling, laddie," Remington taunted. "I'll not be letting you feel up the barmaids after you're married. Be advised though, you'll ride to Mydrias tomorrow, even if I have to tie you and your hangover to the saddle."

"As if that would be necessary." Kamber lifted his head from the barmaid's ample bust and pushed her away. "Damn you, Remmy. You've spoiled my evening."

"Right, boy. It's my disposition that's spoiling all the fun."

* * * *

An onlooker shifted further into the shadows and pulled his hat low over his brow. He gazed at the spectacle two tables away. After a time, he quietly rose and retrieved the prince's ring. He sat back down but his lips never touched his tankard and his eyes never left the drunken pair.

Genia Avers

Chapter Three

Unfamiliar voices pounded against Subena's eardrums and drew her to full alertness. She saw nothing but rock. *Where am I?*

Breathing deeply to invoke calm, she inhaled the sea air. Her mother's accusations came roaring into her consciousness. She'd come to the sea.

Alone.

More pounding. Who had followed?

As clarity increased, panic threatened. For once, she didn't curse her hypersensitive hearing. She tugged on her earlobe. Unintelligible words.

Gads. What now? Didn't her country have enough issues with the crystal shortage? Were her people now at the mercy of invaders?

Hide. She needed to hide. Needed to spy on the intruders and uncover their purpose. How badly had the Mydrian shore been compromised?

She scurried to the top of the cliff, climbing with an expertise lacking among people who'd lived without toil and who'd wallowed in luxury for too long. The sight that greeted her when she looked seaward made her blanch. "Bockle."

Her vision had come true. The invasion was real. Ships bearing Lord Creshin's emblem on their sails hovered on the horizon, marring the water's crystalline beauty.

Being native to Lanatus, the warlord had always resented the presence of the álfar. In the past, Creshin hadn't been powerful enough to act upon his hatred. Had he somehow learned of their predicament and decided to attack?

"What are you planning?" she whispered.

Several crest-boats dropped from the big ship and sliced through the water toward the shore. Subena peeked through a crevice in the jagged rock, knowing the Lanatus Sun-Star above her would blind anyone looking in her direction. She watched, desperate to know what the warriors planned.

The first boat stopped midway between the master ship and the land. Had the rowers seen her?

Subena started to back away, but the spectacle of a cloaked figure rendered her immobile. The hooded creature stood upright in the boat. The body rose into the air and a skirt fluttered in the wind. The lady began to float toward the shore.

Mother of Bockle. She's flying.

Subena dropped her chin to her chest, rubbing her temples with her fingers. Surely she hallucinated. Even the Gatslians couldn't fly. Bockle, even the ancients couldn't fly.

When she dared look again, the lady stood with her feet planted on the beach. Her hands signaled to the boat. The warriors didn't move.

Don't let them come ashore. Subena's countrymen had grown soft and could offer little resistance if a battle ensued.

The strange female scanned the horizon. She seemed to be searching for something—or someone. The lady spoke, but only noise carried to Subena's hidden nook.

The wraith walked closer to the trees at the edge of the beach. She tugged at the hood of her cape, pulling it low over her brow. Subena couldn't see her face, only the imperial bearing of her posture.

The lady uttered a strange sound and held out her arms. A male emerged from the woods. The female opened her arms to embrace him, looking anything but ladylike. Subena ducked behind a jutting stone, trying to steady her racing heart. Nothing made sense. She peered between the rocks again, needing assurance that her eyes hadn't deceived her. They hadn't.

She covered her mouth to keep from screaming. The deep blue color of the cloak identified the garment. That hue could only be produced by a dye created from ansur, a mineral found only on the Mydrian shoreline. The male was a traitor.

A stolen garment? She stared at his silhouette. Maybe not. The cloak suited him like a second skin. He wore the mantle with the assurance of a rightful owner.

A cold shiver raced through Subena's body. Mydrians were loyal but hunger for life made loyal people do awful things. She had to warn the Council.

Subena chanced one more look. Should she tarry in hopes of identifying the Mydrian traitor or rush to alert her people of an impending attack? The Mydrian and the flying lady were no longer visible. Two soldiers had rowed to the shore and paced on the beach. One glanced in her direction.

She jumped back, trying to press her body into the rock. The identity of the traitor would have to remain unknown. How could she warn anyone if she were a captive? Or worse.

She couldn't leave the same way she'd come. The only escape route lay over the second rock face at her back. She'd have to climb higher before she could descend. And risk being spotted.

Crawling with the stealth of a night creature, she reached the top of the summit and peered over the edge. A quick glance assured her no one followed. She scooted over the flat parapet until she reached the opposite summit. She descended the mountainside without making a sound.

When she reached the bottom, her eyes darted in all directions to make sure no one had skirted around the rock wall. She doubted any of the ship's warriors had time to cover the distance by ground, but she'd no experience with people who could fly.

Seeing no one, she lifted her skirts and bolted. Her feet didn't slow, but she couldn't resist a backward glance every few meters. If the invaders spotted her, she'd need every skill she possessed to escape the long-legged male, not to mention the flying female.

One last look broke her rhythm. She faltered. Her foot caught on a stone. She fell to the ground, twisting her ankle. Pain shot through her body. She pushed it from her mind. After a silent grimace, she willed her feet to trot again.

Lord Creshin had sailed into forbidden waters with war ships. The interloper's boldness could only mean he was prepared to attack.

* * * *

"What do you mean there were no ships?"

Sitting behind his large driftwood desk, her brother stared, his face masked by an expression Subena couldn't decipher. "The search party saw nothing."

"Jal, I saw the ships."

"You're sure it wasn't...a vision? I mean, you were pretty upset when you ran off—"

"I know the difference between a vision and reality. There were ships."

"And a female who flew?" Jalakin stood, the abrupt motion knocking parchments off his desk.

He walked toward her and placed his hands on her shoulders. "I'm sorry, Bena, I don't doubt you, but others will question your version of reality. Our search team found no trace of the landing party. Even if we could confirm the sighting, we...what do you suggest we do?" Jalakin released her hands and banged his fist against the desk. "We're powerless."

"We must sound the alarm. We can't just let the traitor go...go about his business."

"Suppose we find this faceless male? What then? It'll be your word against his as to whether there were actually any ships." Jalakin leaned against the wall and crossed his arms. "Let's keep this quiet. We've a greater chance of identifying this spy if he doesn't know you've seen him. Unaware, he might wear the cloak in public. Alert him, and he'll just burn it."

Subena bit at her lip, her own frustration surpassing Jalakin's. "You're right, of course. Whether we find the traitor or not, our best hope is to bind the alliance with Gatsle. As soon as possible."

"Funny you should say that. We received a courier from Gatsle this morning. Rothart insists the wedding ceremony take place next week. I'd expected him to stall and I haven't even gotten the Council to ratify the treaty yet."

"Next week?"

Jalakin nodded, his expression dour. "I must admit, little sister, I do not like his demand for haste. Rothart's motives worry me. Not only has the Drow king demanded the union occur ahead of schedule, he's declined all our offers of technology and culture."

"They're not Drow." Despite her protest, she felt like the room had begun to spin. "But I don't understand. If he doesn't want our technology, why would he sign the treaty? There's nothing in it for Gatsle."

"Exactly."

The full weight of her sacrifice felt heavy upon Subena's shoulders. Without being able to offer new wonders to the Gatslians, her mate's people would ostracize her. She'd be more of a freak in Gatsle than she was in Mydrias. Taslin would snort steam.

Bockle. She hadn't told Taslin about the marriage.

"Bena, did you hear me?"

"Sorry, what?"

"I said, you don't have to do this."

"I do. We both know it."

Jalakin puffed out a breath. "If you go through with this marriage, you'll have to remain in Gatsle for at least a year. Those are Rothart's terms."

"A year?" She felt strength return to her limbs. Anything could be endured for a year. After that, she could return to Mydrias as a heroine.

"I'm so sorry." Jalakin shook his head. "I tried to negotiate less time, but Rothart refused. Don't mention the threat from Lord Creshin. We'll look desperate, and we've so little bargaining power."

"You mean don't talk about the flying ladies or things that go bump on the sand. In other words, don't let Rothart think I'm demented and give him an excuse to tear the treaty to shreds."

"I didn't say that."

"No, but that's what you meant."

Subena turned to leave, but one of the papers scattered on the floor caught her eye. She bent over and picked up an image of the most beautiful female she'd ever seen. Glimmering ebony hair framed a dark, angelic face, but it was the eyes that demanded attention. Although the image was mere paper, she felt the hypnotic power in the female's golden glance.

"Who's this?"

Jalakin opened his mouth and then closed it again.

"Don't start keeping things from me now, Jal. Who *is* she?"

Her brother wouldn't meet her gaze. He spoke in a steady voice. "His mistress. The female is Kamber's mistress."

Chapter Four

Subena nodded politely when she really wanted to stand up and scream. The Mydrian Council had discussed the treaty for three hours, but had yet to take a preliminary vote.

Bockle. It's not like it's important or anything.

Each of the four regional councilors debated every line of the treaty as if there was an alternative. Given their precarious situation, ratification should've taken less than five minutes but if the Council was true to form, it would take them another three hours.

She chanced a look at Erwin, the economics minister and her former academics mentor. He stared straight ahead, but the tiny motion in his jaw telegraphed his frustration. At least he'd vote for the treaty.

As Minister of Technology, Subena also cast one vote, and Jalakin's role as head of security ensured another "yes" for the treaty. They still needed one more councilor to vote "yea." As the council chair, the empress didn't have voting power, but if her mother said "no," all four regional members would follow suit.

Bejet, the eastern representative, asked for the floor. Again.

"We've had no interaction with Gatsle in over two hundred years. How do we know we can trust these backwoods animals? How do we know they won't kill Subena? And eat her."

"Bockle help us," Erwin snapped. "How many times must we go over this?"

Subena wanted to hug him.

31

"Erwin," Annika said, with the same amount of emotion she used when asking for mint in her tea, "it will take as long as it takes. Our government's based on open democracy."

The economics minister frowned, but made no comment. Bejet started to drone and Subena wanted to doze. To distract her mind, she looked beyond the floor-to-ceiling circular windows to the crowd outside, searching for a particular deep blue cloak. All council meetings were community forums with the audio piped into the courtyard. Judging by the crowd, almost everyone in the city had turned out for today's session. The traitor might be among them.

Seeing no hint of the cloak in the milling audience, Subena again contemplated Gatsle's motivation. Why had King Rothart insisted on the marriage in exchange for the quartz? Gatsle held Mydrias by Bockle's belly, but the monarch had flat out refused payment of any sort. His only demand—a daughter-in-law?

What sort of game did the king play? Mydrias and Gatsle might share a common ancestry, but the two countries were miles apart in ideology. Aside from pointed ears, rumors of secret hordes of rodents and Gatslian blood feasts abounded. Mydrians had chosen a nobler means of existence and abhorred even the idea of blood sucking.

Maybe the rumors were true. Maybe the Gatslians didn't use crystals.

A familiar high-pitched voice shattered her contemplation. "He wants our little Bena to do what?" Annika grabbed her chest and Subena's attention.

Little Bena? What did she have to do to be taken seriously?

"Hold on," the eastern councilman bellowed. "According to this document, Gatsle law dictates that the prince marry a virgin." He looked up from the document he held. "How archaic. I don't think we even have a Mydrian female who meets this qualification."

Bockle.

There were murmurs as the council agreed. Intense sexuality was one of the few traits that linked Mydrians with their ancient kindred.

"Then there can be no treaty," Bejet said. He stood and started to stack his papers.

Subena? Jalakin's alarm flashed with his mind message.

Her head twisted in his direction, her neck cracking from the force of her movement. Why hadn't she thought to warn Jalakin so he could sidestep the issue?

Of course she hadn't warned him. One did not discuss one's virginity with one's brother—even in Mydrias.

Subena? Jalakin repeated. His mental response reverberated as loudly as if he'd yelled. *We have to address this. It may be grounds for nullifying the treaty.*

It isn't an issue. Subena puffed out her cheeks as she flashed the message.

No jest? Jalakin's gaze sought hers. His royal purple eyes widened in question. They grew even wider when she gave him a slight nod.

The empress interrupted, "Who expects a female of marrying age to be a virgin?" Annika scoffed. "Subena's too good for that barbarian anyway. I say we forget about the treaty."

The spectators began to nod and murmur. "Bejet's correct. We'll have to forget about the treaty if they want a virgin," Kaarl, the northern councilman barked. "Death is better anyway."

Subena knew what she had to do but still she stalled, wanting to delay ridicule as long as possible. No matter how many crises she averted, no matter how much of her time and skills she devoted to being the Mydrian science minister, her efforts earned her nothing but mockery in a country that loved to play. She doubted today would be any different.

There was no other option. She had to expose herself. For the first time, she cursed the open forum that would make her humiliation public.

"I *am* a virgin."

The announcement silenced the noisy room. Every set of eyes riveted to her.

"It seems we don't need to worry about the clause." Jalakin addressed the council, his voice as smooth as a ping on the clearest crystal. "The clause won't be a...eh...a barrier." A few snickers followed his comment.

Sometimes, she could almost hate Jalakin. He and the whole damn council could eat rats for all she cared. She flashed her brother a hostile message: *Forget about my virginity and just get the blasted approval.*

"She lies," Lynette, councilor of the South, stated. "She'd say anything to get the treaty approved."

Another unnatural silence filled the room. Not one person could likely comprehend not sharing pleasure. Subena didn't really understand it herself.

The empress closed her gaping mouth and whined, "Bena. That cannot be right."

She ignored her mother and addressed the Council. "First, I do not lie." She glared at Lynette. The southern councilor shrank further into her seat.

Feeling somewhat mollified, Subena let her gaze scan across the rest of the Council. "Second, Mydrias can comply with the stipulations in the treaty. That said, I will entertain no further discussions about my sex life." She hoped her no-nonsense tone would refocus the group. "Marriage to Prince Kamber will not only give us the crystals that keep us alive, Gatsle's army will keep Creshin and his warriors from killing us. Unless one of you has a better plan, I suggest you hurry up and ratify this treaty."

"But we'll be indebted to those barbarians," someone called from the upper chamber.

Jalakin interrupted the grumbling that followed. "Councilors, listen. We had another death just yesterday. How many of your children will you allow to die?"

A collective gasp echoed through the large hall.

"Worse," Jalakin continued, "Lord Creshin and his organized warlords have already declared war on Mydrias. The alliance little Bena has proposed will join our armies with those of Gatsle and ensure that we've enough troops to keep the peace. Without an ally…"

Subena tried to conceal her surprise. She didn't know Creshin had declared war.

When did that happen? She stared at her brother. He winked before masking his face with seriousness.

He lied. Her saintly brother spoke falsely. Creshin had made no formal declaration of war.

She wouldn't have been able to pull off a boldface distortion of the truth, but Jalakin had done it to spur the Council into action. The cad. The wonderful, manipulative cad. She could almost overlook his use of her nickname in front of the Council.

"Wait." The empress stood, preening and puffing. Subena braced for yet another counterargument. "I still don't understand why my daughter must marry the cur? Can't we negotiate a treaty without sacrificing her?"

"Mother," Jalakin replied, "we're in no position to dictate terms."

Subena flashed her brother a look of gratitude. She doubted, were she in his place, she'd have enough patience to reply as civilly.

Jalakin's tone softened. "Even if we could somehow ensnare an alliance with Gatsle, historically treaties only last when countries are bound by blood or matrimony. King Rothart is adamant about the marriage."

"Whatever for?" The empress's stressed voice sounded unfamiliar.

"It seems the king wants his son to settle down." Jalakin refused to look at Subena.

Kaarl quipped, "If our little science minister's still a virgin, maybe it's time she settles down, too." The room erupted with laughter.

The empress burst into tears and fled the room. Bejet rose to follow.

"Wait, Bejet." Jalakin managed to block his path. "We must vote." The councilor hesitated but returned to his chair.

With the empress not present, the treaty passed by a vote of five to two. As soon as Jalakin recorded the ratification, Subena stormed out the door.

* * * *

The promise of comfort beckoned Subena to the Rosetta Garden where Taslin, Lord Duke of the province of Reklaw, waited. The presence of her lifelong friend would make things better. He'd understand.

Catching sight of him, Subena stopped running and pressed her hand against a tree. Looking at Taslin's profile diminished the humiliation burning in her skin. Seeing his face lessened the dread of a dismal future.

Taslin stood tall and proud, the stuff of female fantasies—wide shoulders, slim hips, and long muscular legs. His dark wavy hair touched the top of his collar and framed a face Bockle had bestowed with granite perfection.

He tossed a pebble into the smooth pond before he turned to face her. Something in his gaze turned Subena's feet to stone. She could practically feel the darts of anger shooting from his body.

Of course he's angry, you idiot. She cursed her oversight. Taslin deserved a full explanation, but negotiations and searching for warships had consumed her time. The opportunity to speak privately with him had never presented itself. Until now.

"Tas, I..." She squashed the part of her that feared Taslin's temper and plastered a smile across her face. Forcing her stiff legs forward, she approached the male she'd once believed was the love of her life.

"You what?" The duke rebuffed her open arms and turned his back to her.

She winced, not sure how to react. Taslin must surely understand. He exemplified patriotism. Shouldn't he applaud her sacrifice, understanding that Mydrias would not survive otherwise?

"Tas?"

Subena touched the back of his arm, needing a connection. Without turning to face her, he methodically removed her hand like a piece of lint. "I got your message. What do you want?"

She slumped onto the bench. Where was the friend she'd known for years?

Although Mydrias didn't believe in royalty, Annika had sent her children to the Royal Academy in Reklaw. Subena and Taslin had formed a childhood bond and had been inseparable for as long as she could remember. She couldn't bear it if he deserted her.

She'd assumed, as she felt sure he did, that someday they would take vows. Once, Taslin actually hinted at an engagement, but she'd stalled, engrossed in testing her blood substitute, hoping it could prolong the life of crystals. When her experiments proved futile, Taslin didn't restate his proposal, but he'd asked her to share his bed. He'd punched the wall when she refused.

"Tas, we'll get through this." They always had.

He said nothing.

"Look, I'm sorry I didn't talk to you sooner."

He spun to face her. "How can you do this?" His bark stunned Subena.

She dug her nails into the bench to steady her body. "I have to do this. I thought you, of all people, would understand."

"Understand? You didn't even have the decency to tell me first. Did it ever occur to you that I'd become a laughingstock?"

She blinked. *Bockle.* The Taslin in her mind was very different from the cold, distant being standing before her. "Laughingstock? Why would anyone laugh at you?"

His face contorted. For a brief second, Subena thought she'd glimpsed hatred, but that couldn't be correct. The day's events had made her overwrought.

Taslin's scowl smoothed into the handsome face Mydrian females loved. "People expected us to wed."

"But we never announced..." Bockle, he'd started those rumors. "I never agreed to a wedding, Tas."

His face remained passive, but hardness glittered in his eyes. "Of course you didn't. But you didn't say no either. What? You didn't want anyone else to have me?"

Pain sliced through her ribcage, as sharp as a sword. She doubled over and grabbed her side. She'd never once seen any evidence that Taslin had ancient skills; otherwise, she'd swear he'd attacked her.

Not possible. If he had talents, he wouldn't have hidden them from her.

Why not? She'd hidden her skills.

Subena straightened and shook her head. She saw evil where none existed. Taslin might be angry, but he'd never harm her.

And his anger was justified. She'd really hurt him. "I'm sorry, Tas. I have to go through with the wedding. I've no choice."

He sucked in air, making a hissing noise. "Everyone has a choice."

"Some choice," she replied, wishing she sounded calmer. "If I don't do this, everyone I love dies from lack of crystals? How's that a choice?"

"There are other ways." He turned away from her again. "Typical little Bena. So consumed in your own games you don't stop to consider anyone else."

"Tas. I'm sorry. There's nothing else we can…wait. What do you mean, 'other ways'?"

He twisted his head to glare at her. After a couple of seconds, he turned away again. "Never mind. Tell me what you thought. I can't wait to hear your rationalization."

She couldn't tell him what she thought because she couldn't think. Days of tension had exhausted her mind.

No, that was an excuse. Being honest, she realized she'd simply forgotten Taslin. She hung her head.

"No response?" He made a snorting noise. "Responding isn't your strong suit, is it?"

Her head popped up, a shot of defiance replacing some of the guilt. He'd always acted so sympathetic when she complained that everyone called her the frost nymph. "This marriage is a political assignment," she stated woodenly, knowing she sounded like she deserved her reputation.

"An assignment with a life sentence. It isn't just your sentence."

Her anger melted. "That's not true. I only have to stay in Gatsle one year, Tas. Then I can get an annulment."

His scowl frightened her. "You really think I'll *touch* you after you've been with that vermin?" He shuddered. "Honestly, Subena. I thought you were at least intelligent."

She jumped up from the bench and positioned herself in front of him, grabbing the lapels of his jacket. "He won't touch me. I won't let him."

Taslin froze. After a second, he laughed. "You're more naïve than I thought. Get out of my way."

She cringed at his mocking cruelty. "Taslin, please. Surely you understand?"

"No." He grabbed her arms just above the elbows. Squeezing harder than necessary, he lifted her up and moved her off the pathway. "Even if that Gatsle pig doesn't force himself on you, I couldn't bear the thought of you belonging to him. The Duke of Reklaw waiting around for crumbs from the wife of a barbarian king? I don't think so. Worse, I won't be with the female who destroyed our hope of returning to earth." He marched away, never once looking back.

He'd deserted her.

"Kamber isn't a king," Subena whispered. She touched her face, startled by the warm moisture on her cheeks. She felt her ears growing into a point, but she didn't have the concentration to change the shape so she pulled her hair over them.

She supposed she hadn't really expected Taslin to wait for her and maybe she didn't even want him to. Still, a friendly shoulder would have been nice.

Genia Avers

Chapter Five

From her second story window, Subena used her index finger to part the heavy curtains and peer at the dark elf. Per custom, she'd avoided direct contact with Kamber since the Gatslians had arrived three days earlier, but curiosity hadn't precluded spying on her soon-to-be spouse.

The tightness of his shirt emphasized the ripples in his chest, making it difficult to look at anything other than his tall, massive frame. He wore long, loose slacks that still managed to cling to his thighs like a second skin. It irked her that his jet-black hair touched his shoulders but still looked stylish.

He should have been reviled. He was, after all, a descendent of the Dökkálfar. Why didn't he look like the evil being he was?

She supposed she understood why the ladies flocked to him—shallow females, anyway. Except for his impish expression, he could've been a mighty warrior in a bygone era. A member of the dark ones, and a monumental jerk, shouldn't look so good.

"Taslin looks better," she whispered, determined to remain loyal despite the duke's rebuff. Taslin would apologize. After he cooled down.

Subena tried to concentrate on her loyalty, but couldn't resist another peek at the prince. Toned muscles flexed as he settled himself on his equestor. The fluid movement drew her attention to the powerful thighs as he sat astride the stallion.

He might look better than Taslin.

Stop. She couldn't think like that. Physical beauty didn't matter. Taslin personified intelligence—that's what mattered. Tas was good. Kamber was Dökkálfar. Evil.

When she tore her gaze away from the fiend's body and looked at his face, he stared directly at her. Amusement flashed in his shining green eyes and contrasted sharply with his stern expression. She'd barely parted the curtain, but if she didn't know better, she would swear he could see her.

His gaze locked on hers. There was something mesmerizing about those eyes, something more than the unusual emerald color. Subena wasn't sure she could have looked away—even if that had been her desire. She felt as if a brilliant light cascaded between them, filled with facets of all things good–calmness, excitement, happiness. Passion.

All that from a single glance. A connection.

He smiled, adding perfection to an already perfect moment. He waved, shattering the illusion.

She jerked her body away from the window like she'd been stung. Her spies had informed her he'd been seen with a floozy just three days before his journey to Mydrias. There'd been no connection between them. None.

She felt a renewed appreciation for the Gatslian custom that forbade interaction between the bride and groom during the week before the nuptials. The only good thing about the dark elf's presence was the army he'd brought with him. Lord Creshin and his ships would think twice before coming onto Mydrian shores now.

"Looking at something?"

Subena whirled. Even with her superior hearing, she hadn't heard anyone enter her chambers. "Forgotten how to knock, Mom?"

"Sorry, dear. I'm a bit distracted. Why didn't you come down for lunch?"

Subena sighed. Her mother understood the Gatsle custom perfectly well. The empress didn't relish the tradition because Mydrias had no similar restriction. "I think the Dökkálfar no-contact custom is archaic too, but I see no reason to insult the people who are giving us crystals."

"Oh, pooh." Her mother's unusual composure proved almost as disconcerting as her impending nuptials. "I still find it most suspicious those creatures would give us access to their quartz mines. I wonder if there's any quartz left in them."

Subena opened her mouth to remind her mother the Mydrian engineers had confirmed enough quartz to last for fifty years, but Annika rambled on in her typical fashion. "And that Kamber wasn't even in attendance. I swear, he's as moody as you are. But that may be a good thing. I think we can bribe him. I bet it won't take much to convince him to duck out on the ceremony. If he calls it off, you won't have to live in that horrid, ancient place and we can keep the crystals they've already given us."

Subena didn't want to marry the cretin, but thinking Kamber felt the same aversion didn't exactly fill her with confidence. "Mother, what scheme have you concocted this time?"

The empress's mouth formed a perfect O. "Concocted? Why nothing, dear. Just wishful thinking. The only thing I'm planning is your ceremony. I might not like the reason for the celebration, but if we must have one, we must have it with style. We'll show these swamp creatures what class is all about."

Subena studied her mother's face, wondering what the empress wasn't saying. Her mother seemed… resigned. Too resigned, but maybe the party had taken the edge off. Planning events was the empress's specialty, and there was no bigger party than a wedding ceremony.

Subena turned back to the window, grateful her future husband no longer stood on the street below. The boldly-colored roofs on the pastel buildings created a kaleidoscope of color that contrasted sharply with her gray mood. Maintenance crews washed the cobbled streets daily and every pristine building twinkled under the heat of the Sun-Star. She'd find no brightness in Gastle and the prospect of waking without seeing that view suddenly saddened her. It was too much.

She had to get away without letting her mother see her distress. The empress would pounce on any excuse to kibosh the treaty. A single tear would be excuse enough. "I'm a bit tired, Mother. Did you want something?"

Her mother crossed the room and wrapped her arms around her. "I'm trying not to think about how much I'll miss you."

"It's only for a year." She lingered in her mother's embrace, touched by her parent's sentiment, and feeling uncharacteristically needy.

"Maybe, but a year's a long time. I fear you'll grow fond of that disgusting Dökkálfar and you won't return. There's something unnaturally appealing about all that dark handsomeness. It's the bad boy thing, I suppose."

Not possible. No matter how gorgeous Kamber was, he spent his days gambling and hunting. Everyone knew how he spent his nights. "It would be easier to grow fond of eating mice."

"I wish you'd get over your fascination with rodents." The empress shuddered.

Subena reached for her mother's elbows, all too aware that simply mentioning mice or rats might be enough to send Annika into one of her fainting spells.

Only the empress seemed steady on her feet. What happened to the simpering parent she'd been last week?

"I've heard the reports about Kamber's nightlife, too," the empress said, rolling her eyes—the same gesture she'd made earlier when Subena suggested white napkins would be fine at the wedding dinner. "A cultured beauty like you deserves so much more."

Subena stepped back to get a better look at her mother. The naughty look on her face was alarming. The empress hadn't worn that particular expression since…well, since her father was alive.

Her father had been special, a pillar of strength and responsibility who adored his wife and children. Subena wanted a mate like that. Instead, she'd be stuck with a cur who'd probably continue to fornicate with every willing female in Gatsle. Her country might have open views about sex, but once vows were exchanged, monogamy was required. Subena felt something akin to hatred for her future spouse. For the first time, she questioned her decision.

"I'm so sorry you had to sacrifice your true mate," Annika whispered.

"Sacrifice my what?" Subena blinked, not certain she'd heard her mother correctly.

The laughter that followed grated on her nerves. "Your true mate. Surely you haven't forgotten Taslin? Although he did desert us rather quickly."

"Taslin isn't..." Tension stiffened her body. She'd known in her heart the duke wasn't for her, but she also knew there was no one else. No living being had ever stirred her passion—only the male from her vision had been able to touch her heart. And that male was merely fantasy.

"Oh, dear." The empress twisted her hands together. "I hadn't thought of that. If this monster keeps you from your true mate, you won't be able to have a child."

She swallowed, feeling spooked that her mother had voiced her own concerns. Most Mydrian couples never conceived at all. Subena blamed the crystals, although she had no proof.

Bockle blessed the more fortunate parents with a single child, which made Annika's four offspring one of the country's greatest miracles. The people loved her mother—even before Jalakin was born. After Subena came along and the twins followed—the only multiple birth ever documented on Lanatus—her mother attained legendary status.

Subena didn't want to be a legend, but she did want a baby. "Even if I find my true mate, that wouldn't guarantee a child, Mother."

The empress gulped. "There are things a female can do..."

Subena cringed. She'd heard rumors about blood rituals that permitted artificial reproduction, but the offspring were seldom healthy. She couldn't believe her mother would even suggest such a thing.

"It's unnatural." As a technologist, she believed nature made reproduction difficult for a reason. Her kind lived for centuries. If it were easy to reproduce, overpopulation would be rampant.

"Don't think about babies now, luv. I'm sure you'll have one. After you've served your sentence and gotten away from that Drow creature."

Subena didn't bother to remind her mother, yet again, that Kamber wasn't Drow. Having four children might make a woman popular, but it didn't necessarily make her smart.

"Maybe," she said instead.

"Not maybe. It *will* happen. We just need to get your marriage annulled first."

"What?" Subena had spent days searching the ancient volumes for a way out of her marriage. And she'd found one, but how did her mother know? She couldn't remember seeing her mother in the library. Ever.

"Despite his foolish announcement, I believe Taslin will wait for you, dear."

"Taslin isn't my true mate."

"Of course he is."

Subena shook her head. "You mentioned an announcement. What announcement?"

"You haven't heard? He's going to propose to Garilee. The girl's mother told me yesterday." The empress curled her tiny hands into fists.

"Garilee?" Subena wondered if the joist beneath the hardwood had slipped. Sure felt like the floor had caved-in.

"Yes. Stupid, airheaded Garilee. She's as bad as her mother. Can you believe it?"

"Mother." Subena hadn't meant to, but she'd used the same reprimanding tone one would use for an eight-year-old child. "Garilee's mom is your friend."

"That's not true. And Taslin'll ruin everything if he announces an engagement."

Subena sighed. Taslin had already ruined everything— just not in the way her mother supposed. He'd destroyed a longtime friendship. "Don't be crass."

The empress pursed her lips. "Isn't it enough that I must sacrifice you to Gatsle? Must you also rebuke me?"

Subena wished the petty, whiny words coming out of her mother's mouth surprised her. That too was probably her fault. Her actions might save her people, but she'd hurt her mother in the process. She vowed again to be patient—even though it might kill her.

"I've told you before and I'll say it again," her mother snipped, "if you don't want to marry the prince, you don't have to. We'll find a way to survive without the Drow

46

crystals. I'll make the excuse and tell everyone I forbid the marriage. We can talk to our legal counselors and find a way to extract you from this treaty. However noble your heart, luv, you shouldn't sacrifice yourself."

Unable to face her mother, Subena turned away. "Of course I want to do this. It's the only way. Rather it's the best way."

"I'm so sorry."

Subena swallowed, feeling overcome with melancholy. Desperate to change the mood, she asked, "Are the rumors true?"

"Could you be more specific, dear? The universe is full of truths."

Subena turned toward her mother. "Was that sarcasm?"

The empress dabbed at her eyes with a dainty handkerchief, a tiny smile lighting her face. "It might be. What rumor are you asking about?"

"Is Jalakin truly planning something as ridiculous as a freedom party? I thought those went out with—well, before the ancients left earth."

Her mother huffed a long sigh and propped an elbow on the arm of her chair. For some reason, a flush covered her skin. "Well, yes. The ladies wanted to give you a party, too—with a pleasurer—but you got so angry when I mentioned it, I canceled the festivities. Have you changed your mind?"

"Of course not. That's not what this—"

"Then it's no big thing, dear. Let the boys be boys."

"No big thing?" Annika was definitely up to something. "Mother?"

The empress looked away, but not before Subena saw a smirk.

"Mother..."

"Dear," Annika spoke softly, "our Mydrian waltzers are renowned, even to the barbarians in Gatsle. To us, dancing is culture. To Gatslians, it's...well, foreplay."

Not good. "What are you planning?"

The empress smiled her most practiced smile. "Nothing. It only made sense to stage a performance. It'll all be very tasteful. No one can blame us when certain males behave like animals."

47

"Waltzers?" Subena tried to uncurl her fingers, but they seemed glued into fists. She had little doubt her sleazy groom-to-be would fall prey to her mother's diabolical plan. Annika would cry foul, and justifiably so, but the treaty would be null and void. So would Gatsle's promise of more quartz.

"You have to cancel the Waltzers."

Her mother looked at her thumbs. "Can't. It's already on the schedule and we don't want to disappoint our guests."

It wouldn't do any good to argue with her mother. The lady might be flaky, but once she set her mind on something, she couldn't be easily deterred. If Subena managed to get Jalakin to cancel the Waltzers, her mother would try something else—possibly something irreversible.

"I suppose you're right." Subena wanted her mother to go to bed believing her silly plan would work. She'd have to find some way to keep Kamber from falling victim to her mother's scheming, and inadvertently ruining everything.

"Of course I am. The Gatslian party wanted to see the dance, so I arranged for Dilena to perform. There's no reason to get yourself into a stew."

"What stew?" Jalakin asked, pressing his lanky frame against the door.

"The freedom party. Doesn't anyone knock?" Subena tried to make eye contact, but Jalakin seemed distracted.

He threw up his hands. "This party thing sounds lame to me, but Mother insisted."

"Mother insisted?"

He nodded. "But I agreed. If you're going to have to live with Gatslians, I figured I could help smooth the way, make a goodwill gesture. You know, start undoing centuries of mistrust." Her brother, ever the diplomat, had no idea what their mother plotted.

Jalakin laughed, clearly oblivious to her tension. "Maybe you should've danced. According to the Waltz-Master, you're the best dancer in Mydrias. I don't see how that's possible since you have two left feet, but I can't contradict him since I've never seen you waltz." He looked at her, waiting for a reaction.

Not a bad idea. Dancing was her one extravagance—one she hadn't planned to share with anyone—but desperate times called for the dance of the doomed. She kept her expression impassive, knowing she couldn't telepath her plan to Jalakin without alerting their mother.

"Seriously, Subena," he said. "You can't be mad about this party. Allow him this last night of freedom."

She wanted to argue, but a glance at the time monitor indicated only two hours until the scheduled dance—barely enough time. It might involve using ancient skills of persuasion, skills forbidden by Mydrian law, but what could they do to her? Send her to Gatsle?

"I'm not mad," she replied. "Just don't let my fiancé embarrass me."

Suspicion flashed in Jalakin's eyes. Subena lowered her head and hurried away, leaving her mother and brother in her chambers. She didn't want Annika to sense her brother had reason to be alarmed.

Genia Avers

Chapter Six

Dilena stared at her with vacant eyes. Subena felt a wave of guilt. Not about Dilena. The female wouldn't be harmed and wouldn't remember a thing. She felt uneasy about deception, period.

"Surely, there's no need to worry about a little trickery when one's fiancé is a sleazy barbarian," Subena whispered, pushing self-reproach from her mind. She didn't particularly care if her future husband ogled a Mydrian waltzer on the eve of their wedding, but anything more than ogling would give her mother a reason to dissolve the treaty. Subena didn't intend to let that happen.

A knock on the door turned Subena's body into a block of stone. Had someone missed Dilena?

"Subena?" The voice belonged to her mother's assistant.

Her body regained some of its elasticity. The assistant couldn't possibly know about Dilena.

Subena yanked the bed curtains closed to hide Dilena's sleeping form and rushed into the sitting room, a mere second before the door opened. The assistant stuck her head in the door.

"Porala," Subena wheezed, positioning her body so the assistant had to back into the hallway. "Do you need something?"

"Actually," the empress's assistant looked at her through narrowed eyes. "I need you. Everyone is waiting."

Subena'd forgotten about the planned dinner with her future in-laws. *Bockle.* She couldn't attend now.

"Please convey my greetings and make apologies for my absence." Subena didn't have to make her voice sound weary. She felt weary. "I have a killer headache."

"Subena, you're going to have to—"

"Thank you, Porala." Subena stepped back into her bedroom, wishing she could save the quartz without being rude to everyone she knew. She closed the door and hurried to get dressed. Before she completed her preparations, another knock sounded.

"Porala," she snapped, grabbing a robe to cover her costume. "I told you, I have a headache."

She'd scarcely unhitched the latch when the door flew open. Subena jumped backward, barely avoiding being struck. Jalakin's large frame blocked the light which filtered in from the sitting room. The fury etched into his features sucked the very life from the room.

"Porala says you aren't coming to dinner." His voice echoed, eerily calm, but his wrath wrapped around every word. "What's the matter with you, sister? This treaty was your brilliant idea, but you're acting like a spoiled brat."

"It's not what you think." Before she could say more, a rustling noise captured her attention. Someone was coming.

"Then what is it?"

"I have a headache." Subena didn't lower her eyes. Not daring to speak aloud, she flashed Jalakin a message. She had to make him understand there was more at stake than a compromise of the diplomacy he prized. "You will come down and eat with the Gatslians, even if I have to carry you." She huffed a breath. Jalakin's anger obstructed her communication. Her brother stared down at her, his purple irises turning black as he gnashed his teeth. What was wrong with him?

The sound of footsteps on the stairs barely registered before Annika's voice rang out. "What's happening in here?"

"Our little Bena is hiding," Jalakin snarled, turning toward the empress. "She needs to get her butt downstairs and quit being a snit. Mydrians are superior beings. We should act like it."

"I'm not being a snit." Glaring at Jalakin, she wrapped her robe tighter around her shaking body and willed him to understand. He blocked her telepathic plea.

"See? Being a snit." Jalakin threw up his hands before he whirled. "I'll repeat myself. Bena, you wanted this damn treaty with Gatsle. Why are you trying to destroy it?"

"I'm doing no such—"

"You most certainly are."

"Jalakin, don't be so harsh," the empress interceded.

"Harsh? She'll insult Rothart if she doesn't show. Do you have any idea what that Dökkálfar and his army can do if we tick him off? Subena's already missed one planned event. If she stalls again, the king might cancel the second quartz delivery and you know how desperately we need it."

"The only way we could insult that fiend is if we run out of brandy," Annika said, winking at Subena. "Let's go, Jalakin."

Was that a glint of amusement in the empress's expression? Gads. Her mother thought she was trying to help get the wedding canceled.

"Please convey my regards to the Gatslian queen," she whispered.

Jalakin harrumphed. "Women. Winsome didn't bother to show either."

Subena stared at him. She hadn't heard that.

"It's a long journey," Annika interceded. "I'm sure Winsome would be here if she could."

Jalakin crossed his arms across his chest. "Everyone says the king and queen can barely abide each other. That should make it easier for Subena to return after one year."

She jerked her head toward her brother. "Where'd you hear that?"

"Come on, Jalakin," Annika cooed, interrupting before her brother could reply. "Let's go so Subena can rest."

"But mother, she doesn't need to rest because she doesn't have a headache."

"If Subena says she has a headache, she has a headache. We won't make her greet her future family if she isn't feeling her best. She has sacrificed enough." The empress tucked her arm around Jalakin's elbow and pulled him toward the door. Behind his back, she winked at Subena again.

Jalakin looked as though he wanted to argue, but he allowed the empress to guide him through the door. Subena heard him mutter under his breath, "Exactly how is being a princess in the planet's most powerful country a sacrifice?"

She intended to flash her brother a reassuring message, but Annika released her son's arm and pushed him gently toward the stairs before she had the chance. "Go ahead, son. I'll be right down." She half closed the door and flashed a beautiful smile. "Hopefully, you won't have to show up for the ceremony either, luv."

* * * *

Kamber watched as the Mydrian emperor-in-training rose. The regent simply stood, unmoving, until every elf in the crowd stopped talking. Kamber frowned, wondering what it must feel like to command that kind of respect.

"Welcome." Jalakin abruptly turned to his right. "Hold on."

"What now?" Kamber groaned. He knew the Mydrians were trying to entertain him, but he didn't want to celebrate his forced nuptials. He just wanted the night to end.

"Shhh."

Had Remmy actually shushed him? He pushed his shoulders back and stared at his old friend. If he weren't so bored, he might muster enough enthusiasm to be offended, but his brain felt fried.

When Jalakin had surprised him with a freedom party, he'd been honored. And horrified. With his reputation, the last thing he needed was a lap dance—even one under the guise of a cultural experience.

Monotony had long since killed any hopes he had of enjoying his last evening of freedom. After almost a week of tedious political gatherings, his party had turned into another droll event with more blah, blah, blah. Even Remington's ribald toast had seemed contrived and clichéd. And every bit as embarrassing as he'd feared.

He could scarcely believe he'd arrived in Mydrias only six days earlier. It seemed like he'd been in an abyss of dull for at least a month. Playing big brother to Nally and Quika,

54

Subena's thirteen-year-old sisters, had provided his only semblance of relief in a week of hell. Thank the God of the Mountain the girls were too young to have been tainted by the Gatsle-Mydrian hostilities.

He'd had one moment of hope when he'd spotted the beauty in the window. He'd felt something powerful, although he didn't understand exactly what he'd experienced. He'd hoped the charmer he'd spotted was Subena, but the eye color was wrong. Instead of the fabled blue eyes Remmy had droned on and on about during the trip, he'd been ensnared by a depth of silver beyond comprehension.

"Gentlemen," Jalakin spoke when the crowd quieted. "For your pleasure, and for the groom's last pleasure..." The Mydrian waited until the laughter trickled off. "For Kamber's last hurrah before he dons his ball and chain...and knowing my sister, we all know where she'll put the chain." Jalakin rubbed his crotch.

The crowd cheered. Kamber did his best to make his smile look genuine. The Emperor-in-Training actually had a sense of humor. Who knew?

"Joking aside, we are very proud of our famed Mydrian waltzers. In honor of the prince, I present one of our very best. The one, the only..."

Nothing happened.

Genia Avers

Chapter Seven

What am I doing?

Subena chewed on her thumbnail and tried to swallow the self-doubt rising in her throat. The music hadn't started. Still time to halt her deception, but that would mean questions: *Where is Dilena? What were you thinking?*

She peaked through the curtain and saw a large male— probably Remington. She knew all about him. Her spies indicated he not only accompanied the prince during his official duties but actively participated in the nights of debauchery. *Pond scum.*

Kamber sat next to Remington. *Double pond scum.*

She only wished the second scum wasn't so easy on the eye. Even his scowl didn't diminish the appeal of his striking features. What did he have to scowl about anyway? It wasn't like she could demand fidelity.

She'd been more careful after the window incident, but she'd continued to spy on her husband-to-be, searching his eyes and his manner for hints of cruelty or ambivalence. She'd been unable to detect the expected traits, but the dark ones were renowned for their acting abilities. She'd seen kindness, intelligence, and a great deal of sadness. Subena decided her intuitive skills didn't work on the Gatslians, because she didn't sense any evil.

Without warning, Kamber's jade eyes lifted, examining the stage curtain. She jumped back. The damn Dökkálfar always seemed to be aware of her scrutiny. Every single time.

The music started. Too late to back out.

She checked her mask to make sure it wouldn't come loose before she steeled her shoulders and took the ready position. Whatever she wanted to prove with her little stunt, it was show time.

"Ready, Dilena?" someone whispered from the left wing.

She started to raise her hand to indicate she was in position, but doubts accosted her. Did she want Kamber to be pleased? Lustful? Bored? She knew he could be easily seduced—why did she need confirmation? Life would be bad enough without knowing with a certainty that her husband had desired another on the night before their wedding.

The stage manager hissed, "Dilena, what's wrong with you? We have to start."

Subena whispered, "Stop the music. I've changed my mind."

The manager held her hand to her ear. "What?"

She groaned. The manager couldn't hear her above the orchestra but she dared not speak louder. If anyone on the other side of the curtain recognized her voice, Jalakin would kill her.

She waved her hands frantically, trying to signal the stage manager to kill the music. He nodded and motioned to the conductor. The curtain started to rise.

Bockle. The stage manager had misunderstood.

* * * *

A blast of music echoed through the great hall. Energy invaded Kamber's body.

It made no sense. He had no enthusiasm for the dance, even though every living male had heard about Mydrian waltzers. In the past, he might have felt privileged to watch the sensual spectacle, but now, it didn't seem right somehow. Being aroused by someone other than his intended on the evening before his vows was just wrong.

The lights dimmed and the curtain rose. A spotlight appeared.

The creature of his fantasies started to move.

What the...

He dug his fingernail into his palm, believing he must be asleep and dreaming on the very comfortable Mydrian bed linens. He forgot his boredom as a fabulous nymph floated across the floor. The agony of his impending nuptials evaporated and he allowed the movement to mesmerize, tantalize.

He felt connected. Every fiber of his being came to life.

He shifted in his seat, grateful for the dinner table that hid the evidence of his body's reaction. He wondered if the female held the rest of the Gatsle party equally enraptured, but he couldn't take his eyes away from the dancing creature long enough to find out.

Her face was hidden by an exotic mask of blue and purple feathers, but the smoldering eyes peered directly at him from two embellished slits. Silver eyes. Hypnotic eyes. The eyes from the window.

He sat straighter. She wore more clothes than the females in his country did when they went about their daily activities, but the dancer moved with such fluidity, the fabric of her garments clung provocatively, as if she wore nothing at all. Every flick of her wrist and every shift of her hips sent waves of seduction crashing into his body. Each movement proved more alluring than the last.

He wanted her.

The crowd faded from his consciousness and she danced for him. For him alone. The lady rolled her shoulders and Kamber wanted to kiss her breasts. She gyrated her hips and he wanted to pull her body against his erection. He'd been the target of seduction most of his life, but he'd never been so thoroughly spellbound. A goddess had descended to reward him for sacrificing his life to the drudgery of marriage. If only he could pursue this dancing beauty, life would be bliss.

He gulped when the music ceased. He didn't want the dance to end. Ever.

As he focused all his energy on the bright lights that evaporated the darkness, he saw spots. If he didn't get a grip, he'd mimic a prepubescent boy and explode.

Kamber stared at the curtains for a long time. His sexual need didn't diminish. It grew. The waltzer had disappeared but his arousal remained.

He heard laughter, but it took several seconds before he realized that it was Remington who hooted. When he turned to look at his old pal, Remmy laughed at him, not with him.

"What's so funny?"

"You." Remington chuckled again. "I do believe Mr. Righteous is lusting over the waltzer when he's to wed someone else in the morning."

His friend had never spoken truer words. As much as he wanted to be angry at Remington, he could only be irritated with himself. He hated his father because of secret trysts, but for the first time, he had an inkling of how Rothart must feel, trapped in a marriage he didn't want.

"God help me, Remmy, I don't know how I'm going to do this."

Remington stopped laughing. "Relax, laddie. I was only razzing you. Maybe it won't be so bad. If Subena's truly the most beautiful female in Mydrias, she must indeed be spectacular. Seems beyond comprehension, but your bride will be even more alluring than the little dancing girl, who is thus far, the most gorgeous creature I've ever encountered."

Kamber felt his face turn crimson. He, too, felt he'd met a goddess. As asinine as it sounded, he felt like he'd fallen in love.

Not possible. It had been lust—the purest and simplest kind of lust.

"How do you know she's gorgeous, you big, dumb, lummox? The dancer wore a mask." To him, that hadn't mattered in the least.

Remington chuckled. "Wasn't looking at her face, laddie. Even so, if your bride is more beautiful—"

"Subena may be beautiful, my friend, but I doubt she will be one-thousandth as sensual. Everyone I've met respects the empress's daughter, but even her admirers hint that she's a cold piece of stone and cares only about her technology projects."

The big male shook his head. "Can't be right. She's willin' to marry the likes of you to save her people."

"Maybe." Remington had a point, but it made Subena's coldness and self-sacrificing seem worse somehow. She could care about the masses, but never him. "She must be uptight. Even her sisters begged me to teach her how to have fun."

He growled as he thought about the female to whom he must pledge faithfulness. "Like she'd let me teach her anything. I'm to be shackled with a brainy mannequin who scorns the likes of me."

"Be fair, prince. You're no prize."

His jaw grew more crimson. Remmy spoke the truth, but he'd hoped to find a mate who would see something good in him.

Remington chuckled, grating on his already sour mood. "I've hit a nerve, laddie. I hope you haven't been lamenting getting rid of that vicious little tart you left behind."

"I haven't." *Not once.* The scratches Rekita had carved into his back prior to his departure had only recently healed—and he healed quickly. He'd started to avoid her, both physically and in spirit, long before his trip to Mydrias. Maybe it was because of her infernal complaining about his mandatory marriage or her latest hints about a pregnancy—as if that were even possible. She was not his true mate.

He'd tried to tell Rekita it was over when he departed, but he wasn't sure she'd listened—she never listened. To comfort her, he'd ended up sleeping with her again. *Colossal mistake.*

When he returned to Gatsle, he expected her to be yet another of his many problems. He cursed his privileged life and the albatrosses it placed around his royal neck. "I need some air."

"What's your rush, laddie? The night's young and you aren't shackled yet."

Kamber grabbed a glass from a passing attendant and drained it, wishing the weak Mydrian brew was stronger. People called his name, but he headed for the doors, desperate to get away from the entertainment chamber.

He stood on the balcony and gazed at the stars for several minutes. The celestial bodies glimmered as wondrously in this foreign land as they did at home. However miserable his marriage might be, he could not regret his trip. Nor did he resent the treaty between his country and this beautiful land. The people he met surprised him. They radiated with warmth and showed him a carefree existence his own people could never have imagined. If only he'd been in a better humor to appreciate Mydrias.

An open alliance with the country would create new opportunities for education and medicine for his people. Like his father, he'd denied that Gatsle needed such things, but now, he could see differently. Maybe the females in Gatsle could learn to dance.

That damned dancing girl again. He needed to purge the temptress from his mind.

Hellation. He doubted he'd ever be able to rid her from his thoughts. Without speaking a single word, she'd ensnared him completely. He suspected she'd be the one in his mind as he shared his wedding night with his new bride.

He picked up a small stone from the balcony, intending to toss it into the pool below when Remington slapped him soundly on the back, knocking the pebble from his hand.

"Are you still moping?"

"Gads, Remmy. Am I never free of you?"

"No, you lucky cur. I'll forever be nearby to kick your ass and save you from yourself." The large elf rumbled with mirth, his voice deep and melodic. "What's more, I have a surprise for the lonesome lord."

Remington's chuckling penetrated his gloom. Some of his melancholy melted.

"A surprise? Let me guess, you've found a replacement and I'm no longer the future king of Gatsle?"

"Even better, lad. I've found the female. And I saw no tattoo on her wrist, so she must be single."

"What female?"

"The dancer, you dolt. Don't pretend you don't wish to see her again."

Dread quickly replaced Kamber's initial delight. "I can't take another to bed on the night of my wedding ceremony."

"Not on the night of your wedding, silly boy. On the night before your ceremony. Have one last fling, laddie. You deserve it." Remington slapped him on the back again, knocking the wind from his lungs as he gave a hearty cackle. "You're lucky I didn't decide to pursue her me-self."

The big male stopped laughing and his eyes widened. "I've heard all the ladies in this country dance like that. I can't even imagine such a heaven. Maybe we should live here after you wed."

Kamber smiled at his friend's tomfoolery. "Pray tell, old man. How did *you* find her?"

Remington stretched his six foot, eleven and one-half inch frame and his massive girth grew even taller in pretended outrage. "You think old Remmy cannot get a lady's attention?"

He chuckled. "Seriously, Remmy. How'd you find her?"

"'Twas simple. I just asked one of the attendants if I could speak to the dancing lady. The lass went and fetched her. She's waiting in the main courtyard."

"The attendant?"

"No, you blasted fool. The dancer. You best not keep her waiting."

Genia Avers

Chapter Eight

Kamber hid in the shadows for several seconds, watching the dancer as she lingered near the fountain. Her face glowed in the moonlight; she was lovelier than he'd imagined a female could be. Definitely the same person he'd seen in the window.

Her beauty startled him when he'd seen her from a distance—even with a mask. At closer range, she made him dizzy. An abundance of long beautiful hair curled and danced around angelic cheekbones. Full lips that begged to be kissed pursed in an expression he did not understand. She seemed sad.

He could relate.

Kamber wanted to touch her, but touching would require moving and he feared movement would break the spell. He felt content to stare, to drink in her exquisiteness and forget about wedding ceremonies, wars, and treaties. Looking at her would be enough.

He hadn't made a sound, but she jerked her face in his direction. Had she sensed his presence?

Not possible. Mydrians possessed no ancient skills.

"My lady." He approached her, took her hand and raised it to his lips. She had a well manicured, but not pampered, hand. He saw a slight scratch on one finger and one nail looked shorter than the rest, as if recently broken.

The lady uses her hands. He suddenly felt curious about what she did when she wasn't dancing.

As his lips touched her skin, jolts of energy coursed through his entire body. He felt himself becoming aroused. She jerked her hand away as though she'd touched a flame.

Ah, she felt it too.

"There's no need to call me 'my lady.' We have no caste system in Mydrias."

Her voice echoed like a song, as delightful as the rest of her. "What shall I call you?"

"It matters not. Your man said you wanted to see me, Your Majesty. Pray tell, what do you want of me on the night before your wedding?"

He stepped backward, surprised by her hostility. The Mydrian people were the friendliest he'd ever encountered, most surprising given the centuries of hostilities between the countries. Even folks who didn't know he was a prince had treated him with great courtesy. Why was this female so frosty?

He assumed Remington had already arranged an interlude and he'd decided he would make love to her. *One last pleasure.*

The dancer didn't seem amenable.

Kamber shifted, trying to regain his footing. He didn't know how to react after his renowned charm had failed. "I-I simply wanted to tell you how much I enjoyed your dancing." What was wrong with him? He never stuttered.

She smiled, making him feel like a star had fallen to the ground for the sole purpose of dazzling him. Perhaps he'd only imagined her hostility.

"That's all? Then I will bid you goodnight." It took Kamber a moment to process her words. He couldn't believe she'd already started walking toward the building.

"Wait." He hurried to her side.

The look she flashed made him regret his impulsive plea. "What do you want, sire? Surely you do not expect a female loyal to the empress's daughter to share a romantic evening with you? With her fiancé?"

She'd just expressed his exact hope but the look of revulsion on her face squashed his ardor. She couldn't know that he'd planned to seduce her. Could she?

"No." He didn't recognize his own mumbling voice. "Of course not."

Unexpectedly, the dancer smiled, disarming him again. She moved closer, stopping only inches from his body, and lifted a slender arm. She stroked his cheek, her touch light and enticing.

"Really? When I was dancing, I could have sworn you wanted me." Her eyes briefly darted to his lower tunic. "Yes, I'm sure you wanted me."

He wanted to kiss the smirk off her face. He cursed his groin for falling under the influence of the fickle female. Never in all his thirty seasons had anyone made him feel so inept. "Yes, I wanted you. Rather I want you. But..." He paused to gather his thoughts. She raised an eyebrow.

"But..." Kamber tried again. "That doesn't mean I would act upon my desire. You're the most beautiful creature I've ever seen. Curiosity consumed me, that's all. Please forgive me if I've offended you." He cursed his weakness again.

She studied him for several seconds. "Curious? Tell me, prince. What is it you are curious about?"

She'd made him feel unworthy, yet he still wanted her. He wanted all of her, not just a quick sating of his lust. Not just a mere conquest. He wanted her—for keeps.

He certainly couldn't say that. Nor could he say that her lips made him so curious he wanted to cover them with his own. He dared not tell her that his hands were curious about the feel of her silken curls or that he wanted to know if her breasts would feel as amazing as he imagined.

Kamber gulped, hating himself for his hunger, yet unable to focus on anything else. Only one option remained. He must speak the truth.

"I'm sorry, my lady." He couldn't believe the way his voice rattled. "I marry tomorrow and when I saw you tonight, I realized I must give up on finding someone as beautiful as yourself. Lest you think I'm blinded by lust, and there is that in abundance, I sense you are even more beautiful on the inside. For a few minutes, I wanted to be...alone with you. I was curious as to how *that* would feel."

He looked directly into her mesmerizing eyes—eyes with a luminous quality that challenged the splendor of all the moons. He watched, willing her to understand. She lowered her lashes, effectively shutting him out.

After a few seconds, she raised her head and returned his stare. "So you do not wish to marry our princess, my lord?"

"Regrettably, I do not."

"Is there someone else?"

"Not really." He wondered why he hadn't just said "no."

"Not really?" She laughed but she didn't sound amused. "So the things we've heard about you are true?"

"What things have you heard?"

"You are renowned for your...prowess. 'Tis said you kept your mistress, even after your engagement. And now, you flirt with me." She shook her head, sending her hair into a fan that seemed to catch and reflect the iridescence of the moonlight. "You see, my lord, you cannot escape your reputation, even in Mydrias."

He transferred his weight from one foot to the other. Embarrassment gave way to irritation. "I cannot see anything wrong with sowing a bit of wild grain while I am single. Since you're from a society that touts open sexuality, I find it strange that you'd judge me for a few bachelor trysts."

"A few trysts?" She held her stomach and sniggered. "If Mydrias had a warship for each female you've...eh, encountered...Lord Creshin would never be a threat."

The injustice of her statement made him bluster. The dancing lady burst into giggles. When her laughter subsided, all trace of emotion left her flawless face. "And yes, in Mydrias, we believe sex is a natural and normal part of life. But even in our culture, prince, we do not tolerate promiscuity."

"Promiscuity?" He struggled to maintain his composure.

Her lips curved upward, her smile radiating with rebuke. "Perhaps I am being unfair. Count the number of lovers you've had over the last year. If the number is less than twenty, I will apologize."

He was too aware of her scrutiny as he tried to do a quick tally. He didn't like the numbers. *Am I promiscuous?*

"Less than forty?" she inquired.

Maybe he was promiscuous.

"So tell me, do you intend to keep your mistresses after you marry?"

68

"It's none of your business, but I do not." His neck muscles grew stiff. "In spite of what you've heard, my lady, I hold marriage in high regard. I shall not be unfaithful after I've spoken vows."

"Really?" She'd turned away and shadows hid her face, but he sensed her doubt. "So you are not like your father?"

"What the..." Kamber closed his mouth. He hadn't concealed his surprise. His negotiation skills were renowned, yet he couldn't hide his emotions from a dancing girl. "You are well-informed." He turned from her and leaned over the wall. The fragrance of lavender no longer smelled sweet. "I assure you. When I'm married, I'll be very different from my father."

She studied him intently before she spoke softly, "But you're more than willing to make love with me this night?"

He grinned, the playing field again familiar. "I have not yet said my vows."

"Alas sir, vows or not, I doubt you'd find anyone in Mydrias willing to sleep with another's fiancé. I, for one, would not disrespect the bride-to-be."

Kamber squirmed. He felt like a naughty schoolboy, but his lust belonged to a grown male. She leaned against the wall and propped her chin on her hands. "I will confess, I'm curious about you too, prince. Why is this marriage so repugnant to you? Surely a future king doesn't expect to be able to marry for love?"

The hostile tone no longer coated her lovely voice. He wanted to talk. Nay, he needed to talk. "No, I didn't expect to marry for love, but I'd hoped. I suppose I'm not ready to give up on the idea."

"And you suppose Subena's ready to give up on love?"

He sighed. "I regret to say, I've not considered her ideas about this arranged marriage. She is..." He paused, aware he needed to carefully choose his words. "I've been told she cares more about her work than about people, but it seems she'll go to any length to protect Mydrians. Since she engineered this oh-so-brilliant treaty, I supposed she didn't care about love."

He expected sympathy. When he glanced at the dancer, he saw clenched fists.

"Maybe, sir, you're misinformed."

He nodded his head, still wanting to please the female by his side. "Maybe."

"It bothers you that our science minister takes her work seriously? I suppose it must bother her that you never work."

"That's not true. I—"

"I suppose you would prefer that she spent her time dancing rather than experimenting with new energy sources?"

He turned and placed his back to the stony wall. "It would be nice if she did both."

"Then you will have no objections if she wants to create more schools in Gatsle?" The dancer wore her smug expression again. It should have put him off but didn't.

"I don't care what she does as long as she stays out of my hair." He realized, too late, that he'd said too much. This female would certainly be well acquainted with the empress's daughter. Perhaps even a best friend.

Her sarcasm confirmed his fear. "Gee, you're too kind."

"Are all people in this culture so outspoken?"

"I like to think we are," she replied. "In Mydrias, people are encouraged to speak openly—even if they are speaking to royalty." She glared daggers at him. "Maybe because we believe in equality, we don't take visiting royalty very seriously here. Tell me, prince, do the people in Gatsle tell you what they really think?"

Instantly he became defensive, unable to stop himself from shuffling his feet again. No female had made him that uncomfortable since his nanny. "I don't know," he replied.

"Shouldn't you know? You're the future leader."

He looked directly into her face, a fierce anger rising within him. The battle that waged between his temper and the increasingly painful swelling beneath his lower tunic made rational thought impossible.

"Perhaps," he snapped, "we Gatslians are not as advanced as your country. Perhaps we care more about living life than analyzing it."

Unable to stop himself, he grabbed her. Before she could protest, he kissed her deeply on the mouth. It was only when his fury had subsided that he realized she'd responded.

He jerked his head upright, still needing her body against his, but struggling to maintain some semblance of dignity. "I appreciate your time, but I'll keep you no longer."

Leaving her open-mouthed, he fled from the garden. He couldn't afford to let her see the too obvious result of their contact.

Genia Avers

Chapter Nine

Subena grabbed a pillow from her bed, covered her mouth, and screamed. She couldn't believe the prince had actually requested an audience with her. Only because he thought she was someone else.

He'd almost gotten to her when he'd spoken about the beauty inside. For a brief second, she thought he understood her—and she'd hoped. Hoped someone had finally seen beyond the mask required of her station. Hoped she'd found someone who might understand her heart beat more furiously with just the possibility of real love. She'd prayed someone might actually patch the hole created when she couldn't save her father. Fool that she'd been, she actually believed her future husband might be that someone.

"The nerve of him, looking for a hay-tumble when he's to marry me in the morning," she whispered, pounding her fist into the pillow. "The bloody sod judged me. Without knowing anything about me."

She ignored the tiny voice that insisted she'd purposely seduced him. Unable to face another rejection, she had to hate him, had to hate the mess her life had become.

Staring out her window into the silent streets, she wanted to strike something but nothing resembled the prince's head. She poured another glass of ale instead.

Placing the silken pillow on the windowsill, she pounded one more time, trying to soothe her anger. Thanks to the boorish Dökkálfar she was fated to marry, sleep would be impossible. If only she could think of a way to cancel the wedding yet still obtain the crystals.

The nagging voice issued another reminder, "He said he'd be faithful once he married."

He lied. Of course he lied. A male didn't learn to kiss like that by being faithful.

She tried hard to push away the memory of his kiss. For the briefest of moments, she'd responded. And discovered the power of his intoxicating lips. As kisses went, the contact surpassed anything she'd imagined and she hated herself for that moment of submission. She hated the Gatslian for fanning a flame Taslin could never ignite.

The kiss might've been a thing of beauty, except Kamber hadn't meant the blasted kiss for her. He'd been enamored with his dancing girl. Even that she could've accepted, but like everyone else, he'd judged her—in his mind, Subena and the dancing girl could not exist in the same body.

She picked up the pillow and hurled it at the wall. Feeling no better, she downed her ale and poured another glass.

* * * *

At some point, she must've fallen asleep because her mother's voice frightened her into consciousness. "I can't believe you're still sleeping. Have you changed your mind? Shall I tell them you're ill?"

Subena wiped her eyes, trying to remember why she needed to awaken. The empress looked regal in a gown of clingy mauve silk.

Ah crap. Her wedding day. "No, I'll dress quickly."

"I'm sorry I failed you," the empress repeated. "I was so sure that Gatslian whoremonger would want Dilena after she danced, but that blasted girl went straight to her chambers. No one ever listens to me anymore."

The minute her mother left the room, Subena covered her head with what was left of the pulverized pillow. If she dozed for just a minute, maybe she could convince herself she'd done the right thing. At least Mydrias would have an abundance of quartz.

Her mother's shriek jarred her world. "Subena! You still aren't dressed? Let's call off this ridiculous ceremony."

She blinked. "What time is it?"

74

"A half-hour after you said you'd get up." The empress took a hard look at her. "Oh sweetie. Have you been crying?"

"No."

"But your eyes…"

"Too much ale."

The empress nodded. "That does it. No wedding day for you."

Subena shook her head and immediately wished she hadn't. "Mother, we need those crystals. I *will* get married. Please don't make this day any more difficult than it is."

The empress did something she rarely did. She stood still for several seconds. "You're determined to do this?"

Subena started to nod, but remembered the pain the movement would cause. "Yes."

The empress bit at her lip. "You're like your father, you know that?" Annika turned away and swiped at her eyes. "I'll find some eye drops." Her mother rushed from the room.

Subena smiled. Annika might hate that her daughter was getting married to a Gatslian, but there'd be no red eyes in any ceremony planned by the empress.

She crawled into the big tub and let the warm water soothe her tired body. Falling asleep on a windowsill did little for one's spine. She glimpsed the magnificent dress the empress had hung on her armoire. And closed her eyes again.

"Wake up! You're going to drown."

Subena jumped, bumping her head on the back of the tub. Bockle. Had she really fallen asleep again? In the tub?

"I understand you didn't sleep, honey, but unless you want me to call off this farce, you'll have to act like you're among the breathing. This may not be the wedding of our dreams, but we can't have you looking like someone's going to chop off your head."

"The way my head pounds, it feels more like the funeral of my dreams. I may never drink ale again." She grabbed the towel and covered her chest. "Wait, did you just make a joke?"

The empress had already scurried out of the room. Subena dragged herself into a standing position, every muscle and instinct screaming, "Stay in the tub." She almost sat back down in the beckoning water, but her crystal caught her eye. The glass shone as brightly as the day the crystal had been created. Most crystals weren't so perfect.

The day wasn't about her. It was about the substance that would sustain her people until she could find a better solution. She dried her body and tugged on her undergarments, trying not to poke her finger through the flimsy fabric.

"Why bother?" She looked down at her reflection. The skimpy bridal lingerie hid nothing and emphasized her intimate areas as if she wore nothing at all. She resisted the urge to tear the silky material away from her skin, instead sinking down on the padded bench to pull on sheer stockings. After securing the lacy garters, she opened the box and pulled out a shoe. Her grandmother's crystalline slippers.

"If only you were here, Nana." If only the male from her vision were waiting at the altar.

Fighting back tears, she admired the footwear. Shells gathered from the Lanatus Sea had been intricately molded into a heel. Tiny straps made from strings of delicate pearls crisscrossed over a sole decorated with diamond dust. As a child, she thought the shoes were the most beautiful things she'd ever seen. She slipped them on her small feet and stood, not surprised they fit perfectly. She and her grandmother had been alike in so many ways.

The door flew open. Subena wrapped her arms over her naked breasts. "Bockle, Mother. Do you ever knock?"

Her mother rushed in, shaking her head. "You still aren't dressed?"

"Whoa. Who told you?"

Annika clicked her tongue.

"Sorry, Mother. You know how cranky I am when I haven't slept."

"Pretty much the same as when you have. Let me help you with that corset."

Subena watched as her mother visibly put on a happy face. She'd waited so long for the empress to stop mourning her father, Annika's new attitude almost make the day joyful.

"Two jokes in one morning, mother? Still, I won't wear that…"

The queen jerked the towel away before Subena could protest. The empress took the undergarment, wrapping the corset around Subena's body. "Hold still."

"I am not wearing this thing." Subena tugged at white fabric interlaced with metallic threads, but her mother kept tightening the strings. Every pull pushed her breasts higher.

"It's tradition." The empress reached over her shoulder and fluffed Subena's hair. "Besides, your dress won't fit without it. Now smile. Your sisters are aglow with romance. If you must go through with this abominable plan, put on a happy face for them."

Subena rubbed her temples. If only her mother could run a country as well as she could manipulate a daughter. The empress spun her around as if she were a child's top and lifted her chin with a firm hand. Annika pulled a bottle from her pocket and poured a drop into Subena's eye.

"Ouch. That stings."

"This'll put the sparkle back in your eyes. Can't have them looking plain old gray." The empress released her chin abruptly. Subena's head banged against the edge of the chifforobe.

"Ouch."

"Those drops don't hurt that much." The empress flicked her wrist. "Sit down. I'll style your hair."

Subena's head ached. "You don't have to do that. I can brush it." The last thing she needed was her mother tugging at her scalp.

Or seeing her pointed ears. Drawing upon her inner magic, Subena rounded each helix.

"Nonsense." The empress pushed her into the chair at her dressing table and proceeded to pile Subena's silvery hair in an intricate design. Each pull with the comb made the ache in her temple pound with renewed vigor. Subena closed her eyes, trying to distance her mind from the fire covering her scalp.

When Annika finished curling and pinning, the empress stepped back to admire her handiwork. "It won't do."

"What do you mean? It's fine."

Annika didn't respond. She pursed her mouth and began to methodically remove every pin.

"Do you have to yank so hard?"

"Where's my tough little girl?"

Her mother twisted her head back and jerked another pin free of a snarled curl. "Be still. It won't hurt so much."

Finally, all traces of hairpins had been removed. Subena lifted her fingers to massage her throbbing hairline, but the empress pushed her hands away.

"Let me, love. Close your eyes."

The brush soothed. Her headache started to recede.

"Open your eyes," the empress commanded. "You look beautiful. The silver matches your eyes."

Subena blinked. Her long locks shimmered, catching every ray of light. The empress had pulled the tendrils from her face and set them in place with a row of gems that held a gauzy veil of iridescent colors.

Her mother stared at her reflection in the mirror. "Look at yourself. You're gorgeous, little one. I'm sure everyone will forgive your lateness when they see how beautiful you are."

The empress glanced at the time monitor. "This is not the day I'd hoped for, but it's still your wedding day. We must hurry." The empress twisted her back to Subena and started to remove the covering on the gown hanging near the door. Annika lovingly smoothed the silken folds of the gown she'd worn at her own ceremony.

She watched her mother's cheery bravado transform into real joy and envy gnawed at Subena's stomach. If nothing else, her mother was a romantic. If only she could feel that sentiment. If only she could feel anything.

Standing like a fence post, she let her mother slip the dress over her head and arms. The sapphire silk rustled as it fell over her body and brushed the floor. The sensuous fabric beckoned to the touch and shimmered as if woven from the movement of a waterfall. Even so, the beauty of the cloth did little to improve her mood.

The empress sighed. "You take the air from the room with your loveliness."

The person who stared back in the mirror was unfamiliar. Black pearls and tiny diamonds framed the intricately embroidered low-cut bodice. The gemstones glittered with such intensity, Subena almost felt dizzy from the reflections.

No. It wasn't the gems that made her lightheaded. It was the intensity of what she intended to do that made her sway.

The empress didn't notice her hesitation. Annika had already headed to the door. At the entrance, her mother paused. "I'll send Jalakin up to escort you."

"I have to get Grandmother's necklace. I'll only be a moment."

Annika huffed a breath. "Fine. Don't go back to sleep."

After the door closed, Subena retrieved the necklace from her closet and sat down at her dressing table again. She looked at the tiny diamonds that formed the chain of the pendant, wishing again that her grandmother were around to advise her.

"Oh, Nana. How can I go through with this?"

She squeezed the necklace in her fist. The only enjoyment she would have would be the look on *his* face. She could barely wait for the moment when he realized he'd made a fool of himself with a dancing girl who was actually his bride. The sparkle returned to her eyes.

The twins burst through the door, followed by Jalakin.

"The gown is gorgeous," Nally exclaimed. "I can't wait to wear it."

"You can't wear it," countered Quika. "I'm wearing it."

She hugged a twin with each arm, suddenly feeling the full weight of her sacrifice. She smiled, refusing to put a damper on her sisters' excitement. "No more fighting or I'll get new attendants."

"Let go of me, Nal," Quika shrieked. "You'll wrinkle my dress."

"It's my dress," Nally argued.

Each sister darted under one of Subena's outstretched arms and headed for the stairs. The bickering continued as they raced down the stairs.

"Some things never change," Jalakin said, no trace of a smile on his handsome face. "Ready?"

She took her brother's arm, fighting tears. "No, but let's go anyway." She would miss her family so much.

Her brother whispered, "Are you positive you have to do this?"

"Yes."

He sighed. "Then I have to believe things will be all right."

Jalakin is wrong. Things won't be right. Not at all.

Chapter Ten

Kamber wanted to kick something but refrained because people watched. He stood erect and tried to think of anything except the beautiful dancing creature. He thought about the Gatsle crops that were failing, about schools that needed building, and even about how he would keep Rekita away from his bride, but thinking didn't help. As hard as he tried to occupy his mind, he couldn't purge the image of the beautiful waltzer and her smoldering eyes.

What kind of ass thought about another lady on the day he married? Self-loathing washed over him, making him feel heated in the cool chamber.

One of his men approached. "Empress Annika wishes to speak with you. She's waiting in the atrium."

What did she want? Prince Kamber hadn't expected to like his soon-to-be mother-in-law, but he did, even though he sensed she didn't care much for him. The Empress displayed the same flustered behavior his mother did. Maybe losing a husband to death, or losing him to another female, had a similar effect.

He hurried downstairs to meet her, and bowed from the waist. She frowned. Mydrians didn't seem to care much for bowing either.

"My dear empress," he mumbled. When he raised his head, he detected anxiety in her expression. "What's wrong?"

For a fleeting second, he hoped Subena had refused to marry him. If she had, he'd rejoice. He'd still find a way to get the crystals to these people and then, he'd find his dancing goddess. Not necessarily in that order.

He dismissed the idea and his temporary relief vanished. Whatever her faults, he knew from his own sources that Subena, fiercely patriotic and self-sacrificing, would not cancel the ceremony.

"Prince Kamber. How handsome you look." The empress refused to meet his gaze and rubbed her hands together. In only a week, he'd already learned that trying to hurry the Mydrian leader would only fluster her more. He waited for her to get to the point.

She said nothing.

"Does the bride need more time for her dressing?" Kamber asked. The ceremony had already been delayed for a full hour. *Not long enough.*

"No, no. She is ready." The empress paused to bite her lip. "A most bizarre thing has happened." The hand rubbing started again. "You see, no one knows what happened to the holy leader. He's not here and he's not in his assigned quarters. Normally, he's a most reliable cleric. I cannot imagine why he isn't here."

"And the marriage cannot occur without this holy leader?" Kamber asked, narrowing his eyes. It would not surprise him if they discovered Subena had bribed the priest to stay away. Only a minute earlier, he'd actually been foolish enough to believe she wouldn't cancel the wedding.

The empress nodded.

"Let me be forthright," he replied. "Does your daughter wish to call off this ceremony?"

Annika stared at him, something akin to horror flashing in her eyes. "Heavens, no. To be frank, Kamber, I'd like to cancel the ceremony, but Bena's determined to go through with it." She held her hand to her chest. "As a mother, I don't want my daughter to leave our fortress. Now that my husband's gone, my children are my life."

The empress pulled her gaze from her own hands and looked directly at him again. "So help me, if you're not good to her, I'll find a way to hurt you."

Annika seemed to grow taller and Kamber saw beyond her grief, saw a real empress, regal and benevolent. "And," she continued, "what I'm trying to say is we are honest people, as you no doubt already know. Sometimes we're too honest, so you may be assured, if my daughter wanted to cancel the ceremony, I'd simply tell you we wanted to cancel the ceremony."

He waited, doing his best not to smile. She had yet to state the purpose of their talk.

Defiance defined her face before the concern he'd observed earlier crept back over her countenance. "Unfortunately, Father Hisem is truly missing. He's a good friend, so I'm especially worried."

He stepped forward and kissed the empress's cheek. "Then let me help. I have fifteen men who can assist with the search. Is there someone who can direct them?"

She nodded. "Thank you. What should I do about the guests? How long do we let them wait?"

"I'd like to wait for your holy leader, my empress, but the ceremony has been delayed too long. Remington is licensed as a justice and can marry us."

"You want your friend to fill in for Father Hisem?"

He nodded. The empress turned a ghostly shade of pale. "I suppose that would work."

At least some of his tension dispelled.

* * * *

Everything blurred. Kamber hoped to have some time to get his mind right, but all too soon, Remington stood in front of him in ill-fitting robes. If Kamber weren't worried about the end of life as he knew it, he'd tell Remington what he could do with his damn smirk.

He focused on obliterating the dancing girl from his mind, but his body refused to cooperate with his brain. He could feel her. Nearby. The serenity of knowing she was in the chapel competed with the dread that he felt for his future. The combination left him disoriented.

He had a vision of a blue being floating down the aisle, but could tell little about the bride beneath the veil. Her posture was perfect. Everything about his wife-to-be was probably perfect. The notion filled him with revulsion.

The ceremony drifted through his consciousness, hazy and unreal, as if he watched the proceedings from some distant place. He thought he mumbled the correct responses, but he couldn't be sure. He heard someone whisper, "Kneel."

He dropped to his knees at the altar. He fidgeted.

The tiny creature by his side hissed, "Be still." Had his bride actually scolded him during his ceremony? It was surely a sign of things to come.

His head popped up. He lowered it quickly when he realized a councilor prayed to Bockle. When he took his bride's small, gloved hand into his large one, the sweetness of her scent assaulted him. He felt a brief surge of desire. What the hell was wrong with him, lusting after two females? One who despised him, one he despised.

Exhaustion had claimed his body when Remington finally pronounced he was wed. People chuckled. He realized he was supposed to kiss his bride.

My life is over.

He lifted the veil.

And swallowed hard.

Only years of royal training kept him from screaming like a little girl.

Underneath all the fabric, under the netting, beneath the jewels and all the trappings of wedding attire, he found the smoldering eyes of the dancing girl. A wave of pure happiness flashed through him. He'd married the dancing girl.

No, wait. He'd married Subena. *Is she...? Dung.* Remington had gotten the eye color wrong.

Deadly anger consumed him, obliterating his momentary joy. His little bride had deceived him. And he'd made a fool of himself.

Again.

Chapter Eleven

The horrid ceremony and the endless banquet finally ended. Subena's feet hurt and her jaw hurt more. She'd spent so many hours forcing a smile even her teeth ached.

She sat in the suite her mother had arranged for the wedding night, trying to ignore the male standing on the other side of the room. She removed a slipper so she could rub her foot and smiled again, remembering the look on Kamber's face after he lifted her veils. Just wait until he learned there would be no consummation of the marriage. She fought the urge to giggle.

"What's so funny?"

"Nothing." She needed to control her facial expressions better.

She moved to the table and began to eat, relishing each bite. "I can't believe I'm still hungry." She glanced at her new husband who leaned against the door, pleased to see he still looked miserable.

Kamber had been glaring since the ceremony. Judging from his demeanor, she might not get a chance to gloat about the absence of a wedding night. He looked like he'd only touch her to choke the life from her.

That works, too. She grinned, fighting to contain an entire bout of giggles.

Her new husband continued to glare and she continued to eat. If he didn't want any of the sparkling ale or delicious delicacies piled on the plates, that was his problem.

"Are you going to eat that?" She gestured toward the caramel and chocolate concoction on his tray.

"Why are you smiling?" He unclenched his hands and walked over to the table, picked up the dessert, and tossed it into the trash. "You can't deny that you wanted to marry me even less than I wanted to marry you. Why are you smiling?"

"Temper, temper," she purred, pleased that her new spouse raged. She instinctively affected an even more pleasant disposition, knowing that would goad him more than ranting back at him.

She glanced at the trashcan. "Gee, I really wanted that crumb cake. I do love caramel." She wiped her hands on a linen napkin. "I suppose there's more in the kitchen."

He whirled and raised his fist, stopping it just before it came in contact with the wall. "At least I was honest. You pulled that sneaky dancer stunt like...you're really...something."

"Sneaky? How can you say that?" She smiled, and licked her fingers. "I only danced to entertain you. It really isn't my fault you acted like some equestor in heat." She might have glimpsed a bit of embarrassment but if she had, her new husband quickly masked it.

"You purposely deceived me."

"If someone else had danced, Bockle knows what you would've done, so get over it, will you?" She looked up from the last of her cake and smiled again, enjoying his discomfort. She doubted anyone had ever told him to "get over" anything. More likely he surrounded himself with "yes" people.

When he lifted his glass, his fingers shook. He stared at the ale, seeming to channel his wrath into the glass. Without warning, the glass shattered in his hand. The remaining drops of liquid trickled down his hand to the floor, leaving an ugly stain on the woolen rug.

Having suppressed reactions her entire life, she didn't flinch. "Someone will have to clean that."

His face flushed. He opened his mouth, closed it, and opened it again. A brief knock at the door interrupted any response he'd planned to make.

The prince wiped his hand on the towel that had wrapped the sparkling ale and cracked the door. He blocked her view and she couldn't make out the voice. She heard mumbling.

"No," Kamber responded, "everything's fine. My bride's merely nervous."

Her good mood evaporated. She'd gotten the worst of the marriage bargain, yet she'd been able to retain her good humor. How dare the imbecile blame his temper on her? When the door closed, her façade of composure crumbled. "You ass!"

"Maybe I can have my advisors help you with your vile language."

"Really? Maybe they can also help you with your vile temper."

"Touché."

He walked to the window and she retreated to the settee. The silence became unbearable.

"I'm sorry about the glass." His voice sounded like a plea. "And the cake. I'll find you another piece if you really want one."

"Don't bother. I've lost my appetite."

"Look." He slumped against the door. "We both got a raw deal but unless you want to nullify the treaty, you and I must consummate this marriage. Tonight."

"You can't be serious. There'll be no consummation."

His eyes narrowed. Subena fought the urge to back into the wall.

"No consummation means no treaty. Is that what you really want?"

"No. I mean yes." She shook her head trying to sort out the thoughts bombarding her. "What I mean is...of course I want the treaty. I just don't want to have sex with you."

"Now there's a revelation."

She ignored his surly tone. "Since you've mastered the obvious, I'll say good night."

She headed for the opposite door, the irony of a bridal suite with two bedrooms not lost on her. Kamber stood on the opposite side of the room, but he moved so fast, she saw only a blur. He blocked the door and grabbed her arm before she reached for the knob.

"How...how did you do that?"

Kamber stared at her but he didn't reply.

"Of course," she said, the truth of his speed registering in her mind. "Gatslians have the skills of the ancients."

"Gatslians can't possibly have skills Mydrians don't possess," he snarled. "We're inferior."

"Your whining is rather tiresome. Possessing ancient skills *is inferior.*" She lifted his hand off her arm and dropped it. "Your foul magic is what condemned both our peoples to this planet. Now if you'll excuse me, I'm going to bed. Alone." She glared back at him, channeling her hurt into anger and flashing it at him. She hoped his skills included telepathy so he'd get the message.

His head snapped backward. Apparently, he had the necessary receptive skills.

"You've made your aversion abundantly clear, little wife. But the marriage must be consummated."

Subena didn't try to hide her smirk. "I've read every sentence of the treaty. The marriage requirements are extensively detailed. There isn't a single word indicating consummation of the union is required."

He laughed. The hardness of his eyes didn't match the mirth in his tone. "Maybe not, my sweet, but according to Gatsle law, if there's no consummation, there's no marriage. No marriage, no treaty."

Subena's stomach clenched. *No. No.* She shook her head. How could she have been so stupid? She hadn't even considered Gatslian laws. "That can't be right."

"I assure you, my little ice maiden, it is. We can call for a ruling, but I suspect it will appear as a desperate attempt to delay your bridal duties. You do have a reputation for being...frigid."

How dare he criticize her—she wasn't frigid—she just needed someone who could kindle her fires—someone who wasn't a womanizing slime. Never in her life had she experienced such an intense desire to strike another being. "You...you...equestor's ass."

He laughed again. "Ass or not, you must have sex with me—at least once—or there will be no treaty."

She tried to push him aside but slipped and fell to one knee.

Kamber held out his hand. "Here, let me—"

She jerked her arm beyond his reach. "Don't touch me." She braced for his outburst.

"It's going to be difficult," he said softly, "to consummate this marriage without touching you."

His gentle response surprised her so much, she didn't protest when he lifted her to her feet. He released her, but stood too close, effectively pinning her against the closed door.

He tapped his finger against the bottom of his lip. "Look, I've never made love to an unwilling partner, and I won't do so now. I hope you have some idea how we can deal with this problem."

"That's easy. Let me go and I'll come back to this chamber in the morning. Everyone will make the appropriate assumptions."

He snorted. "My father will require proof. I hope you have some brilliant scheme in that clever little head of yours to produce the…eh, appropriate evidence."

"Me?" Subena blinked, not believing she'd heard him correctly. "You're the one with the experience."

"Experience?" His dark brow furrowed slightly. "You don't expect me to believe you're an actual virgin. Aren't all females in Mydrias experienced?"

How dare he suggest she was less than truthful? Sucking in a breath, Subena ducked, hoping to escape his invasion of her space—and his scrutiny.

Before she could move, Kamber grabbed her arm and held it firm. "I didn't mean that the way it sounded. Even so, I will not be dishonest. I won't pretend there was a wedding night just to satisfy my father's treaty."

"Great." Subena wondered again how her well-planned scheme had gone so wrong. "My husband is a stickler for honesty. Does that mean you'll confess every time you visit your mistress." Bockle, why had she even mentioned the other woman. She sounded…jealous.

Kamber jerked his head back. For a minute, Subena thought he might have looked hurt, vunerable even. But that had to be a mistake. The equestor's ass was arrogance personified and he certainly wouldn't be concerned if she was jealous. Which she wasn't.

He stunned her by kissing her wrist. "As I explained to the dancing girl—and we want talk about that deception—I will be faithful now that vows have been spoken."

His words made so sense. Maybe because his lips sent an unexpected fluttering racing through her veins. Instead of jerking her hand free, she stood unmoving and watched his lips caress her skin.

"You really are a virgin?" he whispered between flicks of his tongue.

She nodded, unable to speak.

"I know you don't like me," he whispered, "but if you'll trust me, I promise to make this...night as painless as possible. If you don't my touch again, I'll honor your wishes."

Painless? It took her a moment to realize he meant sex. Did he really think that was her concern? Shedidn't know which she hated more, him or her body's response to the infuriating imbecile. He might have done the deed a million times, but she'd...waited.

"As painless as possible?" She hoped she sounded tough instead of teary. "I can't remember ever getting such an intriguing offer."

He groaned. "I should've said that better. Can we *please* start over?"

"No." She sniffed. "But let's get it finished. Turn off the lamps?"

Why had she agreed? The annulment would be harder to obtain. Still, not impossible.

He startled her by laughing. She'd liked him much better sullen and haughty. "Now who's making intriguing offers? Does this mean you're actually willing, my little bride?"

"Not willing. Resigned. I'm doing this for the greater good and all that. Just turn off the lights."

"No. I want to see you."

"Please..." He kissed her again—on the mouth, and she forgot what she'd intended to protest. The kiss seem to morph into forever, a kiss more sensual than the one in the courtyard.

Her mind screamed: *resist him*. Her lips didn't listen to her brain. The kiss wrapped itself around her entire body and demanded complete surrender. His lips made her *want* to

90

yield. Submit. Do all the weak things females did for unworthy males.

When he raised his head, she tried again to protest but he pressed his finger to her lips.

"Let's compromise. I will leave one lamp on. Very low. You can close your eyes. Deal?"

No, it wasn't a deal. How dare he reduce her first sexual experience to a business proposition? Didn't he realize it would be easier if he just shut up and did it? She wanted him to take her and be done with it. No, that wasn't right. She wanted the treaty and she *needed* the consummation completed.

She jerked her body away. "No."

"No?" He walked to the first lamp and lowered the flame. He kept his gaze on her while he turned down the second lamp and completely extinguished the third.

He returned, standing too close again and looking far too handsome. For the first time, she had an inkling of what all those silly females experienced when they fluttered about some male not wearing a tunic.

She didn't move. They stood for several seconds, neither making a sound.

The tension crackled and she crackled with it. She had to escape, duck around him and get out of the chamber.

Kamber ran a thumb over the side of her neck, letting his hand slide down to part her robe. The look of desire staggered her.

He wants me? Confusion kept her immobilized. Her empathy skills didn't work with Kamber, but psychic abilities weren't necessary to understand his reaction to the silky fabric clinging to her curves. She felt exposed in her translucent peignoir, but oddly, didn't care. She felt…powerful.

Only she couldn't fall for a male who would never love her. She looked away, knowing he planned to kiss her again. His lips made her stupid and she needed to remain aloof. "Give me a moment." He might claim her body, but she couldn't let him claim her heart.

"Maybe this will help." Kamber reached into his pocket and pulled out a flask. He'd barely twisted the lid when an unfamiliar smell invaded her nostrils, the scent so intoxicating it made her knees buckle.

"Easy..." Kamber dropped the lid, but kept the bottle upright as he used his left hand to steady her.

She clutched his arm to remain upright. "Is that... How is that possible?"

"I see you're a virgin in more ways than one." He smiled a slow seductive smile that combined with the yummy aroma and made her want to tear the clothes from his body.

He wrapped one arm around her waist and held the flask to her lips. She leaned in for a sip. He jerked the flask away.

"Hey. Why did..."

"Intersting," he said, holding the flask just beyond her reach.

Using all her willpower, she prevented her body from lurching toward the container. "What's interesting?" She refrained from adding, "jackass."

"I do believe your ears are pointed. I could have sworn..."

She slapped his hand away and pulled her hair over her ears. Subena blinked her eyes several times, trying to call upon the magic to make them rounded, but her body revolted. She willed the top of her ears round, only to return to the pointed shape of her ancestors the minute she stopped concentrating.

"Most interesting."

She glared at her new husband. "There's nothing interesting about my ears."

"You are ashamed?" he asked.

"No." But she was. How could she not be embarrassed? All her life, she'd been told that evolved beings did *not* have pointed ears. Gatslians had pointed ears and they were barbarians. Mydrians were civilized, with round ears.

Her efforts to keep her ears normal combined with her need to drink from his flask. Everything else blurred.

"So you are ashamed?"

It took a second for his words to register. "Yes. I mean... I don't know."

She turned from him and covered her mouth with both hands. *Mother of Bockle, what's wrong with me?*

"Subena, do all Mydrians disguise their ears?"

She shook her head. "No. I think I'm the only freak."

He spun her around and held her face in his large hands. "You're not a freak."

"I am. Leave me alone." She jerked free of his hold and backed away. Her thighs banged into the edge of the bed and her butt landed on the mattress. "I'm hideous."

"Sweetness, you are beauty personified. You have beautiful ears." He pushed his long black hair behind his ears, exposing his ears. Then he knelt, pushing his body between her legs.

She wanted to push him away, but how could she concentrate with the bouquet of paradise wafting around? "Is that blood?"

"Yes." He poured a drop onto his finger. "Does it offend you?"

She lunged forward, barely stopping before she sank her teeth into his finger. *What is wrong with me?*

"Interesting."

"Stop saying that." She needed to ground her energy. Who knew what her forbidden skills might do if she didn't concentrate.

Kamber smiled and then rubbed his finger across her lips, leaving a taste of the delicious liquid. "I thought Mydrians abhorred blood."

"We do." Or so she'd been told. Only humans had blood and they ranked lower than Gatslians

So why couldn't she control her reaction to the vile substance? Her tongue flicked over his finger and her mouth made a loud slurping sound. A second later, her body contracted, sending waves of pleasure coursing through her limbs. She placed both hands on his wrist, closed her eyes, and sucked on his index finger.

Holy Bockle.

After several delicious seconds, her brain registered her actions and her eyes flew open. She sensed his arousal—without a look or a touch, her mind saw his erection.

A quick glance confirmed her intuition. She released his finger, feeling a flame of mortification wash over her pleasure. She'd acted like a dark creature in heat. Like a sex-depraved ancient.

Kamber grinned lazily, clearly enjoying her primitive display. "As much as I want your mouth on my body, I think we'd better feed you first. I don't want you claiming you were intoxicated with blood lust when you scream out my name in the throes of passion."

"You arrogant jerk. I don't have blood lust and I will never scream your name."

"Perhaps you won't." He held the flask to her lips and tilted it. "You might not scream, but you want me. I don't know how I know that, but you want me. Almost as much as you want to drink from this flask. Almost as much as I want you."

She steeled her resolve, but the contents of the flask cast a sweet spell, making her resistance evaporate into the night. So delicious. She took a gulp, but didn't swallow. She held the warm liquid in her mouth, savoring the sensations that went far beyond taste. Her body filled with life. With magic. With lust.

Kamber pulled the flask back. She grabbed for it.

"Bena, you must go slowly. Your body isn't used to blood."

"How do you know?"

He laughed, a deep, mellow sound that confirmed his amusement. "Mydrians don't partake of earthly essences, remember? Otherwise, you wouldn't need our damned crystals.

Earthly essence? Of course, he meant the blood. The human substance was rumoured to contain the spirt of the ancient planet. Maybe the stories were true. There was clearly something magical in the liquid.

Kamber's laughter died as suddenly as gus north had erupted. Masculine lips found her neck and the light feathery movements of his tongue sent vibrations of pleasure pulsing through her entire body.

"Have you never had any blood sustenance before, Bena?"

She didn't want him to use her pet name, but she couldn't concentrate enough to tell him to stop. She definitely didn't want to tell him about the rat's blood. Under the guise of finding a substitute for the crystal's light, she'd experimented. The rodent essence had been nothing like the powerful elixir in Kamber's flask. Which meant the Mydrians really did keep humans. Disgusting.

Almost as disgusting as her behavior.

"Poor baby." He continued to nibble at her neck between words. "Take another swallow. A small one."

She sipped, thanking Bockle she'd regained a sliver of self-control. The liquid sent fire rushing through her body. The flames sparked and steamed, making her feel more alive than she'd ever felt. Her heightened senses became aware of Kamber. And her own desire. She wanted him more than she'd ever wanted anything.

It had to be the blood. She hated Kamber.

She ran her tongue over her lips, unable to pull her eyes away from his face. Why did she want him?

Did it matter? Bockle, she wanted him. Desperately.

"One more drink," he whispered, his voice gravelly. "Then we must close the flask. I have other things on my mind and I don't want your thoughts diverted." He handed her the flask, seeming to understand she'd regained control of her actions.

"No." She handed the container back to him.

Kamber, nodded, no longer looking smug. He placed his arm around her back and pulled her closer. After taking a swig, he closed the flask. "It tastes like you now."

Another craving blotted out Subena's lust for the liquid—a more powerful need. Her control slipping away. Completely.

Kamber pulled her body against his and covered her lips, tasting of life and desire. Her mind protested, but her body succumbed to his kisses and danced in a heavenly abyss. She pressed her body into his, savoring the hardness of the large bulge pressing against her stomach.

Her traitorous leg encircled the back of his calf and rose higher to wrap itself around him. She thought he growled, but she couldn't be sure. In the middle of the kiss, Kamber lifted her other leg and placed it around his waist.

Still kissing her neck and chest, he lifted her, positioning her body closer to the top of the large foamy mattress. She closed her eyes, trying to pretend she held onto her real love—the male from her vision.

She failed. The only image she could bring into focus belonged to Kamber's gorgeous face.

His hands found her breasts beneath her sheer nightgown. This touch generated a blast of heat, turning flames of desire into an inferno. She experienced a physical pleasure so intense, it bordered on pain. Her nipples hardened into taut beads and her back arched to meet his caress.

His breathing grew shallower as fingers undid the buttons holding the silky negligee together. "Let's get rid of this." His eyes grew wide. "God of the Mountain. Your breasts are perfection."

If she hadn't been gripped by her own arousal, she might have laughed at him.

There was no laughter.

Years of loneliness made the intimacy sweeter. She savored his demanding lust, pulling the powerful emotion into her own and fueling the ache in her center.

His reputation no longer mattered. The treaty seemed like something in another lifetime. She forgot that she hated him and plunged into the moment. Everything vanished as hungry lips found waiting nipples.

Some part of her consciousness welcomed him as the male of her dreams, but she was not ready to entertain that notion. She would only acknowledge she wanted him.

"I'm starting to think this treaty might not be such a bad idea." Kamber mumbled between kisses.

If her brain hadn't been in her breasts, she might have kicked him. "I'm starting to think it's a terrible idea."

He laughed but didn't stop his caressing and nuzzling. The delicious torture continued until Subena thought she might explode.

He seemed to sense the urgency of her need. He lifted her into a sitting position and completely removed the gown. Instead of wrapping her arms around her body to hide from the intensity in his stare, she reveled in her nakedness. Tentatively, she tugged at his tunic, wanting it gone.

He pulled her hands over his shoulders and kissed her mouth, running his tongue over her teeth and gums. Who knew there were so many pleasure receptors in a mouth?

His fingers traced a slow, delicious path from the center of her breasts to her navel. His action distracted her hands, but did little to quell the growing fire in her female parts. She wanted more. More kisses, more caresses, more of him. She might dislike the elf, but her body loved the feel of him.

"Kamber, I…"

He took the back of his palm and made a slow circle just below her navel. She realized she wasn't breathing. Consuming a gasp of air, she involuntarily clutched his shoulders.

"Patience, love."

As if that were possible. The pleasure grew too intense. She wrapped her arms around his back and tried to pull him to her, needing to feel the length of his body against hers. She opened her eyes to find him looking at her with undeniable hunger reflected in his eye. She sensed his restraint.

And had enough of that. "Kamber, please."

The words hurt her pride, but pride didn't ache nearly as much as the desperate need to feel him inside her body. Rising up, she met his lips with her tongue. She could tell the gesture enflamed him.

Still he held back.

She stroked the side of his face with the back of her hand. "Why are you torturing me?"

"Torturing you? You have no idea how much this is torturing me."

"Then you must end our torture."

He grunted and pushed her onto her back. His normally-sure hands fumbled, but her tiny undergarment came away from her body.

Finally.

She closed her eyes. And waited.

When Kamber made no additional move, she gritted her teeth, afraid he no longer wanted her.

"Open your eyes."

She peeked between her lashes, fearing she'd see triumph on his face. Not seeing the expected emotion, she opened her eyes wider to stare directly at his face.

No gloat, only lust. His desire clearly burned as hot and pure as her own. Maybe hotter.

So why did he wait?

He's going to make me beg.

Subena ignored the rational part of her brain that insisted the gorgeous hunk treated her with respect. She ignored logic when it insisted his own lust would not let him insult her.

The battle raging in her mind couldn't compete with the heat enveloping her core. Maybe she would beg. "Kamber?"

He pulled her toward the edge of the bed and placed his large hands on her thighs. She expected him to enter her, but he lowered himself to the floor.

"What are you doing?"

She tried to sit but he lifted her thighs, making her fall onto her back.

"Your first time should be perfect."

Before she could question his intentions, she felt his lips on her. There.

The wonderful, glorious tongue that had done delicious things to her mouth and body plunged into her center. If she hadn't been lying down, she would have buckled from the sheer intensity.

Bockle!

His tongue darted and nibbled around her mound. The licks were first agonizingly slow and then deliciously fast. He nibbled closer to the spot she needed him to reach. He didn't touch it.

She whimpered and wrapped her leg around his neck. Kamber placed his mouth on her folds.

"Holy Bockle."

He didn't respond. His tongue brushed her aching center with long sensual strokes. She grabbed at his head, relishing the feel of his thick, silky hair. The knowledge that she was powerless to resist him inflamed her more.

Subena lifted her body, propelled by an ancient need to grind against his face. Kamber began to massage her with a finger as he licked. He dragged her into a whirlpool of beautiful sexuality, into a world she'd neither experienced nor imagined. Into a world where only Kamber existed and he was all she wanted.

"Ah, ah...ah." She heard the incoherent phrases tumbling from her mouth, but the sound muted as bliss gyrated around her body. Kamber plunged his magical tongue deeper into her. The action pushed her over the edge, sending her mind and body spinning out of control.

She exploded, screaming as pleasure and magic washed over every nerve ending. Rainbows exploded in her mind.

The moment loomed potent, more intense than anything in her life. She would be forever changed.

When the spasms lessened, she stared at him. "What the…" Surely he would gloat now.

No gloat. Only more lust in the blue depth of the eyes that stared back at her. Had his eyes changed colors? They should be green.

"Don't move, love," he whispered. "Give me a second to… Just give me a second."

She didn't understand.

Please don't let it be over. How was it possible to want more after she'd experienced heaven? On an unfathomable scale.

Her insides ached. For him. She closed her eyes, willing him to thrust his manhood inside her.

"Open your eyes, Bena," he ordered. "Try to control your magic—it's too strong. Otherwise, I may not be able to control mine."

Magic? What magic? He acted as if her body commanded his.

She shook her head. She would think about that later.

"Touch me," he whispered. A request, not an order, but commanding all the same.

She complied.

And gasped at the size of him. Maybe she didn't want him inside her.

"Don't worry." His voice sounded tender, caressing. "I won't hurt you."

She tried to speak but Kamber placed his fingers on her lips. "Shhh."

Without warning, he pushed a finger deep inside her. Subena felt a slight pop followed by a sharp sting. He removed the finger quickly and continued his caressing. The pain vanished.

She tried to speak, but couldn't. He'd erased her virginity without causing any discomfort. Why had he done that? His simple act of selflessness confused her. This was not the male she'd expected. He'd deprived himself. And her.

"Kamber…"

"Hmm?"

She forgot what she was going to say as his fingers found her clitoris and she felt a gush of moisture. She began to gyrate against his hand. He inserted another finger inside her. It felt full, but she wanted more.

He massaged her growing need as his lips found her neck. She could feel the throb of her veins as they danced in unison with the tension in his body.

Still holding his thickness in her hand, she ran her fingers over the length of him, tugging gently so he would understand. She wanted him inside her.

Desperately.

"Now." She closed her mouth before she added, "Please."

"You're not ready."

She groaned. "I am past ready. Take me, for Bockle's sake."

He removed one hand from between her legs and stroked her cheek. His other hand continued to finger her most sensitive spot. "Trust me, love. Your Bockle has nothing to do with this."

He pulled back, but held her gaze captive as his tongue traced a light pattern over her lower lip. His hand continued to caress below. She made sputtering sounds as his middle finger increased the friction and his thumb pressed against her center.

His tongue moved from her lips to find a hard nipple and the intensity and pressure increased. He was making love to her with his hands and mouth.

Subena stroked his manhood with equal intensity. "Kamber, I…"

He growled. "Soon."

He rubbed her harder and bit at her nipple. The wonderful spasms returned. She screeched as a second orgasm racked her body. In her excitement, she bit his neck.

And tasted his blood.

His manhood spasmed. His liquid covered them both.

* * * *

Kamber staggered. He braced a hand against the wall and tried to regain his equilibrium. When he'd envisioned sex with his new bride, he'd imagined his wanger getting frostbite, but, holy dung, the siren beneath him sizzled.

For the first time in his life, his grin felt natural. Euphoria lived where hope had all but died.

Thirty years of anger evaporated. Instead of an ice maiden, he'd gotten a female so responsive, her teeth had made him come. "You bit me."

"Shut up."

His lips slowly curled upward. A male could get used to a bite like that. He thanked the God of the Mountains.

"Maybe you should do it again," he teased.

Instead of hiding under the sheets, or worse—withdrawing into her shame, Subena crawled closer to him. She gaped at his still erect member. If he were a betting elf, which he was—or used to be—he'd swear he saw admiration in her eyes. For the first time in his life, he felt like a king.

"Maybe I should."

He growled happily. "Now where were we?"

It was going to be a long night. A long, delicious night.

Chapter Twelve

Subena woke and stretched. A groan followed her catlike yawn. Moving her arms and legs reminded her that every part of her body ached. The physical exertion responsible for her tenderness replayed in her mind.

She sat straight up and covered her mouth. She'd bitten him.

Mother of Bockle. She'd bitten him.

And he'd seen her ears.

Flopping back against the pillow, she pounded her fists into the mattress. She'd shamed her people. And herself.

She wondered for the thousandth time, why did she have pointed ears? Her people had evolved—they weren't nasty sprites who practiced evil. Except Uncle Eustin, no Mydrian had sported anything but round ears for centuries.

She placed her hands beneath her hair. The points were back. Calling upon her ancient magic, she willed them to round. It didn't work.

Bockle. She couldn't let her mother see the pointed horrors. Instead of being a heroine, she'd be reviled in Mydrias.

Crap. Kamber would talk. The piece of dung had been so elated that she'd gone primitive, he'd actually laughed about her ears. Out loud. And instead of delivering a well deserved insult, she'd acted like a floozy. Her body flamed with renewed awkwardness as she remembered her brazen behavior.

Every part of her hurt. Even so one look or one touch from him would turn her into a whimpering sex slave again.

The only way she could ensure there would be no encore was to put some distance between her and her new spouse.

Thank goodness the big imbecile was gone. Where was he anyway?

Something nagged at her brain. What?

She tried to isolate the evasive thought, but her mind splintered into a thousand directions. The last time Kamber entered her body, her senses had leaped over the crest into paradise. She'd clung to him and screamed, stopping just short of calling his name. There was something important about that moment—something other than it being the most beautiful sensation she'd ever experienced.

What? She couldn't isolate the memory her subconscious wanted her to see.

She got out of bed and paced, ignoring the sore muscles and her nudity. She knew what she needed to remember. During her planet-spinning climax, she'd seen it. It was at that moment she noticed the birthmark on his chest. Small. Very small. And shaped like a jagged diamond.

She sat down on the bed again, forcing her breath to normal. "Not possible." He could not be the one.

Nothing good ever came from her visions anyway. She picked up a book from the night table and hurled it into the bureau.

The door flew open. She yanked her hair over her ears and lifted her chin. Subena whirled, ready to snap at Kamber.

Instead of confronting her husband's glorious body, Subena stared at her mother. *Great. Just elvin great.*

"What was that racket?" Annika asked.

Subena wrapped her body in the sheet and started the search for her clothing.

"Never mind the racket, you must hurry, Bena. The caravan is waiting for you." The empress stopped dead in her tracks. "Oh great Bockle!"

Subena looked at the bed, feeling her body blush so hot her skin burned. The covers looked like fighting ferrets had nested in the mattress. Feathers floated from one comforter when she moved and covered most of the bed. One sheet was ripped and at least two pillows were missing. "Eh, sorry. I'll get some new bedding."

She wondered if she looked as sheepish as she felt. She chanced a glance at her mother but Annika didn't look at the bed. The empress stared at the wall.

Following her gaze, Subena gasped. She didn't remember what color the room had been, but she did remember a solid hue. In the glimmer of the morning light, the room shimmered. More brilliant than the Sun-Star. A fresco of a water scene enhanced the area above the bed and the remaining walls looked like a vat of precious jewels had exploded, creating the most beautiful abstract she'd ever imagined.

Had Kamber painted the room for her? He must have some amazing magic to finish the painting in so little time. They'd been awake—and otherwise occupied—until past dawn.

"Oh my lord," Annika whispered.

"Don't be mad, Mom. I'll get it repainted." Subena stared at the walls again, hoping her mother would let the color remain. "The room looks rather nice, though." What an understatement. Beautiful, stunning, stupendous were more apt descriptions.

Annika stared at her, eyes wide. "You don't understand, do you?"

"Understand what?"

The empress shook her head. "Never mind. This is just...unexpected. That's all." Suddenly, tears streamed down Annika's cheeks. "Oh, sweetness."

"Mom, what's wrong?"

The empress shook her head again. "Nothing. I just fear you'll never return."

"What? Why?"

Annika continued to stare at the vibrant walls. "I'm guessing you had a good night."

"Mother." Subena felt another blush all the way down to her toes. Gads. She felt wanton enough without her mother asking for details.

The empress laughed heartily. Subena's reddish hue darkened.

"There's nothing wrong with pleasure, luv. Even with a creature like him. His physical body's quite glorious."

Subena wanted to crawl back under the sheet. And never come out.

Her mother placed the garments she carried on the bed but suddenly re-grabbed the clothing, clutching the garments against her chest. Her gaze flicked across the room before settling on the rumpled covers. After a heavy sigh, the empress laid a velvet gown across a nearby chair. "A gift from your prince, daughter. I hate to admit it, but the fabrics are exquisite."

Subena grumbled. Despite their lofty ideals, Mydrians could be seduced with well woven cloth. Even she was not immune.

The dress was exquisite, with a bodice made of the softest orchid velvet; amethyst jewels surrounded a princess neckline. More jewels embellished the dropped waist and a deep purple skirt fell in silken folds. The fabric felt as if it would melt in her hand. The gown was indeed a work of art.

She jerked her hand away. She didn't want anything belonging to Kamber to touch her skin. The male controlled too much of her body already. "I'd rather not wear it."

"Subena." Her mother's normally serene face furrowed at the brow. "Don't be childish. Why would you refuse a beautiful dress?"

"Because I..." She stopped just short of saying she hated Kamber. Nothing childish about that remark. Worse, it wasn't true. She hated that he made her lose control, but she couldn't honestly say she hated him. "I'd just rather not wear the gown, okay?"

The empress whitened and made a croaking noise. She sat down on the bed and wrapped her arms around her daughter. "Sweetie, I'm sorry. I thought...well, I thought...did he hurt you?"

"No."

Her mother leaned back to look at her face. The scrutiny made Subena feel worse. "Did he force you?"

"No." Subena curled and uncurled her fists.

How could she explain? She'd experienced the single most amazing pleasure imaginable but she wished it had never happened. The logic sounded deranged.

Kamber might've been the male of her dreams in the dimly lit room, but in the light of the Sun-Star, he was still an ass. And he probably still thought she was a frigid lump of coal.

She tried to brush her mother's question aside. "He didn't force me. I just don't like him."

"I see."

Her mother clearly did not see. She disliked the empress's smug expression. The woman thought sex could solve anything.

Wrong. No matter how delicious the sex.

Subena started to protest but her mother spoke first. "Sweetness, don't despair. You don't have to go to Gatsle if you don't want to. I think…I think Rothart might just give us the quartz anyway. Did you notice that none of the Gatslians wore crystals?"

She had. The observation piqued her curiosity, making her determined to understand the reasons.

Still, her mother's suggestion to remain in Mydrias was oh so tempting. But she was no quitter. She'd made a commitment and intended to stay the entire year. And not a day more.

She just had to ensure there was no repeat performance of her wedding night. Ever. "I'm going to Gatsle."

Her mother studied her for a few seconds before she nodded. "All right, but if you plan to go today, you'd best hurry. Oh. Another thing." Her mother paused and looked over her shoulder. "That silly priest is here. Said he wants to say goodbye to you. I can't believe he had the nerve to show his face after standing us up on your wedding day."

"What happened to him?"

"They found him passed out near the Rosetta Garden." She empress shook her head. "Silly priest insisted he'd been drugged but apparently he was too stupid to remove the empty ale bottle from his cloak." The empress shook her head and hurried from the room.

"Mother, wait." Annika had already gone. "Father Hisem doesn't drink," she said to no one in particular.

* * * *

Kamber watched Subena walk down the steps—gliding was a more apt description for her movement. A fat braid restrained the hair he'd ensnared his fingers during the night, but tendrils escaped around her face. It seemed even her own hair could not resist the urge to touch her. Too bad her ears were rounded.

He grinned. He'd fix that.

His gaze went lower and he forgot about her ears. The purple gown trimmed with jewels his mother had selected fit perfectly. Modest by Gatsle standards, the dress revealed too much of her breasts and clung too enticingly to her hips. He barely resisted the urge to take her back to the room and ravish her again.

He turned to tell Remington to take charge of his mount, but his old pal gaped at Subena.

Damnation. His new bride would have to wear her own clothes—the Gatslian dress he'd brought revealed too much. He flung the reins at Remington.

"Close your mouth."

His friend ignored him and stepped forward to offer his arm to Subena. "Greetings, beautiful princess."

"Thank you." She smiled at the giant, ignoring Kamber completely. He felt like a cold breeze had blown through his ears and frozen his brain.

What's bitten her on the butt?

Best if he didn't think about her butt. After last night, he'd hoped she'd be more pliable but damned if she didn't seem even more distant than she had during the wedding banquet.

She leaned forward and hissed in his ear. "If you mention my ears, I'll drive a hot poker through your balls."

His jaw twitched, but he contained his grin. Unlike Rekita's harridan antics, Subena's temper enticed him.

She swept past, still holding Remington's arm. The smile she flashed at the big guy would make honey seem sour.

"What a beautiful creature," she purred, rubbing her slender hand over Pollo's head.

Kamber had heard she was an excellent rider but doubted the poor creatures he'd seen in the Mydrian stables could even manage a trot. Maybe if he let her ride a real equestor, she'd thaw a bit. Hell, he'd give her his steed if she'd smile at him like she smiled at Remington.

He started to make the offer when he remembered the romp they had in the honeymoon bed. No, riding might not be a good idea. Not today. The memory made his pants feel tighter.

His princess glared at him, almost as if she'd heard his thoughts. He longed to pull her into his arms and kiss her until the sour look vanished.

A tall male bowed before her, marring Kamber's fantasy. "Dear Subena," the buffoon said. "I am at your service."

Kamber snapped, "Who are you?"

The male ignored him and continued to gawk at his wife. Subena's expression of pleasure fueled more anger.

"Taslin, why are you here?" she asked. His wife didn't seem displeased.

He watched his new bride closely.

"I am to be your escort, my lady," the stiff replied.

"What about your fiancée?" Subena asked, lowering her gaze. Did his wife flirt with the creep? Kamber cleared his throat.

"Forgive me," she said. "Duke Taslin, allow me to present Kamber, Prince of Gatsle. Taslin is resident of Reklaw, but he's a frequent visitor to Mydrias and a dear family friend."

I'll just bet he is. Kamber smiled, gritting his teeth beneath his faux friendliness. His new wife was no doubt well versed in protocol. She knew a duke should be presented to a prince, not the other way around. He'd never been concerned about matters of etiquette and was equally sure he wouldn't care about any other introduction. He'd just formed an instant dislike for the scoundrel.

"A pleasure." Kamber cut off the Duke's response. "The guard escorting us to Gatsle is the most elite on the planet. I assure you, my wife requires no additional escort."

"I could not agree more, Prince." The duke made his title into a slur. "My little minister can indeed take care of herself. However, Annika insisted, and I've always found the empress to be an unmovable force."

Kamber wanted to remove the grin from the duke's face. Taslin turned his back to Kamber, facing Subena. "To answer your question, Bena, I have no fiancée since I've lost you."

My little minister? Bena? Kamber raged at the familiarity.

He spotted the empress walking toward them and stifled his harsh retort. Annika had tears streaming down her face. He wouldn't make Subena's departure more difficult for the empress by protesting something as petty as an escort. He'd take care of the scalawag later.

He pivoted, positioning himself between Annika and Taslin. "Subena, we must go. I'm sure you wish to say goodbye to your mother and sisters."

She hesitated long enough to glare at him before hurrying to her mother's side. Annika clutched her daughter, sobbing as if Subena were going to the gallows instead of Gatsle. After several seconds, the quiet weeping got to him.

He had to get away. "I'm sorry, Empress. We must depart."

Great. He sounded like an even bigger ass.

Subena pulled out of her mother's embrace and flashed him a look that made him want to crawl under the carriage. Gads. Would he ever do anything right in her eyes? Outside the bedroom anyway?

After hugging her sisters, Subena rolled back her shoulders and walked past him. The tears streaming down her face caressed her skin like tender diamonds. Even in sadness, her beauty stunned him.

Without a word, she climbed into the carriage. Kamber reached for the empress's hand but she pushed his arm aside and embraced him. The twins clung to him so tightly he thought he might topple over from the force of their affection.

His throat constricted. "I'm sorry we have to leave. The borders are treacherous and we must pass them before nightfall. I hope you'll visit as soon as it's safe."

Kamber climbed into the carriage, completely ignoring the duke, and put his arm around Subena. She stiffened and leaned forward to avoid his touch.

When the carriage door closed, he whispered in her ear, "Whatever issues you have with me, pretend we're the happy couple for your family's sake. And for the crowds that have gathered at the gate to wish you farewell. I hope you can keep the bug that's crawled up your beautiful little arse from stinging your admirers."

He regretted his words as soon as he'd uttered them.

Genia Avers

Chapter Thirteen

"I'm sorry." Kamber said, meaning it.

"I know," Subena replied.

He closed his mouth—his only option. Unless sex was involved, his wife brought out the worst in him.

Sex was involved, though. Remembering the night, he huffed out a breath. He hoped her icy countenance didn't preclude a repeat session. He gazed at her breasts, barely hidden beneath her velvet bodice. Before he realized what he was doing, he ran a finger down the cleavage.

She slapped his hand away. "Don't."

Cheering erupted outside the carriage. Seeing a way to avoid her withering tongue, Kamber grabbed her hand and raised it. "Wave!"

He hadn't meant to sound domineering. She surprised him when she acquiesced.

"I can't believe they came to see me off."

"Why wouldn't they?"

Kamber stared at her, amazed that she seemed genuinely surprised. He made a note to explore the source of her insecurity. Later.

When the carriage moved past the crowds, the dazed look left her face. She slugged his bicep with more force than a female her size should have. He resisted the urge to rub his arm. He also resisted the urge to twist her arm behind her back and kiss her senseless.

"What did you do that for? I said I was sorry."

"I have a multitude of reasons."

Maybe he deserved that. He had been a bit of a cad. Of course, she'd have heard about his reputation. He should have wooed her, seduced her. Her body had been willing but her mind hadn't. If he'd had an ounce of sense, he'd have noticed that last night.

What was he saying? No sane male would have been able to think of anything but her body after seeing that skimpy nightgown.

He needed to make things right, but he was in unfamiliar territory. He specialized in the clean getaway, so he reacted from instinct and retreated to the opposite side of the carriage. He stared out the window, past the mass of green foliage to the distant mountains. There had to be some way to make peace with his new bride. When he turned to talk, Subena was asleep.

Not a hint of a snore escaped her luscious lips and her face looked so peaceful she could easily be mistaken for an angel. Had he not watched her sleep the night before, he would suspect she faked her slumber. As gently as he could, he lowered her upper body onto the seat and placed his cloak underneath her head.

After several kilometers, she sat up. Kamber hurried his words. "It's going to be a long ride. Can we declare a truce? Please."

Distrust flashed in her silvery eyes. His charm had never failed with any female before, especially when he was sincere. And he was very sincere.

"Look," he tried again, wishing he had a more eloquent opening. "I've never lied to you. I suspect we're both incapable of lying." The truth of his statement surprised him, but he needed to address the current situation before pondering the meaning. "I mean it when I say I want to start over."

"Do you?" She didn't look like she believed him, but how could he tell? He knew so little about her.

"I do. I know you love your country as I love mine. Let's make this marriage work so the treaty can work."

When her face softened, he pushed his advantage. "I'd like to give you a real wedding gift. Would you like a necklace to match the dress you wear so beautifully?"

"No thank you." The softness disappeared from her expression. "The dress is quite enough."

He stared, knowing he'd botched another truce. What female didn't want jewelry?

"Okay, no necklace." She must like something. What?

He remembered the joy in her face when she'd rubbed Pollo behind his ears. "How about an equestor? Would you like a colt for your bridal gift?"

She rewarded him with a real smile—the first he'd earned outside the bedroom. He felt quite bedazzled. How bad could it be when he had a wife who preferred equestors to jewels?

"Truly?" she whispered.

"Truly." He grinned, exuberant that he'd finally done something right.

"But equestors are so rare."

He shrugged. "The next colt is yours."

"Thank you." She wrapped her arms across her chest and pretended to sleep.

A few seconds later, her eyes darted open. "Where did... Where did you get that blood?"

He grinned, not quite ready to share that secret. "In time, I will show you." She had reacted to his treat, but that didn't mean she was ready to accept Gatslian ways. At times, he felt uncomfortable himself.

"Fine, be that way." She twisted her head and looked out the window. His bride was rather cute when she got prickly.

She turned her gaze toward him again, no trace of hostility in her serene face. "Why don't you wear crystals?"

He huffed out a breath. Just when they were making progress, she wanted to talk about their differences.

"They..." He hesitated, searching for the right words. "Crystals are nothing more than pretty glass to us."

He chanced a look at her reaction, pleased to see no judgment in her eyes.

"I don't understand. I thought all álfar needed the magic of the earth's sun. Even though you're Dök...eh, Gatslain, you're still álfar, right?"

He grinned. His wife had grown up in Mydrias, but appeared to have no prejudice, even if she found the terms uncomfortable.

"Dökkálfar is not a dirty word, Subena."

The imp grinned at him. "If you say so."

Kamber found himself smiling back. "I say so."

The smile vanished from her beautiful face. "But the Dökkálfar caused our banishment from earth. Every race of álfar suffered because of *your* actions."

He put his arms behind his head and leaned against the carriage wall. Having an honest wife had its drawbacks. "Yes, we've heard that legend in Gatsle, too. But dark doesn't equate to evil. You're a logical being, Bena. Think about what you've heard. We were banished because of Dökkálfar tricks? For creating skin rashes and causing bad dreams? Does that make sense to you? The punishment doesn't fit the crime."

Instead of arguing, she looked thoughtful. "Then why are we on Lanatus?"

He didn't allow his gaze to waiver. "I don't know."

She sighed. "Elfin arrival on Lanatus was probably celebrated by Gatslians. This planet doesn't seem to pose a threat to the *Dökkálfar*."

He smiled but the gesture felt fake. "The planet does pose a threat to us. Just a different sort. Our ancestors from earth lived underground, in caves. The sun had no effect on our people. Instead, the earth's core provided our magic."

"And is there no substitute on Lanatus?"

"No. Not for the earth's core. But we've discovered a substance that provides the life essence our magic needs. An essence that doesn't cause damage like your crystals do."

Her body went still. He sensed the anger flare. "I know the crystals cause damage, but what options... Wait, what provides the life essence for Gatslians? Blood?"

To her credit, no look of revulsion crossed her face. After her experience with the blood, he shouldn't have been surprised, but he felt astonished all the same. Partaking in substance deemed inappropriate usually didn't preclude judgment. His respect for Subena grew.

Probably a mistake to feel anything other than lust. A lady of Subena's character would ultimately reject him.

"And is your...substance plentiful?" she asked. "You don't fear a crisis like the crystal shortage threatening Mydrias?"

He puffed out his cheeks, exhaling slowly while he tried to determine what to reveal and what to hide. "We already face a shortage—but it's not yet a crisis."

"Yet you do nothing?"

Every part of his body bristled. She displayed a hint of the judgment he'd expected sooner. "I know you think I don't *work*, but I've been trying to find a way to increase the supply. I'll share my secret when I make some progress."

Would he do that? Could he share anything with an uppity Mydrian? "And what of you, princess? Where is your crystal?"

She glanced at her neck, seeming surprised the glass didn't hang there. "I am not as...reliant...upon the crystal as other Mydrians. I have rarely needed its power. As you know, I am...different."

She said no more but her gaze met his. Something had closed and he could no longer peer into her mind. He yearned to know what could possibly account for her insecurities, but even a dunce like him knew this was not the time to probe.

The carriage moved swiftly across the countryside, the innate object seeming to recognize the need for speed. The need to end the intimacy.

Neither spoke. Kamber's heightened senses reacted to Subena's every move. No matter what passed between them, his physical need of her would not abate. He scarcely restrained from reaching for her, but he vowed to regain her trust before he touched her again. Without trust, she would resent her own responses and dislike him even more.

Resistance proved more difficult than he'd expected. Her scent was enough to make him hard. Whenever she sighed, he'd notice her lips and want to devour them. If he ventured a glance in her direction, the nipples pressing against the velvet softness of her dress increased his desire. His arousal had become torture by the time they finally reached the inn.

He'd barely mastered his libido when the innkeeper led them to their rooms. His control crashed and burned when she asked for a bath.

"Ah, damn."

"Did I say something wrong?" she asked, seeming oblivious to the images her request conjured in his overheated head—both of them. "Is water scarce here?"

He shook his head. How could a female so intelligent and politically savvy be so naïve about men?

Chapter Fourteen

Subena sensed Kamber watching her. As her husband, she supposed he had that right, but she wanted to be alone. She needed to think about the blood, about the possibility the Dökkálfar weren't responsible for the elfin exodus from earth.

And Taslin.

She'd hoped to mull over the duke's presence in the carriage, but Kamber's proximity precluded rational thought. Taslin wouldn't have volunteered to escort her to Gatsle if he didn't still care. He would've had to request special permission from the Council. That was not a spur-of-the-moment action.

That was good, wasn't it? Legally, she was Kamber's wife. She had no intention of being unfaithful—not before the marriage was dissolved—but Taslin's presence would be a comfort. A friend would make her year in Gatsle easier to bear.

Maybe her feelings for Taslin ran deeper than she realized. She needed to tread carefully until she could decipher her emotions. She couldn't risk hurting him again.

Kamber didn't make a sound, but his presence distracted her thoughts. The Dökkálfar made it impossible to think. "Go away."

He approached the tub, as usual totally disregarding her wishes. She did her best to cover herself.

"Let me wash your back, love."

"Said the spider to the fly. No."

He took the washcloth, ignoring her reply, and massaged the back of her neck with the cloth. "I promised to be honest, can you handle it?"

"Not now. Go away." She hoped he wouldn't heed her words. If he touched her...

She turned to glare. The breast her arm covered slipped free.

"Thanks for the view, my sweet. Is that an invitation?"

She splashed water at him and tried to think of something vile to say, but he removed the cloth from her neck and slid it down further.

He chuckled, deep and throaty. "As I was saying before you distracted me, my perfect little morsel..." He kissed her hard and she lost her breath. "I believe I was talking about being honest. I want to wash your back, but I want to wash the rest of you, too. Then...I have other plans."

* * * *

Kamber didn't want to leave the arms of his bride but he carefully removed her arm and crept out of bed. After dressing, he went in search of Remington.

His old pal laughed when he saw him. "I told you it wouldn't be so hard." Remington shook as he chuckled. "Or maybe it was so hard."

Kamber felt his grin clear down to his boots. "I need a favor."

After he made arrangements for additional equestors, he sent the caravan on its way. No one but Remington and the innkeeper had any idea the newlyweds weren't in the carriage.

Kamber crawled back into the downy bed, inhaling the pleasant smell of jasmine and the musty smells of the night's lovemaking. After a short nap, he proceeded to slowly and methodically wake his little wife. His plans for breakfast in bed evolved into lunch in the inn's great room as morning passed all too quickly.

Over fresh dumplings, cooked in tart applesauce, he talked to Subena about the upcoming trip. "We should arrive in three days, unless we have another, um...delay." He waggled his brows.

She punched his arm. "Tell me about your home."

"Our home," he corrected. "I think you will like Vomont Castle." He leaned over to kiss her nose. "It has several wings and it's filled with paintings and antiques. There are many places to hide." He smiled suggestively. "I think every ancestor added to the labyrinth of secret passages. As far as I know, I'm the only person who knows where most of them are. My father was definitely never interested."

"Why not?"

Kamber allowed the familiar anger to consume him, but only for a second. "I don't know. When I was ten, my grandfather showed me a couple of trap doors that led into the passages and I was hooked." He laughed at the memory. "Barkley and I spent most of our youth looking for entrances to other passages. Ronan seems to be following in our footsteps. According to folklore, an underground tunnel runs from the castle grounds to the open fields. I never found the fabled tunnel, but I did find some other hidden passageways. If you're very, very good I'll show them to you." He reached over and ran his index finger along the edge of her jaw.

"No thanks." Her face turned deathly pale.

"What's wrong?"

"I...I don't like tunnels." Her hands started to shake.

He took her tiny fingers and pressed them in his palms, trying to still her trembling. "Want to tell me about it?"

"No."

He smiled and brought her hands to his lips. "Was it the maze?"

"Who told you about that?" She pulled her hands away and sat on them. "My sisters, of course." She looked embarrassed.

"Subena, it's okay. Everyone has at least one phobia."

"Really. What's yours?"

"Oh, no. I'm not giving you that much ammunition. I'm just relieved you're not perfect. Flawed sod that I am, I'm already undeserving."

She didn't respond to his teasing.

"I'm sorry," he said. "I shouldn't have mentioned it." He picked a silken strand from her shoulder and idly rubbed it against his check.

She didn't seem to notice. "My parents had just cut the hedges into patterns," she whispered. "I've never liked dark places so I refused to go in the maze. The next day, Jalakin called me a baby, so I ran into it, just to prove him wrong."

Kamber felt his lips curve. So she'd been stubborn, even as a small nymph.

"The Sun-Star had almost set and I panicked." Subena had a faraway look in her eyes.

"What happened?"

"I got lost. I ran wildly, not able to see where I was going. My mother had several potted urns scattered throughout the hedges and I bumped into one. It toppled over and the dirt spilled on me. It was really nothing, but I thought I was being buried alive."

He pulled her into his lap and held her, understanding the horror a child would feel. Being buried alive was one of the few ways to kill their kind.

His touch seemed to vanquish her horror of the past. Until she realized she'd let him comfort her and wiggled out of his embrace. "Behave yourself."

"Why? You weren't so prickly last night."

"About that." She pulled her long tresses into her hand and twisted them into a knot. "I was drunk last night. The marriage has been consummated. We can't do that again."

He sucked in his lips to keep from grinning. Being inexperienced, she didn't understand she suggested the impossible. "Why not?"

Before she replied, a guard stumbled into the room. He fell to his knees, wheezing and coughing.

"Is he all right?" Subena whispered.

"Breathe, man," Kamber ordered.

After a few seconds, the young soldier sucked in a mouthful of air and rasped, "They attacked us. Remington sent me to warn you. I came as fast as I could."

While he quizzed the lad, he watched Subena march across the room. Able to hear both conversations, he heard her order the innkeeper to send a runner for reinforcements. He said a silent prayer of gratitude for his sensible bride.

Kamber didn't wait for more details. He raced from the dining hall to the stables and led his equestor out of the stall. When he reached for his saddle, he felt a hand on his shoulder. How had Subena reached him so quickly? Not possible. *Unless...*

"I know your first thoughts are for Remington's safety," she said, "but think about what you're doing. You can't challenge the attackers alone. I don't especially like you, but I'm not quite ready to be a widow yet."

"Not quite, huh?" Despite his urgency, her words stung.

He knew she was right about pursing the attackers solo, but he wasn't in the mood for logic. It didn't apply when Remington faced danger. "Remmy's my friend. I'm going."

"I like Remmy, too, but we need a plan. My friend, Duke Taslin, is also missing."

Anger blinded his reason. *How dare she mention that popinjay?* "Duke Taslin? Is that all you care about?"

"No, I..."

He didn't wait for her response. He hopped astride Pollo and rode.

After a few minutes, he slowed the equestor to a trot. Subena had been right. He needed a plan. He didn't know the area and he had only a small weapon. What if the attack had been a ploy to get to her? He'd left her alone.

He'd been a damn fool.

No. Only Remington and a couple of guards knew Subena remained at the inn. He'd look for the carriage.

Kamber wrestled with his decision, but continued down the road the caravan had taken. Who would attack them? And why?

Maybe someone didn't want the treaty to work, although that didn't make sense. The only person who'd benefit by having the treaty canceled would be Lord Creshin. While the warlord might go after Mydrias, he'd never be foolish enough to risk the ire of Gatsle. At any rate, Creshin wouldn't attack him personally.

Rekita was furious about his marriage, but she couldn't pull off an attack of this magnitude. Could she?

He saw three riders in the distance and reined in Pollo. Kamber waited, prepared to attack, ready to retreat. He could take on three swordsmen, but there might be more men behind the ones riding toward him. He wouldn't risk that.

He backed Pollo into the tree line, ready to take the animal off the trail. He halted. There was something familiar about the large bulk of one of the riders.

A weight lifted from his shoulders. "Remington!" He spurred his equestor forward, thanking the God of the Mountain.

He leaped off and slapped the big guy on the thigh, spooking Remington's mount. Only his skill kept the animal from bolting.

"I've never been so glad to see an ornery, cantankerous, old cur in my life. What the devil happened?" Kamber asked.

"A sniper was hidden in the trees. He killed the carriage driver. Once the driver fell, we were ambushed from both sides of the road. Everything got crazy after that. I'm guessing there were about twenty or twenty-five masked men. We regrouped, but we were only able to get off a couple of shots before half of the attackers fled north. The rest went south."

"Both directions?" Kamber asked.

Remington nodded. "We tried to follow the ones headed this way, but we lost them in the glen. Then we rode back to the carriage and found it destroyed. We have to face facts, laddie. You and the princess were the obvious targets. You should have been in that carriage." Remington's head popped up. "Kamber, where *is* the princess?"

"She's fine. How many men did we lose?"

"The driver and two of our guards. One of the Mydrian escorts was also killed."

"And Reklaw?" Kamber spat as he said the name.

"I'm not sure what happened to him. The guards scattered when the sniper fired, but I think he rode with the team toward the south. Hell, he was the least of my worries. I'm sure we killed a couple of the attackers, but when we got back, the bodies were gone. Whoever did this, didn't want us to know who they were. Where did you say the princess was?"

"She's safe. I left her at the inn."

Remington uttered a long groan that sounded more like a bear's roar. "And you think she'll stay put?"

Kamber felt itchy. He growled before mounting his equestor without another word.

"God's breath, Kamber. Sometimes I think all your brains are in your balls."

Genia Avers

Chapter Fifteen

Subena paced the length of the inn's great room before she turned and repeated her march in the opposite direction. "I'm going to kill him."

She stopped moving. Since her engagement, it seemed like she'd done little else except pace. They couldn't leave the inn until the reinforcements arrived. Hopefully, that wouldn't be long because she felt useless standing around. Reinforcements wouldn't have to travel far. They were a long way from Vomont Palace, thus still close to the Mydrian border. Thank Bockle, Rothart had left a large contingent to protect her country from Creshin's warships. A few soldiers from that detachment wouldn't be missed.

A commotion in the courtyard disrupted her pacing. She hurried toward the noise.

"Please stay inside, my lady!" the innkeeper yelled. "Let me send someone to see who it is. Princess, please!"

She ignored the plea and rushed to the courtyard, stopping in her tracks as the riders approached. When Kamber dismounted, she ran to him, throwing her arms around his wide, road-stained shoulders.

Her relief lasted only seconds. The fury of being left behind to worry about his rash actions returned. She stepped back and whacked him across the arm.

"Damn, Bena. Why'd you do that?"

"Because you're a monumental idiot. You ride off alone. Leaving me here *alone*. Who knows what could have happened. To either of us. Your one redeeming quality was *supposed* to be your military prowess and you act like you don't know the first thing about strategy."

"She has a point." Remington chuckled.

"Get your things," Kamber ordered. "We're leaving."

"The hell we are." Her nostrils flared. She took a deep breath. She couldn't unleash her fury at Kamber in front of the guards. "We *have* to wait for the reinforcements from Mydrias. You may choose to be rash with your life, but I won't." She whirled, knowing she couldn't look at him any longer without really losing her temper.

As she started up the steps to her room, she heard Remington chide the prince, "I couldn't have said it better myself."

* * * *

Subena paced across the room once more. When she became aware of her action, she stilled, determined to contain her emotion, and save the inn's carpet. Her resolve lasted for all of five seconds.

It would be useless to talk to Kamber. She'd speak with Remington. Suggest that they take alternate routes to avoid another ambush. She suspected the big male would already have come to the same conclusion.

Thank Bockle there would be no more time for spending lazy days at inns on this journey. When Kamber's mouth was on her body, it was impossible to remember he was a barbarian at heart. Or that she had a brain. Or that she really didn't want her husband to touch her.

"Taslin." She hadn't asked if he was safe.

She rushed from her room and toward the great hall. Remington would know about the duke's whereabouts.

She collided with Kamber halfway down the stairs. "Going somewhere?"

"I'm looking for Remington."

"Why?"

She hesitated. "I wanted to ask about Taslin. Is he safe?" She hadn't expected to see the duke again until her year in Gatsle had ended, but some stroke of providence had made him her escort. Things might not be the same, but she really needed to know her friend hadn't been harmed.

"And why would you ask Remington and not me?"

She blinked, not sure of the reason. "Is Taslin okay?"

Kamber's jaw hardened and his lips formed a straight line. "You refer to Reklaw?"

"That's what I said. Taslin."

"You refer to the coward who didn't stick around to defend the carriage. Your carriage?"

"Taslin isn't a coward."

Kamber grabbed her chin with his free hand, squeezing it with gentle pleasure. "You're awfully quick to defend him, Bena. I'm going to assume your concern doesn't hide tender feelings for the arrogant ass. Not that you need to worry. Snakes usually manage to safely slither away."

Surely Kamber couldn't be jealous? Before she could protest, Kamber pressed his lips against hers. The kiss was harsh and demanding, almost hostile, but his body radiated raw sensuality. When he released her and walked away, Subena hung onto the railing to support her weakened knees.

She shook her head, trying to reconcile Kamber's words and actions. Taslin wouldn't leave the carriage during an attack—her husband had to be mistaken.

Genia Avers

Chapter Sixteen

Subena shifted in her seat and swore she'd never ride in another carriage. They'd driven toward Gatsle for six long days in the newly acquired coach. The dust was the worst, had been since they left as soon as reinforcements arrived. Odd she'd notice the dirt given the trip had been laden with apprehension and discomfort.

She'd worried about Taslin until they received word, via messenger, that he and a contingent of Gatslian guards had reached the midway checkpoint. The Duke had met the caravan there.

"Dungweed," Kamber murmured upon hearing Taslin's story about chasing a wayward attacker toward Gatsle.

The duke ignored the prince in his customary diplomatic way. Not unexpected behavior from a warrior who'd spent a lifetime fighting, but Taslin's behavior proved puzzling. He'd pulled a dagger from his pocket bearing Creshin's shield and tossed it to Kamber. Subena didn't want to believe he'd tossed the knife *at* Kamber. "He got away, but dropped this."

"Likely story," her spouse snarled when he'd returned to their coach. "And no one to corroborate it. Why didn't he stay and protect you? He didn't know you weren't in the coach."

Yes he did. Subena wasn't about to say that. Taslin had to know she wasn't in the coach, otherwise, he would never have left her alone.

"You mean like *you* stayed to protect me at the inn?" she challenged.

Kamber snorted and left the carriage. He'd ridden Pollo for the remainder of the day.

Her defense of Taslin drove a wedge into their honeymoon truce. She didn't care. Much.

Kamber had been frosty during the days and aggressive during the nights. She'd sworn she wouldn't be seduced, but when her husband finally came to bed, after spending most of his night on watch or scouting the roads the coach would take the following day, she welcomed his embrace. Each morning she awoke to a smirking Kamber—and more vibrant tinting on the inn room walls. She'd suspected their sexual escapades had something to do with the explosion of color, but she'd never heard of such a thing. And didn't dare ask Kamber.

After she searched for her clothing, she went in search of a paintbrush. Once the walls were white again, she'd get into the coach.

She stared out the carriage window, hoping they'd arrive in Gatsle soon. Kamber reached for her hand again. She let him encircle her fingers. His conversation might annoy her, but his touch was comforting.

"We'll be there soon."

She doubted it. Remington had heeded her advice, taking detours and retracing the route to make sure no one followed. Because of the extra miles, they were now on day six of their four-day journey.

* * * *

Damn. Kamber banged his head against the back of the carriage wall.

The sweet relief of being home dissipated. Beyond the snarled branches of the centuries old trees, a raven-haired hellion waited for their coach. Rekita.

He'd meant to tell Subena, explain about his former mistress and her scary temper, but he'd spent most of his days scouting to make sure no threats loomed in wait of their convoy. When he took the rare moment to ride inside the coach with his wife, he hadn't risked spoiling the mood by discussing a fling gone bad. He thought he knew a lot about the fairer sex, but after only one week with his wife, he felt

132

certain he knew absolutely nothing. Even in his ignorance, he knew their tentative truce was too fragile for a discussion about an old girlfriend. Now, his procrastination had come home to haunt him.

Pushing worries about Rekita from his mind, he glanced at his wife and his insides took a strange trip. Pride wasn't something he experienced often, but he was proud of Subena. He could tell she was nervous, but he doubted anyone else would guess. She looked stunning, regal. His people would see only her surreal beauty and the haughty lift of her chin. He saw the subtle way she bit at her lower lip. How could a creature so beautiful and so accomplished be so insecure?

Kamber reached over and took her hand. She flashed a look he interpreted as appreciation. Once she realized what she'd done, she jerked her hand out of his clasp.

I will fix that.

The carriage door opened. Kamber wrapped an arm around Subena's shoulder and placed his lips firmly and lingeringly on her neck. He hoped Rekita would see his gesture and take the hint, but mostly he wanted to kiss his wife.

Subena pulled away. "Must you molest me every time there's a crowd? Are you some kind of exhibitionist?"

His lips curved upward. Strange that he should find her snarky nature so entertaining.

He tightened his grip on her arm. Rekita had made her way to the carriage steps wearing a top that revealed most of her breasts and exposed all of her midriff. Her skirt hung low on her hips, barely concealing her pubic area. He wished she would cover herself.

He tried to hold onto his wife's arm as they descended the carriage steps, but the passage was too narrow. Remington held out his hand to help Subena. Kamber had no choice but to step back to let his bride descend first. After she reached the bottom step, she and Remington kept walking.

The moment his foot touched the ground, Rekita pushed around Subena and jumped on him. "Kam, darling! You've come back to me." She wrapped her arms around his neck and interlocked her long legs behind his hips.

Shock rendered him motionless. The crowd noise hushed. Everyone stared.

"Get off me," he hissed. Heads began to look the other way.

Subena turned toward him. He watched her face transition from shock-to-rage-to-disgust.

"Subena, wait." He tried to push past Rekita, but the she-devil gripped him tighter and planted kisses all over his face. His parents and brothers stared, mouths gaping. No one, except Rekita, moved.

He looked toward Remington. "A little help here."

His old pal shrugged. His you-got-into-this, you-get-out-of-it expression held more censure than sympathy.

Subena hadn't moved. She just glared.

"Subena, my love," his father's voice boomed. "I'm so glad you're safely here."

His bride jumped. A mask descended over her face. Only Kamber saw the murderous look she cast before she turned her head toward his father. His mother flashed him an equally deadly stare.

While he struggled to push Rekita away, he heard his wife thank Remington, and caught a glimpse of her when she took Rothart's proffered arm. "The palace is beautiful, sire. I can't wait to see the inside."

His father took Subena's hand and brought it to his mouth. "The palace, and all of Gatsle for that matter, pales in comparison to your beauty."

Kamber's mouth dropped open. He'd never seen Rothart act so diplomatic. Or seem so enamored.

He didn't see what happened next because Rekita freed herself of his vicelike grip and hopped astride him again. He tilted his head to see Tam, his youngest brother, tug on Subena's skirt. His wife extracted her hand from the king's grasp and squatted down to shake the little guy's hand.

"Tell me King Rothart, who is this handsome elf?"

His brother giggled, "I'm Tam. I'm five. You're pretty."

"Let go of me, Rekita," Kamber hissed, hoping no one else could hear. "Or so help me, I'll have you locked up."

"Sounds kinky." The she-devil's reply echoed for all to hear.

"Princess Subena." Rothart spoke louder and bowed with a flourish—more animated than Kamber had ever seen him. "May I present my youngest and oh-so-important son?" The king winked at Subena, before he glowered at Kamber over her shoulder. "He's also my well-mannered son."

Kamber gave Rekita another shove, this one less gentle than the first. When she clung to him, he peered over her shoulder, hoping Subena would see his disgust over the she-cat's behavior.

"I'm honored sir." Subena's eyes sparkled at Tam. "I'm glad you're a prince, Master Tam. I was most afraid that you might be a pirate."

The boy giggled and grabbed her hand.

Blast. He knew it couldn't be good that his wife acted like he didn't exist. He shoved Rekita again, but the witch had a steadier grip than most of his swordsmen.

The king held out his arm for Subena's other hand, effectively shielding her from Rekita's sideshow. The threesome marched toward the palace. Young Tam twisted his little neck to stare at Rekita, who remained plastered against Kamber despite attempts to eradicate the vile female from his body. "You're much prettier than *her*," Tam yelled. "If I were Kamber, I'd wrestle with you."

The boy giggled. Subena withdrew her hand to tussle his spiky hair. As they walked away, she put her arm around the little tyke and never once looked back.

Rekita had stopped kissing him to stare after Tam and Subena, but the blasted harridan still clung to him. "Dammit, Rekita. I said let go."

He yanked his arms away and she fell to the ground with a thud.

"Geesh." Rekita smoothed her hands over her tight skirt. "I'm guessing your surly attitude must be due to sexual frustration. Did the ice maiden actually freeze your pecker?"

"Get away from me before I have you arrested."

She moved aside, a smirk on her face. He jumped up, but Subena and his family had disappeared into the castle. He glared at Rekita. "Don't ever do that again."

"Oh, boo hoo. We both know you won't do anything." She tugged at her revealing top, giving him a glimpse of both nipples. He threw his cloak over her and stomped away from her, toward the castle.

Kamber passed Taslin, who leaned against a tree, idly playing with a twig. "Does Subena also get to keep a pet?"

Kamber wanted to ram a fist into the buffoon's gut. With effort, he willed his arm to remain at his side, knowing he couldn't risk another spectacle.

"Who would have guessed?" The damn duke laughed. "I certainly didn't expect entertainment in this backward hellhole."

Chapter Seventeen

Subena knew, despite everything, that she belonged in the big drafty castle. It was damp. It was dark. It was ancient.

And she loved it.

Even the theatrics Kamber displayed with *that creature* didn't diminish her fascination with the old building. The structures in Mydrias were shiny and modern—and very predictable. Her country had nothing like Vomont Castle with its air of mystery. The fortress ranked as one of the oldest buildings on the planet. There were rumors of ancestral journals hidden within its walls. She couldn't wait to explore every wing.

"Miss. You follow." A maid tapped long fingers on the railing.

Subena stifled a groan. When she'd told Queen Winsome she could find her own way, she'd planned to wander through the corridors instead of going directly to her room.

"You best hurry. The family 'ess holding dinner while you fresh up." The servant's dress was an ugly brown, but the attire didn't detract from her striking features. Her black hair glimmered, making the gown she wore look even more dismal.

"You don't have to wait on me," Subena replied.

"Waiting on you is my job."

Subena frowned. "Thank you, but if you just tell me where the room is, I'm sure I can find it."

"Dis' way, please. You want to get me in trouble?" Without waiting for an answer, the bossy female spun and marched up the remaining stairs. She headed down a long hallway, only glancing over her shoulder once to ensure Subena followed.

"She doesn't act like a servant," Subena muttered. She would dismiss her—politely of course.

When she reached the doorway to her chambers, the sight that greeted her made her forget her intentions. The room contrasted sharply with the rest of the castle. A skylight in the gilt ceiling reflected light from the Sun-Star, intensifying the spectrum and giving the illusion she'd landed on a cloud. The furnishings were sleek and luxurious, yet simple enough to stop just short of being ornate. Beauty surrounded her.

Yet she felt completely alone.

"Miss?"

Subena blinked, remembering the black-haired maid who still hovered. The female pointed toward a smaller door. "You can wash in there." To Subena's annoyance, she curtsied. "I'll take care of your things while you wash, miss."

"Just leave the trunks by the bed, please. I'll take care of them later. And thank you."

Subena hurried into the private room and locked the door. She ran a cloth over her face, wishing she'd more time to study the plumbing; she'd read it worked with ancient, but effective, locking mechanisms. With difficulty, she resisted the urge to look under the cabinets.

After unsuccessfully trying to get a comb through her hair, she wove it into a braid and hurried from the powder room, glad to see the nosy black-haired creature had gone. "Thank Bockle."

The family had already gathered in the great hall when she'd descended the grand staircase. A stunning male with thick black hair and emerald eyes stepped forward to greet her. The young male was a shy copy of Kamber.

"It's a pleasure to meet you, Subena."

His shoulders weren't nearly as wide as those of his big brother, but the mesmerizing eyes and the crooked grin were an exact duplicate of her scoundrel husband. Except there was an air of innocence about the younger vision she found appealing. Subena experienced an instant connection.

"I'm Ronan." As he bowed and held out his arm, his tunic gaped, exposing a tiny birthmark on his chest.

Subena gasped. *No.*

What had she done?

"Are you all right?" Ronan's eyes exposed his emotion—concern.

"I'm...I'm fine." Was she? Subena didn't think so, but she'd had years of experience faking it and immediately shifted into public mode.

"Kamber has told me so much about you, but I expected you to be..."

"Younger?" Ronan prompted. "I'm not surprised. Kam treats me like I'm barely out of the nursery, yet I believe I'm older than you." His dazzling smile sent Subena's brain into a tailspin.

Was he... the one? From her vision?

"I think you know everyone else," he said, pulling out a chair for her.

Which was good, because she really needed to sit down. Ronan pulled out the adjoining seat, his nearness creating a sense of confusion.

Tam wrestled free from Queen Winsome's arms and planted his little body in the chair. "I get to sit by Bena." He grabbed her hand and kissed it. Then he pushed against Ronan's arm. "Move."

Ronan shrugged, but smiled as he took a seat near Barkley and Mettia. Subena thought he looked disappointed. Relief washed over her. He and his disturbing birthmark unsettled her completely.

Everyone talked at once. Subena nodded, following very little of the conversation. She'd met Kamber's second brother and his wife at the wedding party so fortunately she didn't have to remember names. She couldn't remember ever being so rattled.

She sensed Ronan had the same sweet soul as the male in her vision. She'd married the wrong elf.

She assumed the vacant seat next to her belonged to her wayward husband. No big surprise he hadn't shown. Rothart's absence, however, did puzzle her.

She heard angry voices. Her dinner companions continued to chat, as if they'd heard nothing. Subena thought Winsome's jaw looked pinched when she asked Barkley to pass the bread.

"Kamber's in big trouble," young Tam announced in a serious voice. Subena resisted the urge to giggle, but Barkley lost his composure and spat out his wine. Mettia chuckled. The tension evaporated.

King Rothart joined the group a short time later, his face an unnatural shade of red. "Pray forgive my tardiness." He didn't sound like he cared about forgiveness. He slumped into his chair. No one said a word.

A few tense seconds later, Kamber skulked into the room. He sat down without looking at anyone.

Tam yelled across the table, "Did you get put in time-out?"

Even Rothart smiled. Conversation resumed.

As apple dumplings were served, the king proposed a toast. "To Subena." He smiled and everyone lifted their glasses. "I'm delighted you're here, my dear. I applaud your wisdom in authoring the treaty." He glanced at his eldest son. "I'm sure you could have gotten a better deal but we've gotten the bargain of a lifetime."

"But she got me!" Tam stood in his chair so he could hug her.

She pulled the young boy into her lap as the king continued, "I'm off to see Lord Creshin tomorrow. I hope my offer of the Quokon Islands will appease his thirst for war and peace can reign once more. I believe Creshin wanted Mydrias for the spice, cilosange. Our kind has no use for the stuff, but Creshin loves the weed. Quokon has trace supplies of it and the island should appease his pride."

Subena forgave Rothart for all his rumored flaws. Maybe she could talk the king into letting her attend the meeting with Lord Creshin. For all his notoriety, she'd never seen the warlord.

"Father," Ronan interjected, "did you expect me to come with you?"

Rothart lifted his glass and stared at his wine. He didn't reply for several seconds. "I thought you were keen on finding the escape tunnel. Until we're assured of peace, I'd feel better knowing our enemies cannot slip into the palace."

Subena sensed an underlying tension to Rothart's words. What really spooked the king?

"As you wish." Ronan seemed disproportionally disappointed. Subena tried to imagine how it must feel to actually yearn for adult responsibility. She'd worn her mantle of reliability for so many years, she only wished to be a child again. For all her mother's faults, meals in Mydrias were pleasant affairs.

"Tell me about that tunnel," she said, hoping to divert Ronan's disappointment.

"There's a legend that says a tunnel under the castle grounds leads to the outside wall," Ronan explained. "I've been looking for it for a long time."

"If anyone can find it, son, it will be you." The king seemed to change moods, smiling indulgently at his second youngest son. "Perhaps Kamber can spare an hour or two to search with you." Rothart glared at his oldest son, making it clear that Kamber had better find time.

"I'm sure he has better things to do." Ronan crossed his arms over his chest.

"Maybe I can help you." Subena smiled, wondering what possessed her to speak. She hated tunnels.

"That'd be great." Ronan's smile made her feel suddenly flustered.

"I'm not sure that's such a good idea," Kamber said, speaking for the first time since the meal started.

"I think it's a great idea," she countered. Personally, she didn't think it was even close to being a good idea, but roaming around the countryside seemed infinitely better than letting her husband order her around. Maybe he could use the time to rendezvous with the Reck-ass female.

"It's not safe," Kamber said quietly.

Ronan snorted. "She won't exactly be unprotected."

"You were attacked, Subena."

She swallowed hard, knowing she needed to contain her temper. "You mean *your* carriage was attacked. I'm sure Ronan can protect me."

"That's not—"

"Silence," the king interrupted. Under normal circumstances, Subena might have felt sorry for her husband. Clearly no father-son bond existed between Kamber and Rothart. But Rekita had destroyed normal for her. As well as any sympathy she might have felt for her spouse.

"No one would dare harm her on Gatsle land, Kamber. Besides..." Rothart paused to smile at her. "Any female who can ride Pollo can clearly take care of herself. I wouldn't be at all surprised if Subena and Ronan are able to find the secret passageway, whereas you and Barkley have failed."

"You rode Pollo?" Ronan stared, eyes wide. "I'm impressed."

Subena nodded, not wanting to bask in the glow of his praise but basking all the same. Kamber had let her ride the steed twice during the trip. She suspected he'd only offered because he thought Pollo would dump her in the dirt. Instead, the equestor had responded beautifully to her slight commands.

"Father, why do you continue to encourage this folly?" Barkley wiped his mouth and threw down his napkin. "We've searched every inch of the castle grounds. If ever there was a tunnel, it has long since caved in. Or worse, will cave in. Someone's going to get hurt."

Weird. Both Kamber and Barkley seemed to resent their father whereas Ronan and Tam clearly idolized him.

"Subena, how about tomorrow?" Ronan asked. She sensed eagerness beneath his cool question. She hoped his eagerness to find the tunnels spurred his invitation and not some developing crush. If Ronan was the male in her vision, she'd met him too late. She'd have to discourage anything other than brotherly affection.

"Sure." On second thought, was a crush really so bad? Ronan appeared to have all of Kamber's good traits and none of his bad. "I'll help you look for the opening, but I'm not going in any tunnel."

Ronan smiled triumphantly, but the tension intertwined between the king and his two oldest sons continued to hang over the table. Winsome fidgeted.

"Subena, I understand Duke Taslin is a friend of yours." The queen's voice surprised her. She hadn't spoken during the entire meal. "This first supper was family only, but he is welcome to join us for future meals."

"No." Kamber growled. "He is not welcome."

Winsome smiled at Subena. "Gatslian men are notoriously jealous."

The king turned red-faced. "If Winsome says the duke is welcome, he's welcome. Have you no manners, Kamber?" He glowered at his oldest son.

Kamber rose and left the room.

Genia Avers

Chapter Eighteen

Back in her suite, Subena opened the doors to an adjoining room. Given the size of the bed, she guessed the space belonged to Kamber. She slammed the door, relieved to find a lock. Her first night in Gatsle would be spent alone—not exactly as she'd planned, but after the coach scene, what choice did she have?

She rubbed her temples, trying to erase the image of Rekita's lips on Kamber. The fury she'd suppressed since her arrival came roaring back, giving her a massive headache. "How could he?"

And why did she care so much? She was leaving in a year, right?

She picked up one of the delicate china cups she'd brought for Queen Winsome, intending to hurl it at the wall. *What am I doing?*

Controlling her temper hadn't been a difficult task before Kamber, but now she seemed to be angry all the time. She'd almost destroyed an intricate work of art in a fit of pique. Her rage cooled, but she refused to listen to the nagging voice on the edge of her subconscious.

Kamber did try to extract himself from her grasp.

"He didn't try hard enough." She reveled in her fury, not ready to admit something about the scene she'd witnessed didn't ring true. The doxy from Kamber's past had latched onto him in front of everyone. There had to be a reason she thought her behavior would be acceptable.

If she really wanted to go home, why didn't she just go? After meeting Rothart, Subena felt certain that the king

145

would give Mydrias enough quartz to support the populace—whether she stayed or not. Bockle, she could even save face after the attack, using safety as an excuse.

"No." She would not admit defeat so easily. And her resolve had nothing to do with the chemistry drawing her to Kamber. She'd stay busy and forget the gigolo she'd married. There was much she wanted to accomplish. The mystery of the blood beckoned. The temptation to find a replacement for Mydrian crystals was too powerful to ignore. And she'd stay two years if it meant she might stumble across the ancestors' texts.

A knock echoed on the other side of the bolted door. "Subena, open this."

"Go away."

"Unless you open the door, I'll just keep yelling. If you don't care if the entire palace hears our conversation, neither do I."

"I don't care what anyone hears. I didn't do anything wrong."

Kamber pounded on the door again.

"Damn, him," she whispered. She did care.

She unlocked the bolt. He almost fell into the room.

She backed away when he reached for her. "Don't you dare touch me."

"I did try to get away from her."

"How did you…"

He grinned. "If you're going to talk to yourself, you might want to remember that my hearing is very sensitive."

She resisted the urge to stomp her foot. "What do you want?"

"I brought you a present." He pulled the same flask she'd seen on their wedding night out of his pocket. She'd partaken of the blood two more times, but she wouldn't do it again. Not until she knew where it came from. She also had a niggling suspicion she didn't need it any more than she needed the crystals.

"Where did you get that?" she asked.

"It's a secret, but if you agree to a truce, I'll show you tomorrow."

"A truce?" She snorted, torn between the need to smack him over the head with the flask and the urge to rip off the lid and slurp the warm, velvety liquid. "Keep your secrets, keep your flask. Keep Rekita for all I care. After the way you humiliated me, I want nothing to do with you. Nothing."

Maybe she'd reacted too quickly. She might not need the creamy nectar, but it could possibly save her people. Her response also reeked of a tantrum.

"I thought you said you'd forgive my past." Kamber said.

Subena turned away, not wanting to look at the hurt reflected in his expression. "We're not talking about the past, we're talking about your present. I do believe you said you wouldn't cheat on your wife."

"You silly wench," he snapped. "I didn't cheat on you. The she-devil accosted me. If you'd bothered to look, you'd know I didn't do anything."

"Really. You didn't exactly push her away. No decent female would create a scene like that unless a male had made her promises he didn't keep." She lowered her voice. "And don't ever call me a silly wench again. The only silly thing I've ever done is agree to marry you." She stormed from her sitting room into her bedchamber.

He blocked her path before she'd time to blink. "Stop doing that." She cursed his ancient speed as she shoved at him. Kamber didn't budge.

"Rekita isn't a decent sort, Bena. And flirting with Ronan isn't smart. He's far too impressionable."

"Flirting with…" She closed her mouth, not wanting the entire castle to hear her screech, not wanting to admit Kamber's warning had some merit. "Please leave. Now."

He studied her for several seconds, and then disappeared in a flash. She sped to the adjoining door, her speed almost equal to his, and slammed the door.

When her anger abated, she sat down and waited for him to knock again, seeking her forgiveness. She waited longer. He didn't come.

Subena awoke to the sound of a bolt sliding into a lock. "Kamber?"

"Miss, perhaps you should get into your night clothes." The maid in the brown dress hovered.

"The prince. Where is he?"

147

"Last I see him, he was riding toward the village. I locked the door because I...perhaps 'tis none of my concern."

"You're right."

The maid smiled.

"I meant it's none of your concern," Subena concluded.

* * * *

In a noble house near the palace, a lonely male hunched lower into his chair and rubbed his brow with his fingers. He was thoroughly sick of females, thoroughly sick of plotting.

"This is not over." His companion laughed, her beautiful voice transformed with evil intentions.

Why had he'd never gotten involved with her? She frightened him.

Chapter Nineteen

After breakfast, Subena hurried for the stables. She worried briefly about giving Ronan the wrong impression, but dismissed the idea. The attraction between them concerned her, but she could handle that. Right?

"Good morning, princess," the stable-master greeted her. "I'm Arkton, at your service. Prince Kamber suggested you might like to ride Amnesia. She's a spirited little mare and I think you'll like her." Typical of Kamber to think he could appease her with an equestor.

"I know I shouldn't ask, but how did she get her name?" Subena had visions of the animal forgetting to obey commands.

Arkton laughed. "The mare once belonged to Prince Barkley. He could never remember the animal's name."

She laughed and pulled a lump of sugar from her pocket. The equestor didn't have the magnificence of the Pollo, but the little mare pranced, eager to run. She was much finer than anything in Mydrian stables. When the sugar disappeared, she inspected the equestor's hooves and legs. "How is it that you have such a fine stable?"

Arkton grinned. "There've been animals here as long as I can remember. Legend has it Rothart's grandfather bred one of the local mares with a real horse, brought from earth to this planet."

Subena suppressed a smile. Gatslians had a legend for everything—there was no such thing as a *real* horse.

As she habitually did, even with her little pony in Mydrias, she examined the saddle and bridle. In her haste to mount, she almost overlooked the saddle girth. The mare began to step and skitter when she tightened it around her belly. She petted the animal and used "shushing" noises to calm her, but the equestor continued to snort. She unbuckled the belt and took a closer look.

"Arkton, when did you saddle Amnesia?"

The stable-master stopped preparing Ronan's mount and looked at her. "About an hour ago. The prince told me you'd be anxious to ride so I made sure she was ready."

"Was anyone else in her stall?"

The old male's head popped up. She had his full attention. "Not that I can recall. After I saddled Amnesia, several guards needed equestors so I just left her tethered here. Is something wrong?"

"Maybe." She continued to study the strap of leather, trying to make sense of the powdery substance. "Take a look."

Arkton scrutinized the belt. "God of the Mountain." He tugged at his collar. "Mistress, I'm certain this…" He looked puzzled. "I keep my equipment clean. There was nothing on this girth."

"I think it's just dust. Maybe something got laid on top of the saddle. You can replace it, can't you?"

"Of course, princess." Arkton scratched his head. "But that doesn't explain this. Take a look."

Subena leaned over and ran a finger along the belt to gather the dust. It created a burning sensation when it touched her skin. Remba dust. The vile substance coated the girth.

"Poor Amnesia. No wonder you're so jumpy." She patted the animal on her flank. "I'll just wipe her down while you replace the strap. Or get another saddle?"

Arkton stepped back and looked at her, his eyes wide. "I must report this to the prince, mistress. At once"

"Can't your report wait?" She smiled widely at Arkton, feeling guilty about using flummery to get her way. She desperately wanted to ride. No, *needed* to ride. Rekita had tampered with the saddle, no doubt about it. The vile temptress wanted to frighten her and Subena refused to be frightened.

"No. mistress."

She chose her words carefully. "I understand this prank must be reported." Only she wouldn't be allowed to ride with Ronan. Especially after the attack on the caravan.

She stooped to a level she never thought she'd sink to, consciously raising and lowering her lashes. "Only our peoples have misunderstood each other too long, Arkton, and we've made great strides during the last weeks. Our countries are friendly now. Let's not let a prank played by one of Kamber's old flames spoil the progress we've made."

"I don't know." Arkton hesitated.

"If you tell the prince now, he won't let me ride and I really need a good gallop. You can tell Kamber, just don't say anything until we're gone. Please?"

"I don't like this. You could've been hurt."

"Not likely. Any experienced rider always checks the gear before a ride."

The stable-master looked skeptical.

"Please," she implored.

At that moment, Ronan came into view, walking very fast. From the distance, Winsome's voice trailed after him. "You promised, Ronan."

Ronan sprinted as he approached the stables. He dug his heels into the ground, stopping just before he banged into the corral fence. "Sorry I'm late." He grinned. "I've seen twenty-five seasons, but she tries to find a million chores to keep me from the tunnels. You'd think I was ten." He inhaled deeply. "Is Thunder ready, Arkton? I need to go before she finds something else I've forgotten to do."

The stable-master chuckled. "Or discover whatever you've done."

It was clear Ronan was a favorite with most of the staff and Arkton proved no exception.

"Let me get your equestor, Master Ronan. Don't ride him so hard this time, all right?"

Subena watched the stable-master re-check Ronan's equipment. *Good man.*

Arkton kept muttering about making a mistake, but he re-saddled Amnesia after she finished brushing the mare's belly with soft talc.

"I'll give you a twenty minute head start," Arkton whispered, "then I have to tell Kamber."

151

She nodded from her perch before looking over her shoulder at Ronan. "Let's go." She trotted away before Arkton changed his mind.

Subena's thoughts drifted as they rode. The countryside amazed her. There were so many different varieties of trees and wildflowers to examine she hated herself for thinking about Kamber. The brute hadn't bothered to wait for her at breakfast. He probably hadn't even come back to the castle after their tiff.

Blast him.

They stopped at a stream to let the animals rest. Subena half-listened to Ronan as he chatted about his search. "I've looked everywhere for the tunnel. I think if I found it, maybe father would…" He kicked at a leaf on the ground.

"Take you more seriously?" She sensed the frustration beneath his embarrassment. "I know what you mean. Sometimes I felt like my big brother never thought anything I did mattered."

Ronan nodded vigorously, his emerald eyes twinkling. In the light of the Sun-Star, she could see flecks of gold. His eyes were very different from Kamber's. "You were lucky."

"Lucky?" Subena frowned, wondering how she could be *lucky*? How so?"

"You only have one brother." Laughing, Ronan gracefully hopped on his equestor and turned the animal around.

Subena remounted her mare. "Did I tell you about my sisters?" She laughed as she pressed her knees into Amnesia's side, coaxing the animal into a trot. "So how do we search for this tunnel?"

Ronan provided a vivid history of his searches and the techniques he'd used in them. "I think Kamber may have a good idea where the tunnel entrance is, but he won't admit it."

They stopped in a clearing to take a better look at some disturbed ground. Ronan offered her a drink from his flask. Subena shook her head, fearing her control would become an issue should the container be filled with blood. The substance had made her completely lose control with Kamber. If Ronan was her true…

No. She couldn't think that.

152

She started to re-mount, but froze as shivers raced through her body. She smiled at Ronan, hoping to hide her fear from whoever watched from the woods. It wasn't a sound that spooked her, although she might have heard a twig break. The air itself seemed to send an uncanny warning. Alarm encircled her body and sucked the breath from her lungs.

Someone definitely watched. And not someone with their best interests at heart.

"Ronan, don't be obvious, but keep talking," she whispered. "While you talk, scan the area behind me. I think we may have visitors."

Ronan nodded once and followed her directions. He kept talking about the tunnel but his gaze roved over the landscape. He looked down suddenly and spoke softly, "I saw something move. It could be that Kamber's having us followed. Wouldn't be the first time."

"I don't think so," she whispered. "What do you say we race back to the castle?" she said, raising her voice.

She heard a rustling in the woods. Ronan blinked and rubbed his hand over his neck, affecting an air of nonchalance. "I think that's an excellent idea."

"Let's go," Subena said in an even louder tone, almost shouting. She may have spoken too loud. Hopefully, the onlooker still believed they were unaware of any surveillance.

Ronan whispered, "You go first." He unsnapped the sheath to the knife. "I'll cover you."

She didn't have to nudge Amnesia. The little mare sensed her unease and sprinted before she'd gotten her foot completely in the stirrup.

They shot across the terrain, maintaining the breakneck pace for a couple of kilometers. Subena looked over her shoulder. Seeing no one, she reined in the mare. She turned her animal around, trying to look inconspicuous as she checked to see if anyone followed. She didn't see anyone so she brought the equestor to a standstill and listened.

She'd almost dismissed her foreboding when she heard the whinny of another equestor. Ronan reined in his mount and waited with her. "See anything?"

She turned to look at him, jerking her body to one side as her mare sidestepped. An arrow whizzed by her head.

"Bockle!" If not for her ability to react quickly—a skill forbidden in Mydrias—she'd be dead. She waved her arms frantically. "Run, Ronan."

She jerked at Amnesia's reins, spinning the animal about, before spurring the equestor into a gallop. Ronan bolted after her. They didn't stop again until they reached the stables.

Ronan helped her dismount. Feeling winded and out of sorts, Subena let him pull her into his arms while she willed her racing heart to beat at a more normal pace. She lifted her head, spotting an unexpected figure hovering near the stall.

Taslin stood by the stable door.

She jumped away from Ronan. "You scared the wits out of me, Tas."

The duke seemed oblivious to her surprise. "I came to say hello, but you seem...occupied."

"Taslin, I... We..." Why in Bockle's name was she explaining?

"What's wrong?" He stared at her, concern mixed with something else evident on his face. Surely he didn't think the hug she'd given Ronan meant anything?

"Someone shot an arrow," Ronan supplied, looking from her to Taslin. "It seemed to come from out of nowhere. Where'd you come from?"

Taslin rushed forward and took both her hands in his larger ones. "Tell me what happened."

Her emotions twisted into conflicted knots. What was he doing? Taslin had never pampered her before. She'd expected him to tell her to buck up. And Ronan looked like he wanted to punch the duke.

Before she could find her voice to question him, another shadow materialized. "Get your hands off my wife." Kamber emerged from the darkness, his face a mask of pure fury.

"Sorry. Just trying to be a comfort. The lady's quite rattled." Taslin bowed deeply. He didn't seem surprised to see her husband. "Of course, you're probably not familiar with the concept of providing comfort." He winked at Subena and sauntered toward the palace.

She stared, first at the duke's retreating back and then at her spouse, trying to comprehend what had just happened. "Kamber, I need to tell you—"

"Save it," he barked. He narrowed his eyes and held her captive with his glance for a brief second.

"Don't bark at her, Kam," Ronan shouted. "She's been through enough for one day."

Kamber looked at his brother, almost as if hadn't seen him before. Before either of them could speak, her husband stomped away.

"Kamber, wait," Ronan called. He headed toward the door.

She turned toward Amnesia, patting the animal's heaving side. "Men." So much for the attempt on her life.

"Subena." The voice surprised her. She'd thought Ronan had gone after Kamber. She turned to find him staring at her, concern in his eyes. "We're not all like those two. I know my brother's a bit of a jerk, but why didn't you tell him about the attack?" His voice sounded somber. Like someone had died. "I saw the arrow."

She sighed. "Like the macho jerk gave me time to say anything. I'll go find him and explain, but it was probably just someone hunting in the woods." Her words were hollow.

Ronan's eyesight was probably as keen as hers. He would know the arrow had been crafted entirely from silver. A death arrow.

Ronan stared, his beautiful olive skin pasty with red blotches. "No, it wasn't. We have to tell Kamber now. I know we just met, but... I don't want anything to happen to you."

Subena debated her course of action. After the attack on the caravan, Kamber would probably send her back to Mydrias. It would be the first time he and Taslin agreed on anything.

She could avoid any arrow meant for her, but she couldn't take chances with the lives of others. Ronan could have been killed, too. "Let's go find him."

Genia Avers

Chapter Twenty

She was late.

Subena rushed her toiletry. The ladies' brunch in her honor would start in fifteen minutes. She'd searched for Kamber, intent upon telling him about the arrow, but she'd been unable to find him. She should have told Winsome and had her cancel the event, but the queen looked so animated, almost happy—that Subena had compromised.

She hurried to her room, intent upon leaving Kamber a note. A new gown and a rose lay on her bed. As if he could buy her forgiveness. She ignored the garment and scribbled out the note about the arrow.

Task finished, she carried the paper toward the adjoining suite. But the door to Kamber's suite remained bolted. How had he gotten the dress into her room?

She shoved the paper under the door, feeling stupid. No doubt he had a key.

She eyed the stunning dress with distaste. Wearing it would be tantamount to full submission. She'd already given in and accepted a dress on the day after her marriage. If she wore the gown, it would send a signal—her cad husband couldn't do as he pleased just because he brought her gifts.

The fabric beckoned her fingers and tested her resolve. She touched the velvety bodice with its array of colors. The blues, purples and greens intertwined and looked different from every angle, each blending of hues more lovely than the last. Her hand traced over the blue-green gems that embellished the waistline and traveled down to the silky skirt. She could practically feel the divine cloth caressing her hips and legs. Gatsle might not be a modern country, but their textiles were unsurpassed.

"No." She jerked her hand away.

Her husband had much to learn—she had no use for his trinkets. The dress must have cost a fortune. She would return it and use the funds for schoolbooks.

Her mood plummeted as she went through her closet. When compared to the garment on her bed, her wardrobe left much to be desired and it was paramount that she should make a good impression, wasn't it? She lifted the new dress off the bed and held it against her chest. What would it harm if she tried it on?

She slipped the garment over her head. Turning, she glanced into the antique mirror.

"Too much harm," she murmured. The colors reflected in her eyes and the cut emphasized the curve of her hips and the smallness of her waist. As though the gown had been made especially for her.

"What the devil." She'd keep the dress and ask for the funds, too.

I must tell the dressmaker to put the fasteners on the side. She was just trying to fasten the back when she heard her door open. Leave it to her husband to appear the minute she was undressed.

She whirled, ready for battle, holding the dress against her chest to keep it from falling down.

"Here, let me get that."

Subena almost dropped the bodice. She faced the female who'd unpacked her trunks.

"Who are you?" Subena tried to keep the annoyance out of her voice.

"I'm to be your maid, madam."

Madam? Subena didn't care for titles but madam was most inappropriate. Hadn't the maid called her "miss" before? Also inappropriate.

She started to complain but the maid looked so eager-to-please, Subena let the matter drop. And she was late.

"Thank you. If you could fasten my gown I would really appreciate it."

"Yes, madam." The maid practically skipped.

"Just this once. I don't really need a servant." Subena didn't want to encourage her.

There were no personal servants in the Mydrian Palace and Subena didn't intend to have one in Gatsle. She and her sisters had paid assistants to help with social functions and matters of state, but Mydrian females were expected to dress themselves.

"No maid?" The servant stopped fastening and placed both her hands over her mouth.

"No maid," Subena repeated.

"But, my lady...please, they'll punish me."

So now she was "my lady," not madam. "Don't be silly. They won't punish you because I don't want a servant."

"They will, my lady. I'll be sent back to the fields or stables. Let me help you. Please let me do your hair."

Subena caught a glimpse of herself in the mirror. Her long curls were tangled and frizzy after her frantic ride. It would take forever to get a brush through her hair.

"Maybe. But just this once." She'd started to repeat herself.

The maid reached around Subena and grabbed the brush from the dressing table. "Here, sit."

Subena sat. "What's your name?"

"Kelsie." The maid dragged the brush through the snarls. Each tug threatened to make Subena's eyes water. Her want-to-be maid clearly didn't know how to style hair. At least she didn't know how to comb someone else's hair. Kelsie's blue-black tresses looked like a comb would float through the strands without resistance.

"I'll do this. You must have other things to do." Subena reached for the brush, but Kelsie backed away.

"You don't understand. They'll sack me if you're not happy. I'm...different."

"What do you mean, different?" Subena worked to keep her voice calm. She wanted Kelsie out of her room.

"I'm a half-breed."

"Half what?" Intrigued, Subena forgot her annoyance.

"I'm part Gatslian." Kelsie hung her head. "Part something else. They'll use any excuse to fire me."

Surely Winsome wouldn't allow such biased behavior? Subena decided to talk to the queen first. "All right. You can stay until I figure something out. But you're my companion, not a maid."

Kelsie threw her arms around Subena. "Thank you, thank you, thank you."

"Just hurry."

Twenty minutes later, Subena stared at the mirror, trying to find something good to say. "My mother would shriek," she said, smiling so Kelsie would interpret the comment in a positive way.

Her bangs were pulled back from her forehead and secured with so many pins she felt the beginnings of a massive headache. Misshapen braids trapped her pale curls high on her head. She looked like a severe priestess with a beehive on her head. Kelsie waited, one fist clasped in her other hand.

Subena picked up the hand mirror to check the back. The view didn't improve.

Kelsie gushed, "My lady, I assure you, the style is all the rage."

"Thank you. Please go and tell Winsome I'll be right there."

Kelsie furrowed her brows, but nodded and left. When the door closed, Subena gritted her teeth and tore at the pins. Once her long locks were pin free, she attacked the braids. She didn't have enough time to completely remove the plaits, so she left two braids on each side of her face and tied them in the back with a ribbon.

"I look like a little girl." At least the style flattered her face, but she was very late now. She dashed for the door.

When she arrived in the banquet hall, everyone had been seated. Winsome stood to greet her. "Good. You're here."

Subena surveyed the room, wondering if the queen was relieved at her arrival or annoyed with her tardiness. Not one of the ladies sported a hairdo that remotely resembled the coiffure that was "all the rage." Kelsie might be 50 percent Gatslian, but she had zero percent fashion sense.

She spotted Rekita seated at the second table. Years of training allowed her to keep smiling. *What is that witch doing here?*

"Let me introduce you to everyone," Winsome said.

Subena could remember everything in most situations, but a wave of social panic invaded her body. Rekita was quickly forgotten. A whir of faces and names came at her with amazing speed and her mind went blank. Everyone nodded politely and she did her best to nod back. She couldn't escape the feeling she was on trial—and about to be convicted. These ladies would judge all of Mydrias by her actions.

They stared, some biting their lips, some with mouths pursed. Did they expect her to have two heads just because she was from Mydrias?

"And this is..." Queen Winsome paused in her introductions. Subena blinked, bringing Rekita's face into focus.

Great. Just great.

"The quartermaster's daughter, Rekita," Winsome continued, narrowing her eyes. "I trust she will behave today."

A tittering noise echoed in the great dining hall. Whether the guests laughed at her or Rekita, Subena couldn't tell. She did her best not to change her expression when she greeted the evil harridan, but when she shook Rekita's hand, she wanted to jerk her arm back.

A tap on her arm ended the awkward silence. "Master Tam," she said. "I'm so glad to see you." The young boy had no idea how glad.

He motioned for her to lean down so he could whisper in her ear. "Don't touch her. Ronan says she has cooties."

The room had gone silent so Tam's raspy whisper echoed. More tittering sounds erupted. This time, the laughter was most definitely at Rekita's expense.

"Mom says this is a chicken party, but I told her you'd let me stay." The little boy looked hopeful.

Subena looked to her new mother-in-law for approval, her spirit rebounding. "Would it be all right?"

Winsome smiled. "Of course. I tried to explain to Tam that this was a lady's luncheon, also known as a *hen* party, but when he heard the luncheon was for you, wild equestors couldn't keep him away."

Another chair materialized and Tam sat happily by her side. When Subena caught him staring at her food, she asked him if he wanted the chocolates sitting on a golden plate near her place setting. He nodded vigorously and grabbed a candy in each hand. The little boy smiled and popped both pieces into his mouth.

At first, only Winsome spoke, but as curiosity overcame shyness, the ladies of Gatsle bombarded Subena with questions.

She enjoyed herself until Rekita spoke. "The dress you are wearing, princess, is quite beautiful." The way the she said "princess" made the title sound dirty. "I have a gown exactly like it, only in red. With my complexion, I can wear bolder colors." The shrew actually smiled. "I don't generally think much of *imported* goods, but I do like your country's fabrics."

Subena glared at her, confused. "This is Gatsle fabric."

"No." Rekita's second smile emanated pure malice. "It's Mydrian. Don't you recognize your country's goods? I presumed it was a gift from Duke Taslin since I saw it in his carriage."

The apple salad she'd just swallowed returned to her throat. Taslin had given her a gift? Part of her felt thrilled, but embarrassment washed over her. Wearing a gift from another male only a week after her marriage was unacceptable.

The Gastlians stared with open mouths. Winsome became fascinated with her napkin.

"I thought the dress was a gift from Kamber," she said loudly.

"Of course you did," the floozy replied, clearly not believing her. Subena doubted anyone else believed her either.

Rekita leaned forward and whispered so only she could hear. "Kamber *did* give me my dress. Less than a month ago. I conceived that very night."

Spots appeared in front of Subena. She found it hard to breathe. Marrying a skirt-chasing Neanderthal was one thing. Knowing his harlot carried a child was something else.

Rekita flashed an emerald ring under Subena's nose. "He gave me this to symbolize our love. It belonged to his grandmother. You may be his wife, but I have his heart."

Subena swallowed, envisioning calm. She would not give Rekita a reaction.

Tam shrieked.

Subena whirled. Tam held his stomach. The little boy gasped for air.

Only seconds earlier, he'd seemed in perfect health. Without thinking, she lifted him onto a nearby settee. She shouted at the closest female. "Get me a compress for his head. Hurry." Her eyes looked at another guest. "You. Get the healer."

Subena remembered she was in Gatsle. Winsome was the child's mother.

Her gaze darted to the queen. The monarch's bronzed skin had grown very pale. The hand she held over her mouth shook.

"He probably wants his mother," Subena prompted her. "Here, can you hold his head?"

The queen's face grew paler, but she followed Subena's direction. She lifted the little boy into her arms. Subena continued to rub his arms and forehead with the cold compress.

Winsome whispered, "Should we get some backa juice for the pain?"

Subena called upon her empathy, allowing her body to feel what the boy felt. Her stomach churned. The cramping sensation doubled her over.

"No." Her voice rattled. "He needs to empty his stomach. I believe he's eaten some bad food." She looked at another young hovering female. "Bring soapy water."

Genia Avers

Chapter Twenty-One

Subena sat with her mother-in-law, the queen's hand in hers. They'd spoken little during the two hours since Tam had fallen ill.

Winsome looked at Subena, her face ghostly. "I'm sorry about Rekita. She wasn't invited."

Subena blinked, surprised the queen would think of that witch with Tam in grave danger. "It's okay. She isn't important."

The queen nodded. "I didn't know how to get rid of her without causing another scene. I never know how to act around that awful creature."

Kamber cleared his throat. Subena had sensed his presence before he'd entered the chamber. He'd overheard his mother's words.

Ronan and Barkley followed him into the room. "How's the little guy?" Kamber asked, his voice little more than a whisper.

Winsome started to speak, but closed her mouth. She burst into fresh tears.

"We don't know," Subena replied, knowing the queen couldn't talk. "The healer's with him. I think we purged him in time." For Winsome's sake, she didn't add, "But he's so little, we just don't know." Nor did she mention that she'd gotten the faintest whiff of poison.

Kamber scowled. He seemed to understand what she hadn't said.

The next hour seemed like twelve as they waited. Ronan paced. No one talked.

Subena decided she'd join Ronan on his pacing path. Just as she stood, the healer returned.

"Your Majesty," he addressed the queen. Then, the male looked pointedly at Subena. "Did you induce vomiting?"

"I... Yes. Was that wrong?" She didn't know why she asked. She'd done the right thing.

"You probably saved his life. The young lad was poisoned." The healer shook his head. "If you hadn't made him regurgitate when you did... It was a powerful potion. Too much will kill—even our kind."

"Poisoned?" The queen looked as though she might collapse.

The healer nodded. "Do not fear. Prince Tam will be as good as new."

Kamber narrowed his eyes and spoke directly to his mother. "Was anyone else sick?"

"No."

"What did he eat that no one else ate?"

The queen shook her head. The motion sent a tear rolling down her cheek. "I don't know."

Kamber's questions crystallized the hypothesis Subena had been forming. "The chocolates," she whispered.

Kamber spun and met her eyes. "What?"

"My chocolates. Tam ate my chocolates."

* * * *

"You must sleep," Subena whispered.

The queen shook her head. "I can't leave him."

"Then lie on the sofa near the bed. I'll sit by his side."

Winsome hesitated. "You promise you'll wake me if there is *any* change?"

"Of course."

The queen studied her face for several seconds, then walked to the sofa without another word.

After a minute, the soft breath of the queen's sleep could be heard throughout the room. Subena sat on the floor by Tam's bed, watching him sleep. Amazing that the child had become so dear in only two days. She could now understand Annika's distress over her departure a little better.

166

Subena sensed a presence and knew without looking Kamber had returned. He sat on the floor beside her. "Subena, I... Thank you for what you did. If Tam had..."

He reached for her chin, gently turning her face toward his. "I'm worried about you. When the carriage was attacked, it could've been me they were after, but the chocolates were meant for you. We've questioned the staff. No one knows how they got on your plate."

"I gave the candy to Tam." She bit her lip. "I could've killed him." Tears blurred her vision.

Kamber embraced her. "Shhh. You didn't poison the chocolate. You saved his life."

He held her tighter, stroking her hair. "Tam's fine. We have to worry about you now."

Subena stared up at him. Her breath caught, as it always did when she looked into his beautiful eyes. "I'm fine."

"Ronan told me about the arrow."

"I left you a note. Didn't you get it?"

He shook his head and pulled her tighter against his chest. "It will be all right."

The motion pulled his tunic away revealing the jagged diamond birthmark. Her vision had just played out—even the heartbeat was the same. Very real, yet nothing like her dream.

She huffed out a breath, doing her best to quell the dizzy sensation threatening to overtake her. She didn't respond. She couldn't. It was too much—the altered vision, the new place, Rekita's claim, the arrow, the poison.

She wouldn't cry. She tried to sit straighter, push Kamber away, but she couldn't seem to extract herself from his arms. Correction, she didn't want to leave his embrace.

"I figured you'd be too emotional to help me figure this out."

Her head popped. She searched for the appropriate words to spew at the prince, but the sleeping queen and ill child precluded a scathing retort. She settled for an icy glare.

The cad smiled back. He actually smiled.

Her fury abated as quickly as it had risen. He'd tried to make her feel better by making her mad. She closed her mouth and turned away, not wanting him to know his gesture touched her.

"We have to talk about this," he whispered into her ear. "I trust our cook completely and she will personally see to your meals, but whoever did this may try something else. I want you to stay with me or Remington at all times. Will you do that?"

She started to say no, but his point was valid. "I don't know."

"Then I must take you back to Mydrias."

"Isn't that what you want anyway?" She jerked out of his embrace and spun to face him. "If you are rid of me, you can have Rekita."

Her words didn't have the fire she'd intended. They sounded petty—even to her ears. And whispering didn't help.

"For a smart lady, you're sometimes quite stupid."

"You sleep with Rekita and have the nerve to say I'm stupid."

"Touché." His face looked pained. "But it's *slept* with Rekita—past tense."

If only she could believe that. If only Rekita hadn't mentioned an unborn child. Her anger refueled. She grabbed Kamber's ear and pinched.

"Ouch."

Winsome's soft snoring halted. Both she and Kamber froze.

When the sounds of the queen's slumber resumed, Subena whispered, "So you say."

"Say what?" Kamber looked confused.

"That Rekita is past tense. She has…never mind." Fighting with Kamber seemed pointless while Tam struggled to fight off a deadly poison.

The prince didn't speak for several seconds. "I sense we have much to resolve, but your safety comes first. If you don't want me around, promise you'll let my guards watch over you. At least for a couple of days. And…" He waited until she met his gaze. "I haven't slept with Rekita since before our wedding. I never will again."

Her husband had chosen his words carefully—he said he hadn't slept with the harpy, but he hadn't denied that he wanted to be with her. She wished she could tell him what he could do with his help, but fear triumphed over pride.

"I will allow my privacy to be invaded, but only if it isn't you who watches me."

He nodded, his face a mask. "I'll send Remington."

"All right."

Kamber stared at her for several seconds. "Are you disappointed I didn't assign the task to Tail-Spin? I see you're still wearing his dress."

Subena looked down at her clothing. She'd forgotten about the gown. The party seemed ages ago. "I thought the dress was from you."

He grinned. "Are you kidding? I would've given you another equestor." He started to say more but abruptly turned and left the room.

"So where did this dress come from?" she whispered.

Chapter Twenty-Two

Had she been in Gatsle for *only* ten days? Seemed like ten months. In addition to a fulltime bodyguard, Subena was under constant scrutiny. No matter what she did, where she went, people gawked.

The opera proved to be no exception. The lights dimmed, the first act began, yet people watched the royal balcony more than they watched the stage. Subena cursed the skills that made her aware of the inspection. She intensified her efforts to concentrate on the production.

"Do you want to leave?" Kamber whispered into her ear, his breath tickling her neck.

Absolutely. "No." She held her head high, trying to emulate her mother, who'd always been able to work a crowd.

"You sure?" Her spouse squeezed her fingers reassuringly.

She nodded, finding it strange that he understood.

The prince hadn't kept his promise about letting someone else guard her, but as he reminded her daily, he hadn't actually promised. She'd snubbed him for two days but, Bockle help her, she'd missed him. He'd worn her down with teasing and challenging.

The cur made her laugh and she'd softened. He asked for her help with an engineering problem and she'd caved further. Finally, he'd gifted her a baby equestor, Pollina, and she'd completely melted.

I'm too easily swayed.

Worse, her body yearned for him. Afraid of yielding to temptation, she'd kept the door between their suites locked. His "good night" would echo through the walls and she'd toss and turn well into the night.

Her greatest test had come when he'd refused to let her have her crystal. She hadn't needed it, but she knew the light would help her mood.

"That thing will kill you," he'd scoffed.

Kamber had offered her blood instead. He'd dipped his finger into the flask and held it to her lips. She'd tried to resist, but the heady aroma and the pulse thumping in his wrist seduced her completely. After she'd licked his finger clean, he held her back against his chest and let her sip from the flask. His arm rested between her breasts, his breath caressed her neck, and moisture pooled between her legs. When desire threatened to consume her, she'd pushed away and run back to her room like the coward she was.

She frowned. The dillweed still hadn't told her where he'd gotten the velvety liquid. It tasted too sweet to have come from rats.

Subena huffed a deep breath, glad for the darkness that shielded her. While the lights were off, she didn't have to worry she'd do something wrong, something that might make her new people would detest her.

Kamber stood unexpectedly. He bowed from the waist.

"Where are you going?" she whispered. "The scene isn't over."

He flashed a mischievous grin and stepped into the darkness. She refused to look in the direction he'd gone, but every part of her wanted to run after him. That would be rude so she stayed in her seat. And seethed.

Jerk. How dare he leave her alone? He'd probably slipped away to rendezvous with Rekita.

The soprano began to sing, his voice clear and haunting. Unlike opera in Mydrias, this was beautiful. After a few minutes, she put Kamber out of her mind and gave herself to the music, absorbing the sound into her very soul.

Engrossed in the performance, she almost screamed when something bumped her leg. Years of etiquette training kept her from falling out of her chair.

"Shhh, little one." Kamber laughed. The wicked Dökkálfar reclined in front of her, propped up on one elbow. "It's only me so don't make a scene. It won't look good for Mydrias if little Bena doesn't behave at the opera."

She kicked at him. He caught her leg and planted a kiss on her ankle.

"Monster," she hissed. "How did you get down there?"

"I have my ways." He pulled his body into a sitting position, his head just below the balcony wall.

He had ways all right. Blink and he was there. Blink and he was gone.

"Stay down," she murmured, wishing she could yell at him. "You can't just raise your head now. People will think…"

"Now there's an idea." He snuggled his body against her legs.

She gasped at the implication. "What the hell do you think you're doing?"

"Such language," Kamber whispered. He ran a hand over her calf and lifted the hem of her skirt, folding it into her lap.

"Don't." She doubled her fist and struck at his shoulder. The patron in the next box turned to stare.

Subena smiled at the lady and turned her face toward the stage. She couldn't see the performers. Embarrassment made it impossible to see anything. "I said 'stop,'" she hissed.

Kamber chuckled. Then he kissed the back of her knee.

Her options were limited. She could leave the opera box. That would cause a stir and the other theatre-goers would stare again. They might even wonder where the prince had gone.

She could sit calmly and not draw attention to herself. Any attempt to push Kamber away would make too much noise. There was nothing she could do that wouldn't create a scene. That meant Kamber could do whatever he wanted.

"Stop it. Now," she whispered, covering her mouth with her program. "I swear you'll pay for this later."

"Ah, but it will be so worth it." To emphasize his point, the heathen ran his hand over her thigh and kissed her other knee.

173

Maybe she should leave the box after all. She tried to stand, but instantly fell back into her seat.

Not smart. If she tried to move with him kneeling between her legs, she'd fall on her face.

She exhaled softly. She couldn't just let him win.

There was one thing she could do. She could ignore him. Nothing got to an elf like indifference. She might have to endure his touch, but she wouldn't let it affect her.

Why did his hands have to feel so good on her skin? Okay, she just wouldn't let him know he affected her.

He pried her thighs apart. *Mother of Bockle.*

She pushed at his arm, but he was too strong. Before she attempted an all-out shove, she used her opera glasses to scan the crowd. Most people were enthralled with the drama onstage, but a few people still glanced, or openly stared, at their box. She couldn't risk a commotion.

As she contemplated her options, she felt something cold against the edge of her upper thigh and then a faint ripping noise. Her eyes darted to see if anyone else heard.

No one seemed to have noticed. She sucked in a breath. The cad had sliced through her undergarment. What was he thinking?

Oh, mercy. He couldn't be doing what she thought he was doing. Even in Mydrias where people pretended they hadn't seen lovers slip away to the garden or a secret closet, no one would act lasciviously at the opera.

He wouldn't dare.

He would.

The suspense mounted, both on the stage and under her chair. Hands roamed over her bare thighs. A finger stroked between her legs. A tiny squeal escaped her lips.

She slapped a hand over her mouth. How could he?

More important, why had she want him to stop?

Using both hands, he rubbed her with feathery strokes. Subena tried to remember to breathe as his fingers fondled and teased, stopping just short of touching the one spot that demanded contact. She stared straight ahead, doing her best not to slouch in the chair.

He stroked until she thought her skin might catch fire. At last, he parted her and began to probe the moist folds within.

Subena licked her dry lips as they parted, a keening of need surprising her.

The opera seemed like a distant melody, the perfect backdrop for the play being acted inside the box. Kamber teased her thighs with his tongue as his fingers played with her triangle of hair. She wanted more than his fingers, she wanted his tongue, she wanted his penis.

Kamber spread her legs wider. She didn't put up even a token resistance. How did the cur always know exactly what she needed?

Her heart raced; her breasts felt heavy. Her nipples peaked, as sensitive as the flesh between her thighs. Every fiber of her being came alive, became aroused.

"Kamber," she whispered, immediately forgetting what she'd meant to say. He mesmerized her, this male from her dreams. Only better. So much better. "I...ah..."

His mouth began to explore her, taste her. The sensation made her body jerk. She gripped the arms of her chair and bit into her tongue to keep from moaning.

Opera. Remember that.

Mercy. She almost didn't care whether anyone noticed. They might've been on a deserted island, not in the middle of a crowded opera house. Her brain had lost all reason.

Kamber's tongue stroked a heated, moist path across her center. He halted to blow air over her most sensitive spot. Her hips came off the chair, arched forward, oblivious to everything.

His tongue felt like magic as it darted and suckled. How much more of his exquisite torture could she endure without screaming?

She tried to rise from her slumped position, but he spread her legs wider and pulled her hips closer to his mouth. His maneuver pressed her back against the balcony chair as he tasted her.

Oh gads, but he was good. So good. She wanted his body inside her. Not in the theater. *So where?*

Her brain tried to relay the message. *Public place.* Her senses refused to listen. Her hips rose to meet his wonderful, talented mouth, her pelvis grinding against his face. She'd lost all control of her needy body, too aroused to be embarrassed.

Kamber lapped, alternating between thrusting his tongue and sucking on her engorged clitoris. She stifled a whimper. Letting her head loll, she imprisoned his head between her knees.

Zing. The sound reverberated into her ears. The noise wasn't loud, but the reverberation had been so close to her hypersensitive ears it sounded like an explosion. Kamber stopped moving.

He shoved her seat further into the box. His strength tore the bolts from the chair's legs and sent the seat crashing into the back wall. The noise echoed through the opera house.

"What...happened?" Subena blinked, trying to bring herself back into reality. She didn't want real. She wanted Kamber to resume his delicious torment.

"Why did you do that?" she asked, keeping her voice low.

Her gaze darted to the orchestra. The musicians had stopped playing. Everyone stared. "Bockle."

Bless the darkness. She looked down, intending to maim Kamber.

He was gone. Gone.

How the devil did he do that? The ancients were fast, but she'd never heard of anyone who could disappear in the blink of an eye. She'd make him teach her that trick. No. She'd kill him first and make him explain later.

How dare he leave her in semi-quiver? Worse, the dysfunctional idiot had left her to face the crowd. Alone.

The door to her opera box swung open. Two guards rushed in. One grabbed her. The other aimed a weapon into the mass of people.

"What are you doing?" Was sex at the opera a crime in Gatsle?

"Come with me. Hurry." The guard didn't wait for her reaction. He grabbed her arm and catapulted her toward the door.

Subena tried to understand his actions. The guard moved so fast, she tripped. When she stumbled a second time, he lifted her into his arms. Then, he broke into an all-out sprint.

At the main entrance of the opera house, he set her on her feet. She saw her husband running down the cobblestone street.

Please, Bockle. Let the guard be a good guy.

Chapter Twenty-Three

She'd left the door unlocked. Kamber wondered if it were a good thing, or a bad thing.

"You planned that?" Subena glared at him from her sitting room, her face a beautiful mask. Only her clenched fist warned him of the furor awaiting him.

"No...eh...yes. I mean..."

She picked up a painted vase and hurled it at his head.

God, she's beautiful when she's angry. Kamber ducked. Based on what he'd learned of his little wife, he suspected she used anger to mask her fear. Someone tried to kill her, yet Subena hadn't even mentioned that small detail.

"Come on, Bena. You could have hurt me with that thing."

"We both know I couldn't hurt you with a little bit of glass."

Probably better if he didn't laugh. "Why are you mad anyway? Because I gave you pleasure?"

"Pleasure?" She stood, planting her hands on her hips. Her long hair fell over her shoulder, shadowing one eye. She looked delectable.

Whoa. Someone had shot at her. Or him. How could he think of sex now?

"I can think of nothing less pleasurable," she snapped, "than embarrassing myself in front of the entire opera. What if we'd decorated the walls?" She slapped her hand over her mouth.

"So you noticed, too?" he asked, having had suspicions after their wedding night. Being too embarrassed to ask his mother or Remington for specifics, he'd consulted one of his former tutors, the oldest male in Gatsle. The elf said he'd read about passion creating magic, but had never seen such a spectacle.

Still, he hadn't even considered that pleasuring her might add to the Opera House's artwork. Nor had he checked.

So what? If they'd added anything to the dark walls, no one else would know the cause. Right?

"What if someone had seen us, Kamber?"

Judging by the pitch of her voice, the next object she hurled would not miss its target. And she did have a point. He only wished she could see his. "You didn't embarrass yourself. I made sure that wouldn't happen."

"You left me—"

"Frustrated?" he suggested.

"Alone," she snarled. "You left me alone to face the crowd."

He almost smiled. She meant frustrated. That was good, right? And he hadn't meant to leave her hanging. Hell, he'd been in tough shape, too. Still was.

His only goal had been to please her, and okay, himself, too. He could still smell her on his hands. He smiled, feeling the beginnings of arousal.

"Don't you dare laugh at me."

"I'm not laughing at you."

She flashed him a look that should have burned him into a crispy critter.

"How did you get in and out of the opera box so fast?" she asked.

Every Mydrian he'd encountered had been curious about the ancient skills. He'd expected her to be curious, but he hadn't expected a direct question. "I inherited my speed from my grandfather. According to legend, all our kind had great speed in the olden days."

"That wasn't speed," she snapped. "I didn't even see you move. You were there...and then you weren't."

"It's just speed, angel. I can move *very* fast. There are a few advantages to being a backward Neanderthal."

She frowned. "Can all Gatslian's do that?"

"No." It was his turn to frown. Did anyone else have his speed? He didn't think so.

"Just you, huh?" she replied, seeming to read his thoughts. "Why do you suppose our people have lost so many of the ancient skills?"

"Genetics."

Her eyes narrowed.

"What?" he asked. "You think I haven't evolved and therefore can't possibly understand genetics?"

She smirked. "I know you haven't evolved, but tell me what you mean anyway."

He shrugged. "Legend has it our kind mated with humans before they came to this planet. My theory is the human traits became more prevalent with each generation as the two species merged. I think that's the real reason we were banished to this planet. Everyone who wasn't human enough had to go." He didn't add that he thought human traits were most prevalent in Mydrians. He might not be evolved, but he wasn't stupid.

She didn't speak for several seconds. He'd expected that. His Bena thought things through before she reacted. Usually. Some might say that made her a perfect compliment to his tendency toward rash actions. *He* would definitely say that.

"Tell me," she said. "Can you fly, too?"

"Fly?" He chuckled. "I wish I could, but even I'm not that much of an anomaly."

"I never said you were an anomaly." She narrowed her eyes. "An inconsiderate ass, maybe, but I didn't say anomaly. I saw… Never mind."

He'd ask her what she'd seen later. "Call me anything you like, I'm just so relieved you're…" Realization invaded his brain. *She could have been killed.* The blow-dart had been made of silver.

Kamber swallowed hard. He was an idiot. Since she wouldn't let him touch her in the palace, he'd thought if he could get her to climax at the opera, just maybe she'd want him back in her bed.

Dumb plan. Thank the God of the Mountain he'd heard the whiz of the first dart. A few seconds later, he might've been too aroused to notice.

"So relieved I'm what?" Subena persisted.

The extent of his miscalculations embarrassed him. He'd ordered the guards to stand by the door. Only as a precaution.

He hadn't really expected her to make any noise—she had a great deal of self-control—but if she'd screamed at a *critical* moment, he would've opened the door as a signal for his guards to take her away. He'd planted an arrow, a wooden one, in the box and would have reported an attempt on her person—thus a scream would be justified. He hadn't expected the attempt to be real, or to include a silver dart.

But he was the only one who knew about his plan.

If the guards hadn't burst into the opera box, another dart would certainly have followed the one that barely missed Subena's head.

"Why are you so relieved?" Subena's voice sounded insistent.

He shuddered. The weapon made a horrible sound when it lodged into the wall behind them. If they thing had...

"Kamber, talk to me."

He licked his lips, wondering how to explain. After everything, he wanted her so much his mouth wouldn't work right—at least not to talk. When had the ice princess thawed his heart?

She picked up a book, planning to throw it at him no doubt. Even when she was angry, his body reacted to her. Her life had been in danger—was still in danger—and he was aroused.

Kamber forced his brain to control his body. She needed a guardian, not a lover. "Don't throw. I'll explain." Fear for her safety made his voice harsher than he'd intended. He had to make her understand.

Suddenly he understood. Subena could not remain in Gatsle.

She lifted the book over her head. He sped toward her, grabbed her wrist before she saw him move. "There's a real danger... Owww!"

She'd kneed him, barely missing the most important part of his anatomy. His thigh ached and he knew it would be several minutes before he could walk normally.

He flung her onto the sofa and pressed his body on top of her. She kicked and fought like a possessed demon. He thanked the God of the Mountain for her small stature.

She went limp. *Smart lady.*

He lay atop her, his legs holding hers down. He used one arm and his chest to restrain her arms. He had his other hand over her mouth and used all his energy to keep from kissing her. If he kissed her, he'd forget he must convince her to leave Gatsle. And he must do it before he released his hold, otherwise there'd be hell to pay. Dung, there'd be hell to pay anyway.

"Subena, please listen."

She harrumphed into his hand.

"I planned a bit of a diversion." Kamber hurried his explanation. "I didn't think we'd need the soldiers. I stationed them outside the box... Just in case."

He removed his hand from her mouth, but he kept her pinned on the sofa with his body. He waited for the bloodcurdling screech. It didn't come.

"In case what?" Her voice was cold—far more sinister than any scream.

"In case you, you know... You made love noises. You've done so on several occasions." He felt her start to struggle and then go limp again.

The rage left her beautiful expression. "Let me up."

His mirth disappeared. He wasn't fooled by her control—she'd still kill him when he released her. "Promise me you won't throw anything."

She didn't speak but she hurled daggers with her eyes.

"Subena, promise? If you behave, I'll show you where the blood comes from."

Kamber knew she was curious, but she didn't respond to his bribe. "Let. Me. Up."

He studied her face and decided to risk it. Hell, he probably deserved a good slug. She sat slowly, not looking in his direction.

"You know you have to go back to Mydrias," he said.

That got her attention. Her eyes widened and a tinge of pink colored her exquisite skin. She said nothing.

He hoped her change of expression indicated she didn't want to leave Gatsle, but her countenance could also mean she couldn't wait to get away from him.

He waited for her to ask why. She didn't. Instead, her gaze burned into his eyes. His face turned red when suddenly, and inexplicably, his pants tightened. What the hell? How could her anger turn him on?

He turned his back to her, hoping she hadn't noticed. She remained on the sofa, inert and unmoving.

"Subena," he tried again, "I know you're mad, but my stunt saved your life. When you screamed…"

"I did not *scream*."

He suppressed a chuckle. Laughter, of any sort, would be a colossal mistake. "Okay, when you, ah…whimpered and showed me those sexy ears of yours, I heard the dart zipping toward us. After I shoved you, I saw the male who'd fired it, but he'd cloaked his face. I ordered the second guard to help me catch him, but the shooter vanished in the streets."

"If you're making this up to keep me from killing you, I will kill you."

Kamber wanted to laugh and cry at the same time. Somehow, he managed to keep his face expressionless. "I promised I'd never lie to you. I'm telling the truth."

She shook her head, sending her hair swirling around her waist, drawing his attention to her breasts—like his gaze wouldn't go there anyway. "I heard a zing, too, but seriously, Kamber. Why would anyone want to kill me?"

She heard the shot? "I don't know. But someone *is* trying to hurt you. Someone attacked the carriage you should have been in, tampered with your saddle, gave you poisoned chocolates, and now this… I won't take any more chances with your safety. I must take you back to Mydrias."

She paced. He waited, hoping she wouldn't argue with him. He wanted her to stay so badly, she could easily change his mind but she wasn't safe in Gatsle.

Realization struck Kamber harder than a fist. He loved her.

"If someone's trying to kill me," she said, "and I haven't accepted that as fact, we may never know who is behind these schemes if I leave Gatsle."

"What?" he asked, still reeling from his epiphany.

She stopped, reached behind her head, and gathered all her hair with one hand. He followed her movement, fascinated. The motion pressed her nipples against the fabric of her dress.

He turned away. Watching his new bride was too distracting. He needed to be alert, not lust-impaired. "If you stay, you might die. I cannot risk that."

She walked toward him and tugged on his shoulder, forcing him to look at her. "*You* cannot risk it? Since when can't I make my own decisions?"

"You can. Of course you can. But be reasonable. I couldn't live with myself if something happened to you."

"You, you, you. Be quiet and let me think." She marched back and forth across the room several times. "The only person who wants me dead is Rekita."

"Rekita?"

"If you dare defend that harpy, you won't have to worry about my death. I'll be hanged for murdering you."

"Maybe it's Reklaw," he challenged, not really believing the duke would harm Subena. Him, in a heartbeat. Subena? He didn't think so."

"Why would he do that?"

"I don't know. Maybe he thinks if he can't have you, no one else..." Just because he didn't believe his own propaganda didn't mean he could back down.

"There's no way Tas is behind this. He..."

"He what? Loves you? Don't be naïve, Bena. The only person your duke loves is himself."

"Not that it matters, but I was going to say Taslin would only benefit from your death, not mine. He has no sway in Mydrias without my family's influence. No, Rekita is the obvious villainess. She wants you and she wants to be queen." A pained expression doused the angry sparkle in her eyes. "And if it weren't for the treaty, she might already have both."

"Nonsense. I would never marry her."

"Really? Even with your bastard in her belly?"

"Bastard in her..." Kamber's mouth went dry. "That's not possible." He didn't believe he could make Rekita pregnant, but he'd worried about that very thing.

185

"Why not?" Subena's silver eyes blazed. "Rekita says otherwise."

"Because our kind can only reproduce with one's true mate."

She stared at him open-mouthed for several seconds. Then she started to laugh. "Oh, please," she mumbled between snickers. "You can't possibly believe that ancient nonsense. How can you explain all your siblings? Are you saying your parents are true mates? They can barely stay in the same room with each other, yet they have four sons." She looked up at him, horrified. "I'm sorry... I overstepped."

He shook his head. "No, I appreciate your candor, but you're wrong. My father and Winsome didn't reproduce."

She stopped pacing and stared.

He snorted. "Don't worry, princess, your research is not faulty." She'd no doubt studied his family tree. "After my mother died, my father officially changed the records. He believed my birth mother had betrayed him. As in most things, Rothart was wrong."

She didn't reply for several seconds. "Kamber, I'm sorry."

He shrugged.

"I don't understand. I know Winsome and Rothart have been married for—"

"Twelve years," he stated flatly.

"But Tam is only five."

"Tam is adopted. Winsome's sister died during childbirth. Rare, but it happens—even to our kind."

"Bockle, Kamber. I truly am sorry."

He didn't want to talk about his painful history. His father had abandoned the legacy of his one true mate and everyone else suffered. "So you see, the maxim holds. Rekita cannot bear my child because there's no way that witch is...is anything to me."

"I don't know. She sounded so...convincing."

"She's an accomplished liar."

"Maybe, but if she wanted to trap you, Kam, there are ways. Nasty, evil ways, but a determined female can bear a child."

Shit. Rekita might just try something like that.

186

No. Even if Subena was correct, he'd always taken precautions. Especially with Rekita. "That creature does not carry my seed." He crossed his arms. Recognizing his defensive posture, he uncrossed them. "Bena, I would know if she carried my baby."

"How?"

"The same way you knew what had happened to Tam. The same way you know now that he'll be all right. We're both empaths."

She gasped. "How is that possible? You're Dökkálfar. I'm álfar."

"I'm not really sure. I just know I sense things—real things. You and I might sense different things, but we both experience what others feel."

She sputtered again. "How did you... Even if she isn't carrying your child, Rekita has motive for wanting me gone."

"What she doesn't have is enough brains to pull off an assassination attempt."

"She had enough brains to get your grandmother's ring."

"She what?"

"Oh please. Don't pretend you didn't give it to her. I saw it. A perfect circle of tiny emeralds?"

He reached for her, holding her upper arms as he turned her to face him. "I swear to you, I didn't give her the ring."

She pushed his arms away. "Then how'd she get it?"

"The pub. I..." Dammit all to hell. Was he not allowed a single tantrum without consequences?

"You what?" She narrowed her eyes at him. "Never mind. I don't think I want to know. I still think Rekita's involved."

"I agree she's involved, but someone else is pulling the strings. She's not smart enough to do this on her own. I doubt Rekita would attack you outright."

Kamber's mind still struggled, attempting to understand how Rekita had gotten her paws on the ring. He wasn't sloshed when he first arrived at the pub. He would have seen Rekita.

"Let's approach this another way," he suggested. "Who would benefit if the treaty were dissolved?"

"Other than Rekita?" Subena wrinkled her nose. A sure sign anger consumed her. "Creshin and the warlords. Everyone else has more to gain from an alliance between Mydrias and Gatsle."

"So we're back where we started." He watched a myriad of expressions cross her face. She looked at him, all business. At least she'd shut up about Rekita.

"Show me the source of the blood, Kamber."

"What?" His wife was master of the unexpected. Why'd he made that foolish promise? Stupid Neanderthal that he was, he was prone to promising anything to make his surly spouse happy.

"You promised."

He studied her face. She wouldn't relent.

"All right. Let's go."

He was proud of his work, but something told him Subena wasn't going to like his source. Not one bit.

Chapter Twenty-Four

"Kamber. This isn't funny." Subena placed her hands on her hips, so her husband wouldn't see how much they shook. She wasn't mad at him so much as herself. Why had she followed him through a long tunnel into the underground structure? What had made her believe he'd share his secret? It was bad enough he couldn't explain the ring, but to renege on a promise ranked at the top of the maggot scale.

"You're a technologist. Think like one. This is the source."

How dare he imply she wasn't thinking? "You said you'd show me where the blood came from."

"The blood is human, Bena. These are people."

A female smiled at her. "Hi. I'm Lecala. It's a pleasure to meet you." The woman held out her hand. Something about her didn't seem quite normal.

Subena took a step closer. The outstretched finger had a tiny pinprick. A drop of blood leaked, so small only a person gifted with superior sight could see it.

Subena experienced an overwhelming urge to bite her.

"Bockle." The lure of the female grew stronger. Subena jerked her hand over her mouth. She backed away, grabbing Kamber's arm. "Get me out of here."

He wrapped an arm around her shoulders and guided her down the long corridor, up the steps, and into the light of the Sun-Star. "Take it easy. The urge will pass."

How could he know that? He hadn't reacted and he was one who regularly drank blood.

Gads. So did she. Shame tore at her stomach.

189

Subena sank to the ground, filled with revulsion. "They aren't... They can't be... What were they again?"

He squatted down beside her. "Human."

She blinked as she looked at his face, hating him more than she ever had. "You suck the blood from those poor creatures. That's disgusting."

"We're not Vampyr. We don't suck anything." He stood up and turned away from her, his body stiff and unyielding. "I knew I shouldn't have shown you. Idiot that I am, I thought a technologist would understand."

"Don't you dare make this about me," she whispered. "What does being a technologist have to do with abusing those poor humans?"

"They aren't abused," he yelled back. "We keep them alive. We keep them safe."

"Well hooey for you. You keep them caged and you suck their blood. What kind of life is that?"

"Have you suddenly gone deaf? I told you, we don't suck their blood. And they aren't caged."

She wanted to pound Kamber's head with her fist. The blasted elf brought out the worst in her—even in the best of times. This was not the best of times.

"Okay, I'm trying to be calm here." She was so calm, her hands shook. "Let's review. You just used a key to get us into a locked facility that has no windows. How's that not a cage?"

He huffed out a loud breath but he didn't look at her. "The facility is locked to keep others out. By others, I mean creatures that do suck blood, not Gatslians. Our people would never harm the Givers. They're part of us. They're family."

"Okay. Maybe I can see that, but the door's still locked. Looks like a cage, sounds like a cage, uh..." She paused to raise the palms of her hands. "...must be a cage."

"God, you're such a snob." He kicked at a tuft of weeds. "Every Giver has a key. They come and go as they please."

Subena blinked. Was she a snob? Her crystal rationing had led to Alton's death. Did she really have the right to judge Kamber?

Of course she did. Crystals didn't come from innocent things.

She swallowed hard. "Couldn't you at least give them windows?"

"Absolutely not. The Givers are allergic to the Sun-Star's rays. Too much exposure means death to them. And the exposure is cumulative."

"Oh, Bockle." Her stomach knotted. Why was she so quick to judge her spouse? She'd never adhered to any of the commonly held prejudices about Gatslians. Did she want him to be bad so he couldn't hurt her?

"Look." Kamber sat down beside her. "I can see how someone with your background might see the consumption of blood as barbaric, but this is how we live."

"Might see it as barbaric?" She squinted to see if he was joking. He seemed very serious. "Maybe you're too close to the situation. I see people who have no options, no freedom."

He groaned. "Perhaps you're right about the options, but their lack of options is not our fault. They need our protection, which we freely give. In return, they give us some of their blood."

"No. The flask... Have I been drinking from that poor creature?" Subena gagged.

"Get over yourself. The blood you drank on our wedding night was a gift from Lecala. A *gift*. And that poor creature has a name."

Subena kept her hand over her mouth, still not certain she wouldn't vomit. "That means you...you milk them. No wait, I saw marks on that creature's arm."

"The woman's *name* is Lecala. She isn't a creature." Kamber's anger assaulted her senses like scalding water. "And you saw syringe marks. The Givers take their own blood with needles and package it for us. We don't suck it out of them." He edged away from her. Only an inch, but the separation equated to a canyon.

"Why take their blood?" she asked. "Just to get high? I know I shouldn't judge, Bockle knows I've drank enough rat's blood. But I would never take blood from a *human*."

Kamber rose to kneel on one knee, his body facing forward. "The crystals don't work for Dökkálfar, Subena. We're not creatures of light. I told you that. The Givers are from earth—we need an earth type substance to sustain us."

"Can't you just use rat blood?"

Kamber shook his head. "No. At least I don't think so. The humans came to Lanatus with our ancestors. As far back as anyone can remember, they've freely given us blood. In return, we inject our antibodies into their systems. The antibodies not only protect them from infections and possible death, they prevent aging."

Subena closed her eyes, trying to find a calm center. "I need some time to process this."

"Fair enough."

She felt her husband's disappointment, but it was the best she could do. "You called this your work. If the humans have been here since the colonization, what work is required?"

Kamber hurled a rock across the landscape. "No Giver has reproduced in the last fifty years. So you see, we face a survival crisis similar to yours. I've been working on genetics."

"You mean clones?" Subena couldn't control the jolt of excitement that raced through her scientific psyche.

"Yes. But I've also been working on human reproduction methods. The first step is to stop the aging process. If the humans age, they definitely won't be able to produce offspring."

"And have you been successful?"

"Somewhat. We've used our magic to halt the aging process, but I'm not sure we haven't done more harm than good. Magic may scar vital reproductive organs, much the same as the crystals destroy álfar essence."

Subena nodded, for the first time, understanding their survival was intertwined. Human, álfar, and Dökkálfar would have to work together.

"How many humans are there?" she asked.

"Twelve," he said, his voice monotone. "Once there were hundreds, now only a dozen remain."

He stood, his six foot six frame making her feel tiny. "I didn't have much hope that you'd accept me as a husband, but I did hope you'd use your science and help me save the Givers. I guess not."

Subena watched him walk away, her head spinning. She did want to help. Only she had to help.

But could she live with a male who drank blood from people?

Bockle. What was she thinking? She'd drunk the blood herself and unlike Kamber, she hadn't grown-up thinking the practice was acceptable.

She hurried back to the palace, trying to control her warring thoughts. She almost bumped into Kelsie; the maid blocked her doorway.

Mother of Bockle. Could her day get any worse? "What do you want?" Her tone sounded sharper than intended. Her bad day wasn't Kelsie's fault.

"Ooh," the maid responded, her voice syrupy. "Did you and prince have a fight? He's not a nice male, I hear."

"He's perfectly nice," Subena countered. Kamber might be a cad, but damned if she'd let Kelsie deride him. "Can I help you with something?"

The maid drew in her shoulders. "No. I'll go. I thought you might need help."

Blast. Subena instantly felt contrite. "I didn't mean to snap at you. I'm sorry."

"So I can stay?" The maid's face went from somber to glowing in the blink of an eye. Subena wished she had Kelsie's childlike exuberance.

But she didn't and that was that. She was a technologist and as much as she hated it, she knew she'd stay and help Kamber find a solution for the Givers. The blood business made her sick, but she couldn't let the humans die.

"For a little while," she replied to Kelsie. "What do you know about the Givers?"

"Givers? Is that a game?"

A little while might be an eternity.

* * * *

"Let me guess. You've decided to leave the land of the bloodsuckers." Kamber recognized his hateful words for what they were. Defensive. He didn't want his new wife to leave.

"My," Subena scoffed. "When you speak with such refinement and culture, I wonder how I ever confused you with a dick-weed Neanderthal."

He grimaced to hide a grin. He'd miss her sarcasm most of all. "I'll take that as a yes. You're going back to Mydrias. Otherwise, you wouldn't dare cross the gulf between our rooms and enter my chambers."

"That would be a no."

"No?" Kamber barely suppressed the urge to lift her and spin her around.

He felt immediately ashamed. She'd be safer in Mydrias.

"No. I'm here to talk to you about a decoy."

"A decoy?" Kamber replayed her word in his mind, but he had no idea what she meant. "You must be aware that I'm not very smart, even by Neanderthal standards. Are you saying we need a decoy for the Givers?"

She waved her hand dismissively. "One problem at a time. We'll have a serious discussion about the Givers once we find out who's trying to kill us. Call me selfish, but I want to take care of that first."

His lips twitched. "For once, we're in complete and total agreement. Please, tell me about the decoy."

"What if we let everyone believe I've agreed to go back to Mydrias? And we make sure my departure is very public? A single coach would be an easy target."

"Agreed, but how will that help us find the person behind the attacks?"

"We'll have a patrol watch my carriage, from a distance. Maybe even have soldiers hidden in the carriage, ready to counterattack."

He liked the way she said "we," but he wasn't too keen on her plan. "Absolutely not. It's too dangerous."

"If this is about the treaty, it will be equally dangerous for me if I go to Mydrias. Do you really think they won't try to kill me there?"

"I can't use you as a decoy."

"I think it's my decision to make."

Gads, but she could be obstinate.

"We might be married, Kamber, but I don't belong to you and you can't order me around. If you wanted a marionette, you should have settled for Rekita."

"But I don't want to lose you." *Shit. Shit, shit, shit.* He shouldn't have said that.

Subena's mouth gaped.

"Close your mouth." He put a finger under her chin and pushed her lips together. His comment had obviously surprised her, too. "I think your plan's terrific, but I won't let you risk your pretty little neck. I have other plans for it. We'll use a real decoy." His fingers moved on their own volition to stroke her cheek.

She pushed his hand away, but her movement lacked its normal venom. "I won't let others risk their lives."

"We'll use a soldier, one we trust. I doubt I can get any of my soldiers to wear a dress though. If we had to do that, a certain duke comes to mind."

Subena swatted him with her shawl. "Ha, ha." Her voice echoed with sarcasm but her smile seemed genuine.

"Actually, Bena, we can't tell Taslin about this. I know you think he's Lord Wonderful, but if this plan is to work, we can only inform the people who absolutely have to know. For now, that's just Remmy. The guards we send, both in the carriage and as escorts, must think you're actually inside the coach."

"Agreed."

"Could you repeat that? I could have sworn you said you agreed with me. I must be hearing things."

Chapter Twenty-Five

Subena sat in the carriage, rubbing her hands. In between clasping and re-clasping, she reached for the knife hidden inside her skirt pocket.

Four guards had been posted with the carriage, but Kamber's concern affected her. Distrust bloomed inside her body and grew until she suspected everyone.

She patted her little blade, slightly reassured as she peered outside. "What's keeping him?" she asked in a hushed tone. The upcoming carriage ride with her husband scared her almost as much as meeting the would-be assassin. Maybe more.

The coach was too reminiscent of their ride from Mydrias. Her body tingled with anticipation and Kamber wasn't even nearby. God help her when his masculine presence permeated the enclosed space. She might not be able to remain aloof.

Had she truly fallen for a bloodsucking Neanderthal? Okay, so he wasn't really a bloodsucker, but the slur had a nice ring.

What if her aloofness didn't matter? The previous evening puzzled her. She'd enjoyed plotting with Kamber, but when they crawled into the secret hallway, he hadn't attempted to touch her. He'd reacted perfectly when she'd freaked about the dark passageway—too perfectly. He'd held her hand chastely and real concern flickered in the depths of his jade eyes. He'd been polite.

Maybe he's not interested anymore.

She jumped when the carriage door opened. "Bockle. You scared me, Kam."

He tapped on the carriage window to signal the driver. Then he leaned forward, pulling her toward him. His unexpected kiss made her glad she'd been sitting—the contact made her knees weak. His tongue raked across hers before his mouth closed over her lips and found her soul.

She surrendered completely. Cursing her weakness, Subena melted into him, one little kiss making her forget assassins, decoys, and plots. The only thought penetrating her brain was that they were overdressed.

He released her and leaned back into the seat facing her. "Subena, you should've been watching."

"Was that a test?" She fixed him with an icy stare. At least the fool male was smart enough to remain silent.

She detected a flicker of a smile before he turned and stared outside the coach. He didn't look at her again, keeping his eyes on the passing terrain.

She felt foolish. The kiss had probably been a ruse in case they were being watched. He hadn't felt anything. With her bubble burst, she stared at her feet, not knowing what else to do.

The bulge registered with her subconscious before she realized what she'd seen. Her eyes fixated on his crotch. Her spouse's arousal loomed before her, large and unquestionable.

She was oh-so-pleased. She giggled. Just like a silly girl.

Kamber turned his attention away from the window and followed her gaze. "Awkward." He crossed his legs, making his pants tauter at the crotch.

She giggled again. What in Bockle's name was wrong with her?

Kamber spread his legs and leaned forward, his elbow resting on one thigh and his nose almost touching hers. "I amuse you?" he asked, running a finger under her chin.

Her giggles stopped. His nearness did strange things to her insides.

Desire resonated from Kamber's deep green eyes and filled the coach. Her vision blurred. She saw nothing but Kamber.

"Maybe, princess, I should amuse myself."

Before he could make good on his threat, the carriage halted. Kamber swore under his breath and sat straighter. The lover vanished and a soldier rose to full alertness.

He scanned the area before he visibly relaxed. She looked out the coach window and spotted Remington, who'd driven the coach, waiting beneath a sycamore tree. Ronan stood next to him.

"Do you think we were smart to involve your brother?" Subena stared at Ronan, wondering how she could ever have thought he, not Kamber, might be the one for her.

Kamber made a growling sound. "Absolutely not, but he was eavesdropping when I talked to Remmy. After the devilkin got wind of our plan, it was the only way to keep him quiet."

Kamber helped her from the carriage. A perfect gentleman—and perfectly cold. The minutes inside the coach might've never happened.

Ronan smiled at Subena. "I brought the basket."

The younger brother spread the cloth on the ground near the stream, just as they'd planned. Having an festive outing had been Ronan's idea. Subena got the impression he'd never been on a picnic and the plan discussion was a convenient excuse.

"Are you sure you want to be involved in this mess?" she asked him.

Ronan nodded. "Don't you start on me, too."

He refused to look at her, just opened the basket as if she hadn't spoken and set out the food. Like the men, Subena shoveled greens onto plates, but she couldn't make herself eat.

"I'm not complaining about the food, mind you..." Remington spoke between bites as he gnawed on a reptile drumstick, "but don't you think it would have been less suspicious to talk inside the palace? Who's going to believe this? *Me*? At a picnic?"

Ronan laughed, his voice sounding younger than his seasons. "The only thing suspicious about *you* at a picnic is that we didn't bring another coach full of food."

Remington tossed his meatless bone at the younger man.

"I don't care if people know we're plotting." Kamber picked up a berry and tossed it into the underbrush. "They'll think we're planning Subena's departure, which we are. I didn't want to talk at the palace because there are too many hidden passages—anyone could listen."

And we don't know who else has supersensitive hearing.

"But only the family knows about the passageways," Ronan insisted.

"We can't be sure of that," Kamber responded.

No one spoke. They all watched Remington attack a second drumstick.

"Sorry," Remington muttered. "Did anyone want this?"

Three heads shook in unison. "Good." He took another bite and most of the second drumstick was gone.

"What I want," said Kamber, "is a way to make it look like Subena's inside the carriage while she's actually safe in the palace."

A huge ball of food protruded from inside Remington's jaw when he spoke. "Young Ronan's come up with a good plan. He's going to pretend to be Subena."

"No." Subena and Kamber spoke at the same time.

"Why not?" Ronan's jawline stiffened. They'd hurt his feelings.

"Ronan," she said softly, "I couldn't live with myself if something happened to you."

"Nothing's going to—"

"You're not going in the carriage." Kamber tossed another berry into the brush.

"You're brother's a grown male." Remington spoke matter-of-factly. "Hear him out before you decide. You wouldn't like it much if'na I told ye not to do something you wanted to do."

Kamber didn't reply. Subena could tell from the set of her husband's jaw Remington's remark hit its bull's-eye.

"Besides..." Remington swiped at his mouth with his sleeve. "I'm rather keen on seeing the lad in a skirt."

"I'm not wearing any dress," Ronan retorted, apparently not deciphering the twinkle in Remington's eye. "I agreed to a cloak. And I'll pull the hood over my head."

"Fine," Kamber barked, coming out of his pouting coma, "but the minute the carriage passes through the gate, you get out. Understood?"

Ronan glared at his older brother. "I'm not a dunce, Kamber. You don't have to talk to me like that."

Kamber's jaw tensed. Subena watched him work to visibly relax his face. Her husband picked up another berry and tossed it into the air. Everyone watched, the tension mounting, as he repeated the toss and catch, toss and catch.

"Hold on," Kamber said. A berry dropped onto the cloth. "If Ronan gets out of the coach, there won't be anyone in the carriage. We won't have a decoy."

Ronan's grin grew wider. "I'm going to make a dummy out of burlap and hide it in the carriage. When the carriage clears the castle gates, I'll put my cloak on the burlap and position the dummy so it can be seen from the window. Remmy will orchestrate a diversion by having the guards check for snipers. While everyone's running around like drunken equestors, I'll slip away unnoticed. I'll join you and Subena in the woods. Near the old well."

"It'll work," Remington said, picking up Ronan's meat.

"It's an excellent plan," Subena said, trying to appease Ronan. Appease yes, but there was no way she'd let him take her place. "It's just too risky. Why don't I just get in the coach myself and get out at the same spot?"

"Because..." Ronan sounded miffed that she hadn't supported him. "When I take off the cloak, I'll be Ronan. If you're seen outside the coach..."

Subena sighed. His logic made sense. Too much sense. She glanced at Kamber.

"Got any better ideas?" Remington asked.

"No," Kamber admitted. "You're the man, Ronan."

Subena gulped, feeling queasy. She had a bad feeling about the plan.

Genia Avers

Chapter Twenty-Six

Tears streamed down Winsome's face. "I don't see how sending Subena back to Mydrias will help anything. We can protect her better here." She glanced toward Subena. "No offense, dear, but your country doesn't have the best army."

Subena tried to smile, but she wasn't sure she succeeded. "No offense taken." The depression hovering over the breakfast table stunned her. She'd forgotten that only Kamber, Ronan, and Remington knew she wasn't really leaving Gatsle.

"At least wait until Rothart returns," the queen implored. The king had gone to Creshin's land to seek a peace treaty.

Kamber wiped his mouth with his napkin, taking longer than the simple task required. "We've been over this, Mother. Subena's in great danger. We believe the person attacking her is here in Gatsle."

"I want to go with her." All eyes turned toward Tam. He hadn't spoken once during the entire meal.

"Sweetie, I'll be back," Subena said. They hadn't prepared for objections.

Tam crossed his arms. "No you won't." He jumped up and his little legs raced from the room. She made a move to go after him but Winsome reached for her arm. "Let him go."

Subena nodded. Trying to comfort Tam would mean more lies to cover a necessary deception. She choked down the last of her breakfast and retreated to her room.

"Can I help you pack?"

She'd forgotten Kelsie. The maid had to go.

On second thought, she might provide some needed collaboration.

"Thanks. I've already packed, but you could make sure all my trunks are properly tied down on the carriage. I need to make sure I haven't forgotten anything."

The maid curtsied. Her eyes went round. If servants talked, Kelsie would let everyone know that Subena wouldn't be returning anytime soon.

"But miss... Why take everything?"

"I'm not sure when I'll return. If ever."

Kelsie's eyes widened. "Take me with you."

Subena frowned, suddenly feeling sorry for the overly dramatic creature. "I can't. The journey will likely be dangerous."

The maid dropped to her knees and grabbed Subena's hands. "Please."

Subena shook her head. "I promise you, they won't send you away."

Kelsie's sniffling intensified.

"Please stop crying." Subena extracted her arm but the maid didn't leave. She had to get rid of her.

"I'm sorry you're upset, but go now and check my trunks. I promise I won't let them send you away."

The maid still did not move.

"Kelsie, go check on my trunks. Now."

The stare-down lasted for several seconds. Subena felt her expression harden as she looked into the maid's tear-filled eyes. She felt awful, but the maid had to get out of the room. And fast.

Kelsie stood, her chin tucked into her chest. Without looking up, she prodded toward the door.

The moment the door closed, Subena turned the lock. She listened until she heard the click of Kelsie's shoes fade and then whispered, "Ronan, where are you?"

"In here." The lad stepped out of her armoire, grinning as though he enjoyed hiding in dark places. "That was close."

"Too close." Kelsie nearly always rummaged through her clothing.

Subena grabbed her cloak from the arm of a chair and pulled the wig out of the inner pocket. She tossed both items to Ronan. "Put those on. And hurry."

"I'm not wearing a wig," he snorted.

"Then I'll be getting in the coach." She reached for her cloak.

Ronan whirled it away with a flourish. "Fine. I'll wear it. But you better not laugh."

She shouldn't be amused. They were taking a real risk. While Ronan struggled with the fake hair, she peeked out her door, as much to keep from laughing as to make sure no one lurked. "There's no one in the hallway."

She gave her brother-in-law a quick hug. "Go now. Before I change my mind."

Ronan dashed out. Subena ducked back into the room. Leaning against the back of the wooden door, she whispered a quick prayer to Bockle. "Let Ronan be safe."

Two seconds was all she had. Kelsie had taken all her lag time.

She pulled the bag containing one of Ronan's uniforms from beneath her bed. She tried to dress quickly, but her arms swam in the uniform coat making it difficult to find the buttonholes. She had to roll up the pant legs and secure the waist of the trousers with her belt to keep them from falling down.

"Not exactly parade ready," she said to her image as she turned in front of the old mirror. With any luck, it wouldn't matter. She needed to be able to move about the palace thus the uniform was a precaution. If anyone saw her, they'd simply see a junior soldier, no more. Worst case, she'd be seen from a distance. Bockle willing, no one would try to get a closer look.

She unlatched the bolt, walking into Kamber's suite. She closed the door, being careful to lock the entrance to her room.

From behind Kamber's curtain, she watched Remington escort Ronan—a.k.a. her—to the coach. It would've been amusing to watch Kamber's younger brother as he hunched down, trying to take dainty steps in imitation of her own gait if she hadn't been so worried about him.

With her enhanced vision, she watched Kamber say farewell to his pretend wife, even going so far as to plant a kiss on her cheek. Subena chuckled at her husband's audacity. She'd no doubt that Ronan mumbled some choice words in return.

Her husband had publicly announced Remington would escort the carriage to Mydrias. The big male took his position. He'd keep everyone away from the coach.

"So far, so good." Using her magnification glasses, she made out the guards at the palace gate. The soldiers reminded her of ants in a disrupted hill. Gatsle guards swarmed everywhere.

Five soldiers saluted the carriage as it passed. Then, the gate closed. That was her signal to move. If she were going to meet Kamber in his study, she had mere minutes.

If only she didn't have to get there by tunnel.

Kamber had insisted crawling through the palace labyrinth was the only way to guarantee she'd reach the other side unseen. He just didn't understand the depth of her fear.

So why had she agreed? The passageway had been spooky the night before when he'd shown it to her. Without her spouse, the tunnel seemed like the very depths of hell.

She forced her body into the narrow entrance. The dank air assaulted her senses and unmoving shadows took on monstrous shapes.

She closed her eyes, willing her trembling body to be still. "I have a mission." Sucking in a lungful of dusty air, she scurried deeper into the murkiness.

Her body froze. Resisting.

"Okay," she whispered, trying to pump up some confidence. "It's just a little ole tunnel."

She ran, and then crawled, moving as fast as she could. She wished she possessed Kamber's ancient speed skill— she'd already be out of the tunnel.

Kamber would need his speed. He had to race to his study, change clothes, gather the gear, and position another dummy in his chair. A dummy that would look like her prince should anyone peer into the window.

Subena tripped over a fissure in the floor of the tunnel. She fell, scraping her knee and tearing Ronan's uniform trousers. "Crap, crap, crap."

She permitted herself a half-second to rub her leg. Then, she ran again.

Every spider web she brushed against increased her need for oxygen. She stumbled. The folds in one of her pant legs came loose. *I can't afford to fall again.* She stopped to tug the extra fabric into her boot.

Movement. She heard movement.

Subena stopped breathing so she could hear. She waited. A small animal scurried across the floor, the sound of its clicking nails echoing in the cavernous space.

"Mother of Bockle," she hissed. Leaning against the dirt wall, she placed her hand against the mossy surface for support. Dirt particles fell at her touch. A surge of panic coursed through her body.

I have to do this. She couldn't let fear sabotage her mission. *This is a only a passageway.*

She opened her eyes, glimpsing a sliver of light. Just ahead. She'd made it to the south wing. The exit was close.

"Keep moving," she whispered. She needed to take the center passage. She groped at the wall.

Something crawled on her leg. Subena slapped at it without slowing. Her mind kept repeating: *Hurry. Hurry. Hurry.* They wouldn't be able to catch the carriage if she didn't move faster.

 She bumped into another wall. Panic intensified. "Crap." She had to crawl. Her body froze. She couldn't do it.

Don't get crazy.

Self-coaching didn't help. Terror spread through her body like a slow poison. She couldn't crawl. She couldn't go back.

Voices intruded on her whimpering. She sniffed. More voices.

Subena forced her mind to reach beyond her terror. She heard the voices again. Louder this time. Something was wrong.

Very wrong.

She held her breath and crawled. She managed to reach the fork in the tunnel without passing out. She could stand.

Which direction was Kamber's study? *Think.*

She followed her instincts, running even faster than before.

She saw it ahead: the clandestine door leading to Kamber's study.

Thank Bockle.

Subena rushed to the doorway, slowing to ensure stealth. She didn't know whose voice she'd heard.

She placed her ear against the heavy wood. Instinct screamed: *don't open the door.*

"What do you want with me?" She heard Kamber sneer.

"Shut up." Another booming voice resonated through the door. An unknown voice.

Subena heard a loud pop. "Tie him up."

Someone replied, but the door was thick and the masculine accent was thicker. She couldn't make out the words.

"The guards will be here any second." Kamber's voice echoed loud and clear. "You won't get away with this."

"Most of the palace guards have gone with your pretty little wife." The unknown speaker laughed. "Besides, we heard you tell your assistant you were not to be disturbed. We thank you for that."

A loud cackle followed his statement. Several people spoke at once. She didn't understand any of them. Or recognize the voices.

"Who put you up to this?" Kamber asked.

Damn. Their plan had seemed so foolproof when they'd contrived it. She counted at least five different voices. Her heart insisted she barge into the room and demand Kamber's release. Her brain counseled her to wait.

She heard an indistinguishable sound. A flurry of activity.

A noise, maybe furniture being shoved, echoed through the tunnel. Muffled orders. The next thing she heard was "Push him."

"Do what?" That voice was new.

"Forget it, I'll do it myself."

Subena heard a loud thud.

The sinister voice laughed again. "Quick, get out of here!"

Subena heard feet moving across the floor. Fast. She strained to hear more, but no more sounds resonated. She called upon her restraint. She couldn't rush into the room.

A door slammed.

Please let them be gone.

She counted to ten. *Let Kamber be alive. I'll even forgive him for the human blood.*

She listened again. And heard nothing.

After counting to five, she pushed her body against the door. *Ouch. Ouch.*

Stepping back, she shoved her full weight into the wood. The slow swing of the door seemed to take a year.

The sight greeting her took ten years off her life. She sprinted toward Kamber as he dangled from the rafters.

A noose squeezed the breath from his neck.

Genia Avers

Chapter Twenty-Seven

"No!" Her voice echoed but Subena could hear nothing.

"No, no, no." She raced toward Kamber. How could she save him? She didn't have a knife. Nothing to cut the rope choking away his life essence.

His sprained neck would heal, but her spouse would survive only a minute or two without air. Kamber held onto the rope with both hands. His feet twitched and jerked.

"Hold on!" she cried.

Kamber needed something under his feet. She darted toward the oversized desk, ramming her hip against the furniture. Nothing moved.

Adrenaline surged. She shoved again. The desk made a creaking noise. The thing shifted. Maybe an inch.

Another shove. And another. On her fourth attempt, the edge of the desk slid under Kamber's dangling feet.

He stood on the tips of his toes, lessening the tension on the rope. Barely.

She needed something else. *The stool.*

She flung the wooden furniture piece onto the desk. "Place your feet on this!"

Subena jumped on top of the driftwood surface to help. Before she planted her feet firmly, Kamber had his boots on the flimsy stool. She reached up to help loosen the noose, but couldn't reach his neck.

Crouching low, she jumped. Her hand grabbed the cloth shoved in his mouth. She landed on the edge of the desk. After teetering once, she fell.

"Mother of Bockle." She rubbed her leg. Would nothing be easy?

Kamber gasped for air, choking.

"Are you all right?" she asked, righting her body to climb back onto the desk.

"Never better," he croaked. A coughing fit followed.

"I need a knife, Kam. Or a sword. Quick."

"In the desk," he wheezed. "Grandfather's dagger. Bottom drawer."

She found the ancient blade and sliced through the rope binding his wrists, and then handed the blade to him. He cut the rope from the rafter. He stumbled off the stool, sinking to his knees on the desk.

She hopped on the desk and wrapped her arms around him. "Who did this?"

He shook his head. "Don't know. They wore masks. I didn't recognize any of their voices."

He wheezed again. Using both hands, he popped his neck into position. A loud, unnatural sound came from his throat.

"Ouch," she said. His pain would be torturous. For several hours.

"You're supposed to be waiting at the exit." He pushed an errant strand of hair back under her cap. "What are you doing here?"

"Saving your raggedy ass. I guess I can't seem to do anything right."

His lips curved slightly. "When this is over, I'll thank you properly. We have to move now."

Sitting on her hands, she shifted her body to the edge of the desk and gingerly put her feet on the floor. Her right hip hurt like hell, but her pains seemed miniscule compared to what Kamber must be enduring. She hobbled toward the door.

"Subena, stop. Where are you going?"

She turned, surprised. "You need help."

"No one's here. Remember? We planned it this way so no one would know I'm not really in my study." He panted. "I'll be okay."

"You need help. Stop talking."

"Don't think you can go all bossy on me just because you saved my life." He put his fist under her chin. "Actually, be bossy if you want."

She stared at him. Damn fool tried to grin.

He choked. "God of the Mountain, that smarts."

"Serves you right."

"As much as I'd like to bask in your sympathy, we have to get out of here."

"Ronan." She pushed his hand away. "Oh, Bockle. How could I have forgotten him? He's alone."

Kamber nodded. He leaned against the desk, coughing hard. He took a few seconds to regulate his breathing.

"Let me go, Kam. You're not...well."

He waved a hand, apparently smart enough to know he shouldn't shake his head. "Not going is not an option."

After he cleared his throat again, he walked to the armoire. Reaching in, he held up the "Kamber" dummy.

When he leaned over to place the dummy on his chair, Kamber's collar fell forward. Purplish-red marks ringed his neck, about an inch wide. Bile rose in Subena's throat.

"Get that noose," Kamber commanded. "I need you to help me."

"The noose? Are you insane?" She glared at him, understanding he wanted to hang the dummy. "Kamber, that's just sick."

"We can't very well just sit that thing in my chair now. We've got to let whoever did this think I'm actually dead."

"No." He was psycho.

"You have to be strong—Ronan is alone. Remember?"

"You can't make it look like you're...like you've been hung. What if your parents come in?"

"We can't worry about that now. If those thugs look up at the window... My body needs to be visible."

"Ewww."

"Quit being a sissy. We've got to get to the rendezvous point."

"I'm not touching that noose."

"It's just a rope, angel."

She watched with a sinking feeling in her stomach. When he'd hanged himself, or his dummy, he reached for her hand and pulled her into the passageway.

213

After covering a few feet, Kamber yelled, "Wait!"

He darted back into the study and returned almost as fast. They were running down the secret tunnel before she could even think, "Why'd you do that?"

* * * *

Kamber spotted the equestors, tethered to a tree. At the spot where they were *supposed* to meet Ronan.

"Why isn't he here?" Subena asked.

He didn't know. Kamber tried to hide his foreboding. "Ronan will be here. Maybe he's gone looking for us. We are late." He didn't believe that. Not even a little bit.

He watched Subena breathe, waiting. Her stomach caved into her ribcage and then returned to normal. She looked up at him, wincing.

"What's wrong?"

She touched her hand to his neck. Her fingers feathered over the spot where the rope had burned his skin. "Does it hurt terribly?"

He shrugged. "I'm fine, but it probably looks damned ugly in the daylight, huh?"

She didn't reply.

"I'll take that as a 'yes.'"

She shook her head and rubbed her hand along his jaw line. Only his fear for Ronan kept him from pulling her into his arms. He scanned the horizon, looking for his brother.

"Maybe I should find some roots and make a salve for this?" she whispered.

"Not now. I don't want anyone else wandering in the woods alone. We have to wait here for Ronan."

She bit at her lip. He'd seen her angry, he'd seen her determined. He'd never seen dismay etched on her features. He succumbed to his desire and pulled her against him. A burst of new pain seared through his body when he moved his neck. The sting was worth it.

"Who would do such a horrible thing?"

He tried to make a joke. "Didn't you threaten to do the same thing?"

214

She didn't smile. "It's clearly not me they're after. Or not just me. They tried to kill you." Unshed tears glistened in her silvery eyes.

"Shhh."

"What would anyone gain by killing you? Your father's still king and you have three brothers so they couldn't hope to gain your crown." Her last words were barely audible.

"I've been thinking about that," he replied, holding her tighter. "After the chocolates were poisoned, I thought they were after you, but the attack at the opera could've been aimed at either of us. Or both of us. Someone must be trying to break the treaty. It's the only thing that makes sense."

"You're right." She nodded. "I believe the priest really was drugged—to prevent our wedding. But what would ending our alliance accomplish?"

"It would destroy the new cooperation between Gatsle and Mydrias."

"Maybe, but how would our deaths end the peace?"

Kamber reached into his pocket and handed her the note he'd gone back into his study to retrieve. "They put this inside my journal when they were stringing me up. I think it was supposed to be found after my death."

> *You are impossible. I cannot remain married to a lecherous brute. I will never return.*
> *Subena*

She swayed, her skin turning pallid. "Kamber, I didn't write that."

He kissed her open mouth. "Hush, sweets. I know you didn't." If his wife had penned the note, he'd smell her sweet scent on the paper. He'd be able to *feel* the words instead of just reading them.

"It's not even my handwriting," she whispered, backing away to take the note from his hand. She stared at the paper again. "It's pretty close though." Subena continued to look at the page. "And those brutes thought I was in the carriage so they knew no one in Gatsle would question the handwriting." Her volume had increased by several octaves, "Oh, Bockle. Did they really think it would look like you killed yourself? Because of me?" All the color drained from her already pale face.

Kamber wrapped his arms around her again, holding her arms down. "We need to be quiet. I'm not sure we're safe yet."

She nodded, nuzzling her head against his chest. "I wanted to kill you, but I don't want anyone else to."

"Such affection, sweets." He tightened his hold on her. "This is worth having a rope around my neck."

Her body went rigid. She stared into the woods, her eyes unfocused.

"Subena?" He shook her shoulders gently.

"Ronan isn't coming." Her voice cracked. "What do we do now?"

The words were too dreadful to comprehend. "We'll find him," he insisted, trying to sound more confident than he felt. He should have refused to let Ronan get into the carriage. "Let's hope he's still in the coach. Remington can look after him."

She scrunched her face. "I don't think so. He's...he's hurt."

He studied her. "How is it you can feel him when I can't?"

She shook her head. "I don't know. I'm not even sure I feel him. It's very weak, but there's a dull throbbing."

Kamber detached emotionally, attempting to clear thought for Ronan's sake. "He wouldn't just wander off. Whoever tried to hang me probably..."

"You sure you didn't recognize anyone?" Subena asked.

He shook his head, trying to clear the foggy gloom. "No, and it didn't sound like they tried to disguise their voices. Those men may have been paid assassins."

"Creshinite? Anyone from Gatsle or Mydrias would know a rope wouldn't kill you right away."

He nodded, stifling a moan. His neck felt like someone had torched him. "The question is, who hired them?"

"Someone who was able to copy my handwriting," she said.

"I believe this is your stationery as well." He pointed to the paper.

She nodded. "It would be easy to steal my stationery. It probably wouldn't even be that hard to copy my signature."

"That's true, and there's someone who's very familiar with both. Someone who knows you."

"Taslin?"

"That's my guess." He cocked his head to one side. "Quiet. I hear something. Get down."

They waited, huddled inside the trunk of a huge decaying tree. A young male came into the clearing. He rode one equestor and led another. He drew his reins about forty feet from their hiding place. Hopping down, he placed a hand to his ear.

"I can hear your breathing." The voice sounded shaky. Young. "Come out and I won't shoot."

Kamber knew him—Marcossi. Ronan's best friend.

He stepped around the tree. He felt Subena's hand around his ankle. "Marcossi, what are you doing here?"

"I, eh…"

"Answer me." He ordered. "Why are you here?"

Marcossi gulped. "I was looking for you, sir." The lad swallowed again. "I don't want to get Ronan in trouble but…"

Kamber stood straight, fighting the urge to lean against the tree and catch his breath. "You'll get him in more trouble if you don't speak up."

"He was supposed to meet me afterward," Marcossi rushed his words. "Only he never showed."

"Afterward? After what?"

"I know he wasn't supposed to say anything, but he told me about the carriage. About the decoy. He said…"

"He said what?" Kamber wanted to take the young Dökkálfar by his shoulders and shake the words out of him.

"He said to bring equestors. After he got out of the carriage, we were going to follow it."

"Damn." Kamber pounded his fist against a tree. He took a minute to regain his composure before he barked an order. "Go back to the palace. Now. If Ronan shows up, you two stay put, understood?"

Marcossi nodded, still unable to meet his eye. He put his foot in the stirrup and mounted.

"Make sure you stay with the guards when you return," Kamber snapped. "Talk to no one about this except Remington."

They waited to make sure Marcossi headed in the right direction before mounting their equestors and riding as if demons chased them. Subena feared they'd never find the carriage. They'd already lost so much time.

After an hour of hard riding, Kamber slowed Pollo to a walk. He pointed ahead. "I see someone. A half-kilometer that way. Until we know who it is, we can't let them spot us."

She squinted. Even with her skill, she couldn't see what he'd seen, but trusting his ancient sight, she nodded. "Agreed."

"We'll go through the woods," he said. "Stay behind me, but not too close. If they come after me, you ride for help."

They plunged into the trees. Branches thrashed against her arms and face, clutching at her. Something was very wrong. She tried to sense Ronan's location, but she could only sense darkness.

She heard Kamber dismount. He gestured for her to remain hidden. Complying, she watched him crawl toward the road. After looking in all directions, he motioned for her to follow.

She bent low and edged toward him. Before she reached him, Kamber jumped to his feet and ran. Subena didn't know what to do. She darted behind the tree where Kamber had crouched moments before and peered between the branches. The sight greeting her made it difficult to inhale.

The overturned carriage loomed like a beacon of alarm. The large coach looked out of place in the pristine landscape.

"What the..." She scampered toward the spot where Kamber stood, staring at the ground. He didn't turn around when she approached. All his attention centered on deep grooves in the dirt.

"I don't understand," Kamber said. "There were six guards with this carriage, but not one equestor track."

A myriad of doubts assaulted her. Ronan had been in that carriage. She was sure of that. She knew Kamber didn't want to talk about what might've happened to his brother so she remained silent, studying the horizon instead. "Maybe someone pushed the coach down that hill."

He followed her line of sight. Behind the carriage, the road lay flat. About two hundred meters away, the terrain rose sharply. The carriage tracks continued in that direction.

He nodded. "Let's take a look."

Genia Avers

Chapter Twenty-Eight

After they retrieved the equestors, Kamber tossed the reins of the mare's bridle to her. He bolted toward the hill without waiting for her to mount.

"Hold up!" Subena yelled. "You don't know what's up there."

To her surprise, he reined in the big stallion and waited. "You're right. We'll skirt the edge of the woods."

He maneuvered Pollo back into the trees. She dug her heels into the mare. They retraced the path they'd traveled earlier. When the equestors were parallel with the top of the hill, Kamber dismounted. He kept his back to her but she could feel his tension.

"Stay here, Bena. I don't think anyone's laying in ambush, but let me make sure. Too many people I love are missing."

Her heart made a tiny leap at his declaration. Had he just said he loved her?

She squelched her giddy feelings. Ronan was missing. *Concentrate on that.*

Kamber walked toward the hill, projecting masculine strength and determination. Only the clench of his jaw, barely visible, gave any indication of his agitation. When he reached the top of the hill, he gave the all clear. Her little mare trotted to the clearing.

"It looks like the guards scattered," he said. "I'm guessing they headed toward Gatsle." Kamber pointed toward the fork in the road. "Someone must have cut the harness off the carriage."

She studied the scene. She couldn't get any kind of read from the area.

"I think you're right about someone pushing the carriage," he continued. "Look, those prints lead to the edge of the hill, but only the carriage tracks continue down. See? The footprints reverse direction."

"You don't think..." She couldn't complete her question. She didn't even want to believe someone had captured Ronan. But someone had. She knew it.

"I don't know," Kamber said. "I have to follow the tracks but I don't want you with me. It's too dangerous."

"And what would you have me do? Wait in the woods?" She held his gaze until he looked up at the sky.

"Bena, please." He kicked at a rock. "Don't fight me on this."

She softened. "I'm sorry, but I have to go with you. It'll take too long for you to take me back. Since we didn't come here on the road, I'm not sure I can find the way alone. We also don't know what's waiting at the palace if I go back."

He said nothing.

She reached for his arm, "I want to find Ronan as much as you do. And I'm not terrible with a sword."

"Right. Forgive me if I don't relinquish mine to you. I have a fondness for my pointed ears." He managed a slight smile. "Let's go then. If they've taken Ronan..." The words died out as he reached for Pollo's reins. "Stay thirty meters behind me. If there's any sign of trouble, dart into the woods as quickly as you can. Promise me you'll do that."

"We're wasting time. Let's go."

"Subena..."

"Very well, I promise, but I don't know these woods. If there's trouble, I'll do better being on the open road."

He hesitated. "At least promise you'll keep your distance. If something happens, I want you to have a headstart."

"That I can do."

They rode on, tension filling her body. Even the drone of the insects sounded menacing. Subena had no choice about maintaining the distance between them. She used all her equestrian skill, but her little mare couldn't keep up with the speedy stallion. Several times she lost sight of her husband altogether. Each time he disappeared, she found him waiting around the next bend.

I'm slowing him down. She wanted to tell him to go ahead, she'd follow his tracks, but she couldn't get close enough to speak. She didn't dare yell.

The terrain proved difficult. Not only was her equestor slower than Pollo, The little mare didn't have the stamina of Kamber's big steed. After a while, Subena was forced to slow the animal to a walk. Without a rest, the mare wouldn't be able to continue at all.

She came around a bend and found her husband had dismounted. She jumped off and rushed toward him. "Kamber, I should…"

He shook his head and motioned toward the ground. In spite of the chill in the air, he sweated profusely. "They split up. I don't know which tracks to follow. Do you sense anything?"

She shook her head.

"Me neither."

He leaned down and picked up an item from the ground. He turned and held his open hand in front of Subena. A strip of green leather lay on his palm.

She recognized the narrow piece of rawhide. "Ronan tied his hair with that."

"Yes. We go this way."

She hesitated. "Wait. It's possible Ronan would just happen to lose that leather strap here, but Kamber, don't you think it's rather convenient?"

"Not if there was a scuffle."

"Maybe. But I don't see any evidence of a skirmish."

He studied the tracks again. "No, but Ronan knows I'd search for him. Maybe he dropped the leather so we could find it."

"I don't know." She had an eerie feeling they were walking into a trap.

Kamber leaned his head back and rubbed the bridge of his nose as he stretched his neck. "You're right. The strap's probably a decoy, but I have to follow it."

"It doesn't make sense." She voiced her thoughts aloud. "Why would they be after Ronan? He's not even next in line for the throne."

Kamber exhaled loudly. "They weren't after Ronan, Bena. You were supposed to be in the carriage."

She felt her lungs constrict. Her husband blamed her for Ronan's disappearance.

"Okay. They wanted me." Stiffening her back she asked, Even so, why would they take Ronan?"

He winced. "I don't think they were after you exactly. I think someone wants to get at me. Taking either you or Ronan would do that."

Maybe he didn't blame her, but the situation hadn't changed. "Then the strap doesn't make sense. If Ronan's with Remington, he wouldn't need to leave a trail. Unless..." Subena knew she grasped at very thin air. "Maybe Remington tried to divert his pursuers. He left this trail but he took Ronan down another one."

Kamber nodded. "Remmy would do that to protect Ronan. Ditching the coach and taking the carriage equestors sounds like him." He looked around. "If your theory's right, Remmy and Ronan went this way and they're probably safe. I have to follow this trail." He motioned toward the other path where they'd found the strap. "I'm taking you back to the palace first."

"There's no time."

"Subena. We have to go back. Maybe there's a ransom note there."

She scowled at him. "They tried to kill me. They left you for dead. These people don't want any ransom."

"All right," he reluctantly agreed, "but if we don't see anything within the next hour, you're going back. Even if I have to tie you to your saddle and drag you."

Her lips curved into a half-smile. "I love it when you sweet talk me."

He planted an unexpected kiss on her forehead before hopping astride Pollo. She remounted and they galloped at breakneck speed. The little mare ran hard, her sides caving in and out from her efforts.

They reached another fork in the road. Kamber jumped from Pollo's back. She watched him scan the horizon.

A voice emanated from the trees, oozing venom. "Don't move or you're both dead." Blackness engulfed her.

Chapter Twenty-Nine

Kamber froze. He heard the ticking of an assault weapon. They weren't dealing with amateurs. Worse, he had no clue how many guns awaited them.

A sickening voice behind him sneered. "Why couldn't you just die like you were supposed to?"

Kamber spun like a coiled snake. A weapon placed against his forehead halted his attempted counterattack. He couldn't do anything but watch as Subena crumbled to the ground. The assaulter pointed at him was an advanced model, designed to zero in on a target. The bullet would find him, even if he used his speed. Worse, Subena might suffer.

"What did you do to her?" he snarled.

"Just a little skill I acquired in the north. She'll come around soon enough. She'll have a doozy of a headache, but maybe that'll keep her quiet for a change. By then, you'll be dead. I'll swear you hit her. You've probably noticed she believes anything I say. Your demise, therefore, was necessary to insure our survival."

Reklaw pushed the assaulter into Kamber's chest. "You're both too smart for your own good. All that effort to make us think we had to chase the carriage, and your brother gets out and hands himself to us on a silver platter."

"What did you do to Ronan?" Kamber wondered if he dared risk taking the weapon. He decided against it. If he moved too fast, the assaulter might discharge.

"Don't try anything funny or your brother dies."

"If you hurt Ronan, I'll kill you."

The duke laughed. "Sure you will. Of course it would help if *you* were the one holding the assaulter. Or Ronan." He gave Kamber a shove. "Your brother's fine. For now. If I don't show up with you, he dies."

"What do you want?" Kamber suppressed his urge to lunge at the smirking buffoon. Any rash action on his part would lessen their chances of survival. He didn't think the duke would risk being labeled a murderer, but he could also see Reklaw's arrogance possessed an edge of desperation. That made him unstable.

"Enough questions." Reklaw waved one arm toward the equestors. "Yah, get!" he yelled, shooing the animals.

Kamber edged backward, hoping the fleeing equestors would distract the duke. All he needed was a second.

The barrel of the silver assaulter followed. "Apparently you don't understand the words, don't move." The duke glared and patted the barrel. "This baby fires silver bullets. Another step and you're dead. Now throw down your weapons."

Kamber debated making a dive to escape, but Reklaw's assaulter with its heat-seeking ammo would find him. He ditched his own assaulter and dropped his encased sword. "Don't tell me the Duke of Reklaw is going to ruin his sterling reputation by committing murder?" Maybe the popinjay wouldn't notice the dagger in his boot.

"Attacking your carriage didn't ruin my reputation. This won't either. It'll be self-defense."

"You scumbag. No wonder you disappeared after the caravan attack on the way back from Mydrias. You were one of the attackers."

"I may be a scumbag, but you're a dead."

Before Taslin finished speaking, Kamber spun and walked, hoping he'd correctly assessed the duke. No elf with character would shoot another in the back.

He called over his shoulder, "Go ahead, Dukey. Take your best shot." He kept moving, hoping he looked more confident than he felt. He didn't fear losing his neck, he worried about his wife, still unconscious on the ground. He'd be back for her if he lived. If he stayed, he was dead and wouldn't be able to help her, or Ronan.

"Forget something?" Reklaw yelled. "Subena's a means-to-an-end. Nothing more. Either you stay and cooperate or she's dead."

Kamber felt like someone had ripped his heart from his chest. Subena had somehow become more important than life. Even so, if he turned to face the duke, the male would shoot. Subena would be safer if he kept walking. He prayed to the God of the Mountain he was correct, that Reklaw wouldn't harm her.

"Do what you want with her," he mocked, continuing to put one foot in front of the other while praying his sham words were the right ones. "The lady has a bitter tongue. I'm glad to be rid of her."

He needed only a moment of indecision on the Duke's part to get beyond the assaulter's range. Kamber took two steps and then dove into a ditch. He low-crawled, his ancient speed accelerated by pure adrenaline, until he rolled behind a grove of trees.

Hidden by foliage, he remained motionless for several minutes, breathing only when necessary. Once convinced the duke didn't hover nearby, he skirted up a small hill and crouched behind a group of bushes to survey the area.

"Where's Subena?" he whispered to the wind.

Why hadn't the Duke followed? Kamber circled back, stealthy as a forest sprite, until he could view the area where Reklaw held Subena, his love. From his vantage point, he couldn't see her. Nor Taslin.

* * * *

Subena saw shooting stars in a rainbow of colors. She attended a summer celebration, although no such festivities had occurred since her father's death. The shooting stars turned into rocks and pounded at her head. *Bockle.*

She remembered. *Kamber. Assaulter.*

Shit.

Being still as a corpse, she tried to gain control of her screaming brain. Someone wanted to kill Kamber. She had to stop him. Was she too late?

She forced her eyelids open, hoping the hair splayed around her face would shield her eyes from her captor. She saw the back of a pair of boots. The golden spurs were engraved with the Reklaw crest.

And the cloak. *Mother of Bockle.* He wore the dark blue cloak she'd seen on the beach in Mydrias. Taslin was the traitor.

She attempted to sit. Her head revolted as the gyrating pains returned.

She heard a male. Kamber. "I'm glad to be rid of her."

He was glad to be rid of her? She tightened her eyelids. How stupid she'd been to think he'd actually started to care about her.

Worse, the cad was leaving her with Taslin. Just waltzing away and leaving her with a cretin who'd whacked her on the head. *Double cad.*

Taslin raised his weapon. She reacted. She pounced, for once pleased to have the strength of the ancients. Her hand grasped the duke's leg.

The strength of her contact reinforced with the element of surprise sent Taslin tumbling face first into the gray dirt. She scrambled upright. Her aching head demanded she halt all motion, but she gritted her teeth and lunged for his weapon.

Taslin hung onto the assaulter as he fell. He rolled onto his back and jumped up, pointing the weapon directly at her. Behind him, she saw no sign of Kamber. It hadn't been a trick. The cur really had left her. She cursed herself for being glad he'd escaped.

She returned her focus to the male she'd once loved. Rather the male she thought she'd loved. The magnitude of Taslin's betrayal stunned her.

"Go ahead," she hissed. "Shoot me."

The Duke jumped up. Subena backed away.

"Well, are you going to shoot or not?" She assumed a defensive stance.

She'd excelled in martial arts, but Taslin had been one of her instructors. Even if she could summon her strength after the blow to her head, he would counter every move she made.

Frig that. She wouldn't surrender. He'd expect her to use her arms so she kicked his knee.

The move caught him by surprise. He howled with pain.

Subena tried to run, but Taslin kicked his foot out. The toe of his boot caught her in the stomach, the impact so forceful, she fell backward into a ravine.

Once she started her freefall, she couldn't stop. She rolled and tumbled down the mushy hillside. She tried to keep her body relaxed to minimize injury.

With a thud, she landed at the bottom. Wet moss and rotting leaves broke her fall. She took a deep breath. Nothing seemed broken.

"Subena!" Taslin yelled from above. She lifted her head in time to see a shadow on the ledge above.

She hopped, wincing at the pain in her butt. The duke inched his way down the slope. He held onto a small bush.

The bush uprooted. Taslin fell. He flopped against the hillside and disappeared from view.

Genia Avers

Chapter Thirty

From the upper branches of a large tree, Kamber scanned the surrounding area. With his keen eyesight, he could see a long distance but saw no sign of Subena. Or Taslin. Neither possessed his speed, so they couldn't be out of range yet.

So where were they?

He looked toward the ravine. *Surely not.*

The gorge was the only place where he couldn't see clearly. He hoped Subena hadn't been crazy enough to jump.

He felt tightness in his chest. His wife wasn't native to Gatsle and wouldn't know about the danger. He jumped from the tree, dropping ten meters to the ground. Landing in a crouch, he sprang up and ran. The fastest he'd ever run.

He halted at the edge of the ravine, wondering what he should do. He knelt as close to the edge as he dared. Entering the ravine equated to sure death.

"Please," he prayed to the ancient god, although the deity was no longer fashionable. "Don't let her be down there."

He walked along the edge, searching for any kind of movement. If she'd fallen, she couldn't be alive.

His entire world felt void. Meaningless. He held onto a faint hope Subena hadn't fallen. But she and Taslin wouldn't simply vanish. Where else could they be?

He squatted down near the edge to think.

"Bockle!"

Kamber's head shot up at the sound. Subena's voice penetrated his fear-induced trance. He breathed silently, listening.

He heard nothing else. Had he only imagined the voice he wanted to hear?

He raced to the place where the sound had seemed to originate. He blinked his eyes twice, not believing what he saw.

Subena gripped a couple of small branches, trying to propel herself out of the ravine. She'd either not fallen to the bottom, or she'd climbed at least thirty meters.

"Subena." He felt light as air.

She looked up. "Thank Bockle. Help me get out of this darn swamp."

Kamber's gaze darted back and forth. He needed something to extend to her. He spotted a young sapling. He removed the cloak that kept getting in his way and pulled the small tree from the ground, roots and all. He hurried to the edge of the ravine and dropped one end of the tree over the edge. "Grab hold."

"What's wrong with you? That little sprig won't hold me."

"It's a strong tree. Grab hold."

She clutched at the small trunk. He labored to pull her upward. Her foothold gave way and she slipped, dropping a couple meters. Kamber hung onto the branch. He managed to anchor his foot around another trunk, halting his fall into the ravine. He hovered, a centimeter from death, but Subena miraculously held on.

He huffed out a breath. "Are you okay?"

"Yes. No thanks to you. Give me your hand."

Kamber grunted, the sound echoing down the deep ravine. He gave a sturdy tug on the tree and Subena's small body flew upward. She grabbed the edge of the cliff.

"You're almost there, just heft yourself over."

"I'm exhausted, Kamber. Give me your hand."

"Here, grab the branch again." Awed that she was still alive, he wanted to pull her up and into his arms. But he dared not touch her.

How could she still be alive?

Moss dust covered her. Whatever magic had saved her, he possessed none of it. One speck of that dust would kill him.

"Kamber!" Subena screeched. " I'm still angry you left me with Taslin. And I don't give two shits if you're glad to be rid of me. Give me your blasted hand."

* * * *

What the devil is wrong with him?

Okay, she got that Kamber didn't want her, but he was renowned for looking out for the welfare of his men, for ensuring no soldier was left behind, and she considered herself a soldier for Ronan.

Did her husband hate her so much he was willing to leave her in the ravine? His betrayal hurt.

"Kamber, please. I can't hold on much longer."

He looked at her but didn't move closer. He waved the small tree in her direction. "Take this. I can't touch you. You have kellany on you."

What an absolute crock. She grabbed the small sapling again. He puffed once and then pulled her the rest of the way out of the ravine.

She moved toward him. He backed away.

"What's going on?"

"Subena, please. Don't touch me. I tried to tell you, you're covered with kellany moss."

He couldn't be serious. Her eyes blurred with unshed tears. She hadn't cried since her father died. She certainly couldn't let Kamber see her emotion. "First you desert me. Then you won't help me out of the ravine. Now I can't *touch* you because I'm dirty? Frig that." She glared at him, her body stiff and ready for battle. She turned and marched toward the road.

"Bena, please. Ravines in Gatsle are rampant with kellany moss. The stuff is deadly. You know I'd do anything for you, but just the dust from the plant will kill me."

She whirled. "Deadly, huh? What am I, a sarcophagus?"

If he didn't want her to touch him, the least he could do was be honest. She got it. Her skirt was completely green when it should have been purple.

She turned her face and swiped at her cheek. She would not let him see.

"Ah, shit."

"What now?" She twisted her head toward him, expecting to see disgust. She'd probably wiped the slimey green stuff all over her face.

He took another step backward to put some distance between them. "You need to bathe as soon as possible."

The treaty, the marriage, Ronan. She'd managed to stay positive, but Kamber's betrayal zapped her strength. "I get that you're glad to be rid of me," she said, barely able to speak. "So why don't I end our misery."

She lifted her skirt, using the nasty cloth to rub her face.

"Subena, no!" Kamber lunged forward, jerking the dress from her grasp.

He backed away, holding his hand in front of him. His entire arm turned red.

She heard her own gasp. Her vision blurred, but she saw blisters form on his fingers.

"Oh Bockle," she moaned. "You were serious." She tried to get her brain to comprehend. Why was her skin unmarred?

"Hur. Ree." Kamber's words were hard to form. His throat clenched shut. "Bitson rose—rub the petal…"

"Crap, crap, crap." Where had she seen the cursed rose? She remembered. She'd seen the blue flower when she lay on the ground. She hoped to Bockle the petals would do their magic. Kamber couldn't die.

She sprinted to the spot where Taslin had held her hostage. Falling to her knees, she plucked a rose from the vine. "Please don't let me be too late," she mumbled. She scampered back to the ravine's edge.

The contamination had spread. Blisters covered Kamber's entire arm. "Blasteration. Why did he touch me?" she said aloud. She experienced an overwhelming sense of guilt. He'd thought she would hurt herself by wiping her face with her moss-laden gown.

She glanced at the lone flower, not sure what she should do with it. She twisted the stem in her hand. Kamber let out a weak moan. He labored to breathe.

She clenched her eyes shut. "Please let this work."

Being careful not to touch the rose's petals or Kamber, she rubbed the one flower as hard as she could over his hand.

Nothing happened.

Maybe the attar has to contact the skin.

She used a twig to peel off a single petal and then grabbed a fallen branch. She rubbed the petal with the branch until the oil from the rose coated the back of Kamber's hand. She used the branch to flip his hand over and repeated the process on his palm.

"I don't know what else to do," she whispered.

She sat on a rock and watched. Nothing happened. She thanked Bockle, he still breathed. But for how long?

Subena swayed back and forth. Nothing happened.

After a half hour, she leaned forward to check his hand again. The blisters seemed smaller. At least she hoped they looked smaller.

The next minutes felt like an eternity. She examined Kamber's hand, again and again, being careful not to touch his skin. The blisters were less red. She felt certain.

She waited another half-hour, conscious that every second was time not expended searching for Ronan.

The texture of Kamber's skin improved but he remained unconscious. "Wake up," she said softly and reached for his hand. She jerked her arm back just before she touched his skin. "I would have poisoned him again," she whispered to the debris that continued to trickle to the ground.

I need to wash.

She checked once more to make sure Kamber still breathed. He did.

She put her head to the ground, listening for an underground stream. Her grandmother had taught her how to find water during one of her visits to the wilderness palace.

"Who knows?" her grandmother had said. "You might have use of this skill one day."

"One day" was now. She said a silent prayer to the ancients and made a beeline for the stream. She guessed she was about a kilometer from Kamber when she found a pool of water.

She stripped and put her foot into the stream. "Yikes." The icy water made even her blood shiver.

Squeezing her eyes closed, she plunged her body into the stream. Her teeth clanged as she grabbed the petals from the roses she'd gathered on her way to the water. She rubbed the flowers over her body and then squeezed a new rose and rubbed the attar into her hair.

Her body revolted at the frigid temperature, but she stayed in the icy pool. She had to remove every trace of the moss. She couldn't hurt Kamber again.

With her skin scrubbed raw, she moved upstream and doused herself once more in the freezing liquid. She reached for her dress, halting mid-reach. Her clothes were contaminated.

"Bockle."

Using a stick, she shoved the garments into the water and pounded vigorously, doing her best to ignore the numbness creeping from her fingertips into every cell of her body. She used the remaining roses to create more attar for a final rinse. Task complete, she wrung out her garments and laid them on a rock to dry.

The cold she'd ignored during her flurry of activity attacked her body with renewed vigor when she stopped moving. She rubbed her body briskly. Maybe she'd walk out of the woods and let the Sun-Star warm her. Someone might see her naked, but it was a risk she'd willingly take.

Heading for the road, she remembered Kamber's cloak. She could wrap the outer garment around her shivering body.

After donning wet boots, Subena dashed toward the spot where she'd left her spouse. The lure of his cloak spurred her to greater speed.

She'd barely covered a hundred meters when an unexpected obstacle impeded her path. She tripped, almost falling headlong into the dirt.

"Well, well, well. Surely the show isn't over so soon."

Taslin. How had he gotten out of the ravine? She straightened, covering herself as best she could with her arms and hands.

Taslin leered at her. "There's no need to be so modest, my dear. I enjoyed every inch of your delectable body while you splashed in the stream. Had I known you hid such treasures, I wouldn't have been so patient with you, princess.

I would have taken you when I had the chance. If I had, we wouldn't be in this dreadful place today." He laughed, sending cruel chills down her spine.

His eyes fixated on a nipple that peeked through her hand. "Had I known it was a barbarian you desired," he said, "I would've been more forceful."

She couldn't fight him, he would win. It would be simpler just to submit to his lust.

Only one problem with that idea: she'd rather perish. The thought of his touch filled her with revulsion. Worse, she'd have to take another bath.

Her eyes glimpsed the wet clothing and a desperate plan formed in her mind. "Tas, love. Surely you wouldn't mar my skin with your blisters?"

"My blisters?" He stopped circling. Confusion painted his features.

"Yes, you should wash. I'm sure we álfar aren't as sensitive to kellany moss as the Gatslians, but your face is already red and blotchy. If you don't wash soon, you'll blister."

She prayed his vanity would save her. He touched his face, lingering on the scratches that he'd earned on his trip down the ravine.

"What the hell is kellany?"

"It's a moss, deadly to Gatslians. Poor Kamber died after I touched him." She gulped, hoping she hadn't spoken the truth. "Good riddance I say."

Amazed at her own acting ability, she went for the gusto. "He died begging for the bitson rose, so when my skin began to bubble, I bathed in it. As you can see..." She dropped her arms to allow him full view of her body. "No blisters. But you'd better wash. You have the green stuff all over you. Look."

"I didn't fall all the way into the ravine." Taslin brushed his gloved hand over his tunic. "My assaulter caught on a sapling after I'd fallen a few meters. I wasn't in the ravine long and I didn't go near the bottom so I don't have anything on me."

"Doesn't matter," she said, forcing a calm she didn't feel. "The moss grows all the way to the top," she lied. "Your trousers are almost completely covered."

Taslin glanced downward. Seeing the splotches of normal dust, he touched his face, panic marring his handsome features. "What do I do?"

"Well... I've read you must wash the skin thoroughly, otherwise permanent scarring will occur." Now she had his full attention.

"So what do I do?" he repeated, his voice almost a screech.

"Wash thoroughly. Use the attar from the roses. I left a few by the stream. I'll gather some more for you."

Taslin marched toward the pool, undressing as he walked. "Get a lot more of those flowers. Please."

"Sure, love." She moved slowly until she was beyond his line of vision. Then, she raced like a spirit possessed.

* * * *

Kamber watched the encounter, hidden behind the trees. He seethed as the demon duke ogled Subena's naked body. Kamber could not intercede. His strength hadn't returned and his system could not survive another contact with kellany moss. A single touch from Taslin would kill him.

He waited, his patience as frayed as his immune system. His only prayer was to hit Taslin from behind. He searched for a rock. A well-aimed blow might incapacitate the duke without skin contact.

He halted. Subena talked nonsense about Taslin's blisters. The man had no blisters. For that matter, Subena had no blisters either. Was she really unaffected by the poisonous fungus?

His wife called the scoundrel "love." *Damn her to hell.*

And she'd posed for the weasel. Kamber swore he would kill the álfar.

The duke removed his trousers. Was he planning to rape Subena?

The hell with kellany dust.

Chapter Thirty-One

Kamber slipped into the dense foliage and tightened his grip on a small boulder. He charged from the underbrush like a possessed rhinoceros, headed full throttle at the duke.

Subena rushed toward him. He screeched to a halt, barely avoiding toppling his wife. He grabbed her. She fought like a psychopath.

"Bena. Stop. It's me."

When she looked at him, he saw surprise etched on her features. *She didn't know it was me.*

"Kamber." She threw her arms around him. "You're all right. Let me see your hand."

He showed her. "The blisters are almost gone. I think your blistering tirade was worse than the moss."

She looked at him, confusion in her expression. The calm lasted less than a second.

She reared back and belted him across the chest.

"Ouch. What was that for?"

"For leaving me with Taslin. For making me drink human blood. For wanting to get rid of me. The list is endless."

"Fair enough, but for the record, I never want to be rid of you. You washed off the moss?"

"No. I'm just naked for the hell of it. Wait, what do you mean you don't want to be rid of me?"

He laughed and pulled her into his arms a second time. She didn't resist. "I'm going to assume the cold has addled your brain, because I'm fairly certain I spoke loud enough."

Instead of the punch he expected, she nested her face aginst his chest, her body shaking. If he didn't know better, he might suspect tears, but his little wife didn't cry.

"As much as I like the view," he whispered, "I don't want you to become ill. I have plans for this body when all this is over." He removed his cloak and wrapped it around her shivering body, grateful he'd remembered to retrieve his outer garment. He took his time, letting his eyes ravish her nudity.

She nodded, her teeth chattering. "After we find Ronan."

Her simple logic brought him to his senses. He possessed only half his normal strength, his brother and Remington were missing, and they were a few steps away from a madman who bathed in the forest. Even so, his trembling little wife had somehow aroused him.

He cursed under his breath and took control of his lust. "Sweets, I hate to ask, but do you think you can get Taslin's weapon?"

He expected an argument, but instead she dropped the cloak to the ground. "Good idea." She turned and headed back toward the stream.

"Subena," he hissed. "There's no need to do it nude. Cover yourself."

"What?"

"Put the damn cloak on. I don't... I don't... You're cold." What he really wanted to say was he didn't have enough strength to kill Reklaw if the cur gazed upon her beauty.

She glanced at him, smiling, but kept walking. "If that's your only concern, I'm not that cold anymore."

"Subena." He caught the flicker of amusement in her eyes as she paused to face him.

The humor vanished. "Relax, Kamber. I hate this more than you do, but if Taslin sees your cloak, he'll know you're not dead."

"Bena, wait. I don't..."

"Don't what? Don't want Taslin to see me naked? He already has. Don't want to chance contact with the moss again? I'll use a stick to get his clothes and weapon."

"Damn, wife. For once, could you just not argue?" Her logic was solid, his flawed, but he didn't want that gorgeous

240

butt within a hundred kilometers of Reklaw. "Take a stick and knock the weapon down the hill and…"

Blasted female had already entered the clearing. "Subena not listening," he muttered. "Now there's a novelty."

He followed, being careful to remain concealed behind foliage. He needn't have worried. The vain duke scrubbed his skin like fleas crawled over it. Subena gathered more roses and tossed them by the stream. He watched the duke snatch the flowers without a glance at his wife.

No need to say thank you, you equestor's ass.

Subena artfully maneuvered the stick she carried, managing to hook the weapon by its sling. She pulled it into the woods.

She was almost within Kamber's reach when she whirled and walked back toward the water. "Keep at it, Tas. You're looking better already."

The duke's scrubbed, oblivious to anything but his own hide. Good thing. Kamber would hate to kill a naked álfar.

Reklaw didn't notice when Subena used the same stick to fling his clothes into the upper branches of a huge tree.

"Bravo," Kamber whispered under his breath. "Now get the hell away from him."

His wife circled back to retrieve her clothes. She headed in his direction without increasing her speed, holding her damp garments while she dragged the assaulter.

"Where are you going?" Taslin called, a bit of panic in his voice.

"To get more roses for you," she replied, winking at Kamber. "I'll be right back."

Kamber watched her pause, her gaze on the weapon, clearly ready to grab it if necessary, but the duke returned to his scrubbing. Subena kept walking. She balanced the assaulter on the fork of the stick.

He remained silent until she was within a few meters of him. "Subena, put my cloak on."

"I only have two hands, Kamber."

"You can pick the weapon up, just don't touch me afterward. I'm not being a wimp. Another speck of the kellany will kill me in my weakened condition."

"Bossy, aren't you? Why don't I just push this over the ravine?" She pointed at the weapon with distaste.

"There's another stream just across the vale. You can wash the weapon and your hands there. We need some firepower."

"We won't get any firepower from this thing." She dropped the weapon on the ground and pointed at it with the stick she'd used to retrieve it. "See. The barrel's bent."

He bent over to look. "You're right. It's useless."

The duke's bellow echoed behind them. "Subena!"

"Forget him," she whispered. "We have to find Ronan." She resumed her stubborn march, refusing to look at Kamber.

"Bena, why are you still mad? I had to say those things to Reklaw after he hit you. Surely you can see why."

"I'm not mad."

Yeah, right. He waited, wondering how long it would take her to realize he no longer walked next to her. She whirled, perceptive enough to know she couldn't yell. She puffed an exasperated breath before she trudged back to him.

When he was within earshot, she hissed, "What are you waiting for?"

"Taslin."

"Why are we waiting for Taslin? We just got away from him."

"The duke has Ronan. We need to follow him."

"Be reasonable. If he had Ronan, do you think he'd be sitting in an icy pond scrubbing his vanity?"

He tried to ward off the unreasonable anger that swirled like a nasty mist. "He has my brother."

"He didn't ask for ransom, he didn't taunt you about your brother's fate. Gads, he didn't even mention Ronan. I bet Taslin doesn't even know Ronan's name."

Her words made sense, but the green monster controlled his brain. "Lord of Thunder, Subena. Are you defending that slime?"

"I'm not defending anyone, but I know Taslin. He had no intention of killing us."

"Maybe he didn't intend to kill you."

"At the road," she persisted. "He could have killed you and didn't."

"He wouldn't be able to explain why he shot me in the back."

Kamber was all too familiar with the expression on Subena's face. Further discussion would be fruitless. He didn't really have a counterargument so he restrained his anger. "Fine. If it wasn't lover boy, who has Ronan?"

"Let's pray Remington has him. We should hurry." She started walking again.

"Bena, wait."

"Please be quiet. We don't know who might be watching."

He whistled, loud and shrill. He needed his equestor, so he had to risk the noise.

Subena spun to glare at him. "I asked you to be quiet, so you naturally decide to see just how loud you can be?" A myriad of expressions burst across her face in rapid succession. First horror, then ire, and finally, a mask of resignation. She turned away and started walking again.

He waited for Pollo, grinning when Subena moved faster. He couldn't understand why her anger aroused him, but arouse him it did. She didn't understand his whistle, but his stallion would respond. If possible.

He suspected she was right about Reklaw. He hated the damn duke, but if Tail-Spin had intended to murder them, they would both be dead.

Kamber walked slowly. Making sure Subena stayed within his range of vision. He whistled every few seconds. Ahead, his wife entered the woods. She would reemerge soon. She might be mad, but she wasn't foolhardy.

Just as he worried she'd gone too far ahead, he heard a familiar whinny. The big stallion came to a lumbering halt beside him. "Good boy."

Kamber grabbed the reins. As he started to mount, he sensed a vibration beneath his feet. He knelt, placing his ear to the ground. More equestors.

He straddled the large steed and waited until the riders materialized. He hoped the racing animals belonged to Remington and the guards. If not, he planned to lead the possible pursuers away from Subena.

The equestors came into view. The banner the riders carried filled him with unease.

"What are Creshin's riders doing on Gatsle soil?" he whispered to the wind.

He gave Pollo a swift nudge with his heels. The stallion raced down the road. Kamber looked over his shoulder wondering what happened to Subena.

"Stay hidden!" he shouted to the wind. He'd circle back for her once he lost the riders.

"Let's go, boy."

Pollo galloped.

Chapter Thirty-Two

Blasted Dökkálfar.

After all his preaching about stealth, Kamber's whistle could resurrect the dead. The stupid elf could just get himself killed for all she cared. She burst forth, her surge fostered by vexation.

Hooves. Subena reached for a small tree and clutched at a branch. The sound she heard—that of a trotting equestor— didn't make sense.

She felt a surge of panic. Followed by understanding.

Kamber had whistled for Pollo. Perhaps her husband wasn't an idiot after all.

Summoning her reserve strength, she headed back toward her husband. Another sound halted her progress.

More hooves. More than one rider this time.

"Mother of Bockle," she whispered.

From behind her tree, she watched Kamber and Pollo speed across the open field. A group on equestors gave chase.

She hurried to the edge of the clearing and fell to her stomach. Kamber's gaze darted over the landscape, but she didn't think he saw her. He yelled, but she couldn't make out the words over the thundering of hooves.

Immobilized, she kept her head low and peeked over a mound of gray dirt. The riders pursuing Kamber gained ground. The scene made no sense. No equestor could outrun Pollo. Her spouse seemed to be leading the warlord's soldiers on a merry chase. Why? The riders' helmets bore Creshin's emblem.

The riders galloped by and kept running. She wasn't worried about Kamber. Exactly. If he let Pollo run, the steed would leave the pursuers in the dust.

The presence of the riders did concern her, though. Why were Creshin's men roaming freely through the countryside? Had the Gatslian border been breached? What did that mean for Mydrias?

She tried to devise a plan. Taking the main road wearing only Kamber's cloak was out of the question. "Wet clothes are better than no clothes," she mumbled. She crawled behind a thicket and struggled into her damp gown.

Should she wait for Kamber? Would he circle back or head toward the palace?

A huge buzzard squawked overhead. Balanced on one foot to step into her sodden gown, the unexpected noise startled her. She fell on her butt.

From her seated position, she stared, fascinated by the large bloodless bird. Its huge tail feathers were tipped with iridescent shades of blue and purple, but the predatory light in the buzzard's eye proved even more frightening than his hideous face. The flying creature seemed to be an omen.

Her preoccupation with the vulture almost caused her to miss movement in the trees, one hundred meters in front of her. She crouched lower behind her thicket. Finding a small opening, she peered out.

Taslin? *Where is he going?*

He wore nothing except the boots which rose to his thighs and emphasized bulging leg muscles. She kept her eyes averted from his dangling manhood—after a quick look. The rumors hadn't been exaggerated. She could see why the ladies of Mydrias breathed more rapidly in his presence.

His assets held no appeal for her. Even if Taslin hadn't betrayed her, all his masculine glory, enhanced by the brilliant Sun-Star, did nothing. She just wanted to know what he was up to.

She swore under her breath, "Why didn't I toss those damn boots?"

He hopped on a large boulder and shielded his eyes, turning his head in every direction. Taslin seemed to be listening. For what?

Her former friend might not want to kill her, but his interests clearly conflicted with her's. She froze, flinching when he stared in her direction.

He can't see me. The dried vegetation might catch fire from the intensity of his gaze, but she was well hidden. Right?

After an eternity of seconds, he turned his head, seeming satisfied. Taslin leaped from his perch and headed straight for a mass of boulders.

Maybe he hadn't been searching for her. But why rush toward the boulder instead of toward the road?

He was clearly in a big hurry. Subena doubted his rushed movement had anything to do with his nudity. The elf seemed oblivious to his naked state. Was Kamber right? Did Taslin have Ronan?

She struggled to button her dress as she scurried after Taslin, halting when he vanished behind the largest rock. She hunkered, waiting for him to appear on the other side of the huge boulder.

A full minute later, Taslin hadn't reemerged. She stayed hidden, weighing her options. After a moment of indecision, she made her way to the edge of the clearing, just for a look. She stopped every few steps, watching, waiting. If she went any closer to the rock, she'd have no cover.

"What the hell?" she whispered. She stood upright and dashed straight for the big rock.

She reached the large piece of granite and flattened her body on the ground. The stone's bluish surface reflected the light of Sun-Star. The dazzling effects left her disoriented. If she were superstitious, she would have bolted.

No sign of Taslin. It was as if he had vanished in the dancing, mesmerizing light.

Subena crawled forward and studied the dirt around the rock. Taslin's footprints stopped ten meters from the rock. She could almost believe the large buzzard had carried him away.

Not possible. The bird wouldn't be able to lift even a small lad.

She peered closer and noticed that the ground had been disturbed around the rock. Taslin had obliterated his footprints. Why?

She followed the swept dirt. Taslin's attempts to remove evidence of his presence created a path of another kind. One that lead directly to the rock. And ended there.

"Mother of Bockle."

She was no closer to resolving the mystery than she had been before she noticed the freshly brushed earth. What kind of magic did the duke possess?

Disgusted, she flopped down near the slab. She flinched when her thigh hit a smaller rock. She tried to move the stone, but it wouldn't budge. She knelt to get a better look. The smooth rock was dull and looked out of place.

She tugged, but the rock wouldn't budge. Frustrated, she stood and gave it a kick. The jolt pushed the rock forward.

The piece of stone moved. A grinding noise reverberated from the big boulder. She jumped back as the ground opened before her.

The shiny rock functioned as some type of lever. Moving it caused a hidden door to open.

"Could this be Ronan's tunnel?" No matter. Kamber was correct. Taslin was involved.

Subena crawled into the opening without hesitation. If there was any chance she might find Ronan, she had to follow Taslin. Even if that meant overcoming her phobia.

She needed something to place in the opening. If the secret entrance closed, Kamber couldn't find her. Worse, she couldn't get out.

Best to not think about that.

Grabbing another rock, she positioned it as a wedge and jumped down into the passageway.

Dust and mildew invaded her nostrils and a wave of nausea assaulted her. "Mother of Bockle."

Every instinct screamed, "get out," but Subena forced her legs to move forward, to go deeper into the underground passageway. She fought panic. Gads, had she really crawled into an underground tunnel? On purpose?

This is insane. Even if Kamber found the area, he probably wouldn't see the opening in the ground unless he was standing on top of the boulder. There would be no reason for him to approach a desolate rock. Another wave of fear clawed at her body.

"His cloak," she whispered. She'd leave the cloak by the boulder opening. Kamber would see it, sense it. She hurried back to the opening.

She hesitated at the entrance. If she climbed out, would she have the courage to reenter?

Not in a thousand years. Subena removed the cloak and tossed it over her head, looking back for only a second to ensure the garment cleared the door. Taking a deep breath, she tried to plow forward into the labyrinth.

She could do this. She'd gotten through the palace tunnels, right?

That gave her no confidence. How could she possibly conquer her unreasonable fear a second time? And come out unharmed?

She couldn't do this. Reversing her direction, she devised a new plan. She'd find Kamber and he could search the tunnel.

Before she reached the entrance, her empathy ability screamed with pain. Ronan's pain. Something, or someone, had hit him. Hard. Her foot caught. Her shoulder banged into the wall.

"Mother of..." Groaning, she reversed direction again, with one thought. Find Ronan.

When she reached the four-way junction again, she picked the widest passageway and headed deeper underground. After a few meters, she could move without stooping. She ambled forward until she came to another intersection of paths.

She hadn't entered a tunnel. She'd entered an underground horror—a virtual maze. Her body cast spooky shadows in the dim light from the tunnel opening. A light that grew fainter with every step.

Subena kept walking, her faint connection to Ronan driving her forward. The tunnel in front of her disappeared into darkness. She stopped in her tracks.

Had someone closed the entrance?

She spun around, determined to get out. A twinge of pain assaulted her. "Ah, hell, " she murmured, her voice so low she wasn't sure she'd spoken aloud. "I will do this."

She had the skill of the ancients and could navigate the darkness. She moved toward the pain. Toward Ronan. Her senses pulsed with more strength. She forced her eyes to focus. Even so, the walls were barely visible.

Coming to another fork, Subena looked in three directions. She saw only an abyss of blackness. Closing her eyes, she forced steady breaths. Focusing on the direction of the pain, she selected a tunnel. The opening drew her like a magnet, overcoming her need to escape the black hole.

She feared the darkness as though it were death itself. Running would keep her from thinking. She sprinted. After fifty meters, she slowed to a trot. Spider webs covered her face. Dirt fell around her. The filament felt like an avalanche. Even so, she advanced deeper into the passageway.

The tunnel narrowed. She slowed, barely able to take tentative steps. In her mind, she no longer functioned as a reasonable being. She became an eight-year-old girl, about to die in a maze. History repeated itself, but this time, there would be no rescue.

Ronan. Focus on Ronan. Using every ounce of reserve strength, she moved again. A few steps later, she saw walls. Her increased vision encouraged her to push forward.

A muffled noise brought her to a halt. She strained to hear. It could be help. It could also be some horrible creature living in the dank, musty underground.

The sound grew louder. The clear echo of boot heels on the rocky floor reverberated through the air.

Her heart lifted. Then deflated.

It didn't sound like Kamber. Or even Taslin. She could identify both males by the sound of their footfalls.

The clicking grew louder. Subena flattened herself against the wall. Whoever walked toward her probably wasn't a friend.

The sound of heels meeting stone increased in amplitude. The boots paused. She waited.

The clicking resumed but the volume decreased. Only slightly. The person had turned.

He must know the way out. She could follow the sound.

Hope pumped energy into her panic-stricken body. She hurried, ignoring the hard stone that rose up to pound her cold, sore feet. If she reached the opening—no, when she reached the opening—what would she do? She couldn't exactly waltz up and say hello. She would be at the mercy of the monster in the tunnel. Probably the same fiend who'd tried to kill her at least three times. If that person trapped her beneath the earth, she'd simply disappear.

Without warning, light flooded the tunnel. She instinctively ducked behind a wide support column. Her concealed location prevented her from being seen. It also prevented seeing. She heard voices. One of the speakers was Taslin, but the other voice echoed without identity, a blur of murmurs.

She heard sketchy portions of Taslin's conversation. His tone sounded defensive. The muttering continued. Taslin's voice rose.

One sentence reverberated with clarity. "I won't kill her."

Bockle. *Is he talking about me?*

The heated conversation continued but Subena could decipher nothing. Her sensitized hearing enabled her to hear distant sounds, but the conversation echoed and merged with drips, insect noises and other unidentifiable things. She couldn't understand a single word.

A second later, heels clicked again. Two sets. One emanated from Taslin's boots.

Click, click, click. The sound disappeared. The tunnel faded into blackness.

Subena clasped her hand over her mouth to subdue the echo of her moan. Why hadn't she gotten closer? Being discovered had to be better than dying alone in the tunnel.

She rushed toward the spot where she'd heard the voices. Maybe the entrance was close.

After two steps, she encountered a wall. The tunnel forked, but both passageways seemed to go in the opposite direction of the footsteps she'd heard. She sank to the floor, feeling woozy, and put her head between her legs. She teetered on the verge of losing consciousness. Maybe on the verge of losing her sanity.

Get up. She raised her head, wheezing for air. After an imagined eternity, she summoned the courage to stand.

She expelled a breath and stepped forward. And fell into spider webs.

Knowing her panic was irrational didn't prevent her from running wildly. She bumped into another wall. The tunnel closed in around her.

The panic gained on her—she could feel it. She could taste it.

Running faster, she rounded a corner, And saw a dim light. The smell of lighting fuel assaulted her senses. Oil from a torch, in the distance.

Panic retreated. Following the footsteps had led her in a circle. She approached the rock where she'd first entered the tunnel. The opening. She'd found the opening.

Air burned as it rushed into her lungs. Joy. She could get out. She had to wait until the people she'd followed departed. Then, she could escape.

Even better, Ronan was still alive. She'd find Kamber and together they'd search the tunnel.

She remained totally still, needing the oxygen racing through her rubbery muscles. Without warning, the light vanished.

A door closed. A bolt snapped into place.

"No!"

Chapter Thirty-Three

Kamber let Pollo slow. Calculating the best route to circle back to Subena, he almost galloped straight into another posse waiting at the fork.

More Creshin mercenaries? He signaled for Pollo to halt. The stallion reared at the unexpected restraint.

Kamber stared into the distance, puzzled. The riders waiting ahead did not move. Two men dismounted and gestured toward him.

He glanced at the group behind him, surprised to see his pursuers had slowed to a trot. Then, those pursuers abruptly turned. And fled.

He scratched his head. He considered himself adept at field maneuvers, but could find no explanation for what he'd just observed.

He counted the men waiting at the fork. Fifteen riders. Should they come after him, the odds weren't in his favor.

He decided to wait. Let the riders ahead make the first move. Every second he waited was time Pollo could rest.

The soldiers at the fork ceremoniously dismounted. The warriors stood next to their equestors. And kneeled.

What the devil?

Two soldiers got back on their equestors. One hoisted a white flag. The emblem of surrender fluttered next to Creshin's colors. The second equestrian, nudged his mount forward. That rider carried a banner with the Gatsle crimson.

"What do you think, Pollo?" he whispered to his horse, wondering what game was afoot.

He pulled the knife out of his boot but kept the blade hidden. He watched either a peaceful overture, or one of the best tricks he'd ever encountered.

As the riders approached, Kamber realized that the second rider was indeed a Gatslian guard. Was the man accompanying the Creshinites? Or a hostage?

When the riders were within range, both men got off their equestors and knelt. Kamber waited, still not certain the warriors weren't assassins.

The Gatsle guard said, "Prince Kamber. These soldiers request an audience. They are allies."

"Allies?"

The Creshin mercenary nodded, his nose twitching. "We come in peace."

"Sire," the guard said. "We have been looking for you most of the day."

"You have found me." Kamber yearned to ask the guard about Ronan and Remington, but he knew the Gatslian only by sight. He could not recall anything about the man's character, nothing to assure he wasn't a traitor.

The Creshinite wheezed. His hands shook. Kamber had heard the foreigners were afraid of him, but he hadn't believed the tales.

When the soldier didn't speak, Kamber barked, "Come man, my reputation is not as bad as that. State your purpose."

The Creshinite attempted a smile he didn't quite manage. Maybe his reputation was as bad as that.

Kamber looked to the Gatslian. "Maybe you can explain?"

The Gatslian guard grinned as the foreigner continued to sputter and cough. "Sire, allow me to present Sir Dallison. An envoy from Lord Creshin. He carries a letter from King Rothart."

Kamber raised his eyes, waiting until the Creshinite stopped hacking. "Pleased to make your acquaintance, Sir Dallison. Now tell me, for what purpose have you breached our border?"

"Sire." The Creshinite put his fist over his heart. "We do not breach. We come in peace. King Rothart gave us leave to ride into Gatsle. I have his letter." The foreigner fumbled inside his uniform coat and produced a document. He stood, holding the letter.

Kamber waved the paper away, not wanting the man to approach. He no longer suspected a trick, but a Dökkálfar didn't die from being too cautious. "For what purpose do you come in peace?"

"We are on a specific mission, sire. Lord Creshin authorized a special envoy of mercenaries, my men, to pursue and arrest a band of renegades acting without official consent."

Kamber arched a brow.

The mercenary cleared his throat. "We are also looking for Lord Creshin."

"You're looking for Creshin *here*? Why?"

The mercenary paled. "He is missing."

Kamber glanced at the Gatsle guard who nodded as if his head bob would validate the mercenary's story.

"Our lord left last week, his destination Gatsle. He came to your shoreline to escort King Rothart to the summit. He has not returned to our country."

That didn't sound good. Kamber experienced a twinge in his back. Like a sharp bit of steel. And he knew.

He knew with a certainty. Creshin was no longer among the breathing.

Even so, the Creshinite's story didn't ring true. Rothart had departed Gatsle three days earlier. "Where's my father?"

He thought the mercenary looked uncomfortable. "He arrived at Creshin's compound two days earlier. Your king didn't realize our lord had planned to escort him, so he came straight to Creshin's palace. Rothart is waiting there for his return."

Not bloody likely. There was definitely a hole in the story. His father wouldn't hang around for anyone—unless it was a mistress. *Bloody hell.*

Kamber masked his face, determined to hide his anger over his father's dalliances from a foreigner. "Why is there only one Gatsle guard with this party?"

"Sire," the Gatslian guard interceded. "There are four Creshinite parties searching for the renegades in the north, east, south, and west. All of them have Gatslian guards assigned. Since most of the palace guard was assigned to the princess's carriage, we are understrength. Dallison offered to help us with the search."

"Just how are we to distinguish between the good Creshinites and the bad?" Kamber snapped.

"Everyone under our protection carries Gatslian colors," the guard replied.

Kamber nodded. His pursuers had only carried Creshin's banner. "I believe I've just had encountered some of your renegades. They retreated when they saw you—even though you have fewer soldiers."

"Ah," the mercenary answered, "we didn't really expect to find them here in the west."

Kamber didn't allow his gaze to waiver. "Why aren't you chasing the renegades then?"

The Gatslian guard looked more uncomfortable. "I...I wasn't sure what to do, sire. I thought... I wanted to make sure it was really you. Finding you and the princess ranked more pressing than capturing the renegades."

"I see. What of the search?"

Grimness obliterated the relief on the guard's face. "We have had no other success, sire. Not yet. We hoped the princess was with you. We have seen no sign of her."

"Damn." The curse escaped before Kamber could regain his diplomatic poise. "Forgive me, Lord Dallison. I'm sure you understand my distress." He explained that Subena had been with him before he had to divert the renegade Creshinites.

He turned to the guard. "What exactly happened to Subena's carriage?"

The guard winced. "Our soldiers were ambushed sire. Remington mounted a counterattack and one of our guards was hurt. We killed half of the attackers, but the rest retreated. There was no one to interrogate."

"Where is Remington now?"

"He's leading the search party to the north. He'll be greatly relieved when he hears you are well. When he barged into your study and found..."

Kamber nodded, remembering the dummy hanging from his office ceiling. Once Ronan was safe, he and Remington would have a good chuckle and a pitcher of ale—not necessarily in that order. "And Ronan?"

The guard looked confused.

"Ronan was with Remington," Kamber said, not liking the confusion flickering in the guard's expression. "Are you saying Ronan is *not* with Remington?"

"No sir. Remington saw the young prince get out of the coach near the palace. Remington went after the men who attacked the carriage. *We* were not aware the prince was missing."

"Damn." Kamber swore again. This time, he didn't apologize. "Dallison, do you have any idea who's behind these renegades? Do they have any reason to capture my brother?"

"I'm not sure about your brother, sire, but Lord Creshin fears his daughter, Lady Vilavettia, is leading the renegades." The Creshinite raised his hand, seeming to understand he'd crossed a diplomatic line. "Rest assured. Lord Creshin considers Gatsle an ally. Any attackers involved in your brother's disappearance will be severely punished. No matter who's involved."

His meaning was clear. Lord Creshin's daughter would get no special treatment. Only who would enforce any punishment now that Creshin was dead. If only he couldn't explain the leader's demise.

He couldn't exactly say he just *knew* Creshin had met an unsavory fate. The Northerner's were a suspicious lot and wouldn't understand his knowledge. They'd think he had a part in the scheme.

"So what's your plan?" Kamber asked, having too many unsolved problems of his own to worry about Creshin's death. He's offer assistance later. "How many renegades are we talking about?"

"I don't know the exact number, sire, but we fear at least one hundred soldiers are involved in the rebellion. Alas, we do not know why they have come to Gatsle."

"How many attackers did Remington and his men kill?"

"Sixteen," the Gatsle guard replied.

Kamber rubbed his thumb over his chin. "There were about thirty riders behind me. If your intelligence is correct, that leaves over fifty men unaccounted for."

"We'll track down every last one."

Kamber nodded. "I'd appreciate it if you'd search for my brother while you chase the renegades."

Dallison bowed low. "My services are at your disposal, sire."

Kamber grunted his thanks. "I'd join you, but I must find the princess." He nodded at the Gatslian guard. "Stay with them."

Dallison motioned to his soldiers and the mercenaries mounted. He addressed Kamber. "Allow me to leave two of my soldiers with you."

"One will be sufficient. Again, I thank you." He turned toward his soldier. "Guard, I need your assaulter."

The Gatslian complied. Dallison assigned a soldier, Merk, to ride with Kamber.

He waited while Dallison, his men, and the guard rode in the direction of the retreating renegades. He nodded toward Merk. "This way."

He didn't wait to see if the mercenary followed. He circled back, heading to the area where he'd last seen Subena.

* * * *

Panic required too much effort. Subena had clawed at the door until her hands were raw. The slate would not budge.

Giving up on the door, she'd raced through the black passageway, still holding onto a faint hope there might be another opening. She hadn't found one. Despite having the skills of the ancients—heightened senses, empathy, greater strength—she'd failed. She hadn't even found Ronan.

Thank Bockle she'd kept her wits enough to find the entrance again. She sat, waiting. Subena didn't fear death. The thing she feared was entombment. Being buried alive.

Danger stalked Kamber and Ronan was most likely dead. She'd stopped sensing his pain. She mumbled new prayers. Her words were for the men in her life and for the treaty. If relations disintegrated between Mydrias and Gatsle because of her death, all her efforts were for naught.

If only I could leave a message.

Her hope of a rescue had been snuffed with the light. Whoever locked the door would have taken Kamber's cloak.

Her last thoughts needed to be good ones, for she had no doubt she would die. Ancient skills would allow her to heal herself, over time, and she could endure extended periods without air, but neither advantage would be indefinite.

She closed her eyes and envisioned festivals and music. When that didn't work, she remembered Kamber's kiss, his touch. She felt better.

To maintain her lightened mood, she sang. After a few off-key choruses, she stood and swayed to an imaginary beat. In the tight space she danced, moving faster and faster, gyrating and whirling.

Wham. "Ouch."

Her head throbbed from the impact with the tunnel wall. Her breathing grew ragged. Panic returned to take her.

Taking deep slow breaths, Subena exhaled forcefully and rubbed her head. The wheezing lessened.

Then, something large and creepy crawled over her extended leg. Her body jerked, causing her to again whack her head. Large amounts of rock and earth began to fall.

The tunnel caved in.

Genia Avers

Chapter Thirty-Four

Kamber dismounted at the spot where he'd last seen his wife. Her footprints were visible on the terrain.

"Excellent." She'd left him a clear trail.

He remembered the accompanying mercenary and turned to face him. "I'll look ahead. You follow behind and cover our backs."

Merk nodded. Kamber felt strangely comfortable with the foreigner, certain he could be trusted.

He followed Subena's tracks. "Let's hope she's halfway to the palace," he said to Pollo. Only her tracks had veered from the edge of the trees, in the opposite direction from the palace.

The equestor sensed his unease and sidestepped. "Steady, boy. Maybe she thought she found a short cut." He didn't feel as confident as he sounded. A keen sense of direction didn't rank as one of his wife's better skills, but she would have observed the terrain. If she'd strayed from the path, most likely the deviation was intentional. There were enough clues to indicate she expected him to follow.

He dropped the reins and signaled for Pollo to stay. He followed the footprints at a quicker pace, growing more concerned as her tiny footprints led him further into the brush.

Feeling a sense of urgency, he began to jog. Once it grew dark, even he couldn't follow her tracks.

He pulled up short. Subena's prints intersected with larger ones, obviously male. "Damn. We should have taken Reklaw's boots."

"Sire?"

He motioned at the ground. Alarm crossed the mercenary's face.

The guard muttered, "Acabeia." Kamber recognized the northern curse.

A few meters later, the terrain become rocky. The tracks disappeared.

"Where are footprints?" The mercenary asked.

Kamber shook his head. "Good question." Had she been captured? He saw no other footprints, no sign of a struggle.

He studied the terrain and noticed the large boulder. Maybe she'd hidden behind the big rock. He headed toward the huge stone, hoping she'd left him another clue.

As he got closer, he noted the area around the rock bore no evidence of footprints. "Swept clean." He growled, now almost certain she'd been captured.

"Sire." Merk had his head against the rock. "I hear something." The Creshinites possessed no superior skills. Except acute hearing.

Kamber heard it, too, an indistinguishable noise. Maybe Merk could decipher the sound.

"Do you know what it is?"

The mercenary held up his hand. He pressed his ear against a different part of the rock. "You will think me crazy, but the rock screams."

Both men circled the large boulder, tilting their heads to hear better. Kamber stopped moving. Merk froze, too.

The sound of a blade being drawn from a sheath echoed in the oncoming darkness. He spun. Merk drew his sword in a flash.

Kamber lifted his weapon. "Show yourself."

They watched the underbrush rustle and grow still. Kamber relaxed his grip on the assaulter. "If they mean us harm, they seemed to have reconsidered."

Merk held his sword ready. The mercenary circled the rock. From the corner of his vision, Kamber saw him fall.

"Acabeia."

"You okay?"

"Aye. But... What the hellfire? Sire, this looks like a...how you say? Doorknob."

Kamber leaned over him for a better look. "Here." He handed Merk his weapon. "Stand guard while I take a look."

"But sire," the guard whispered, "I don't know how to fire this."

"Whoever is out there won't know that. Just look fierce." Kamber studied the knob, but Merk's awkward stance intruded on his peripheral vision.

He rose and took the assaulter from the mercenary. "Here, hold it like this." He mimicked an aggressive posture.

Merk shifted the weapon and acted ferocious, but the positioning of the weapon didn't look realistic.

"Ah, hell," Kamber muttered. "Let's hope anyone watching doesn't know how the assaulter should be held either."

He turned his attention back to the knob. He pushed and pulled. Finally, a door on the rock opened. As it swung around, the heavy slate knocked Merk in the back. He fell forward. The weapon discharged.

"Acabeia!" Kamber muttered as he grabbed the weapon and re-pumped the mechanism. He used his other hand to help the mercenary stand. "Are you okay?"

Merk tried to speak but liquid flowed from his mouth.

"Shit." Kamber propped the mercenary against the side of the rock and examined the soldier's back. "I think the door crushed your ribs. You feel dizzy?"

Merk shook his head. Kamber knew he lied.

"Can you hang on for a bit? I must find the princess."

"Go," Merk spat.

"Excellent." Kamber stopped before he patted the soldier's back.

Rocks and dirt covered the entrance. Kamber studied the earth, barely able to see. He backed away from the door.

Subena cannot possibly be in there. His little wife would not have gone underground without a fight. Did someone force her inside?

Behind him, Merk's breathing rattled.

Everything okay?" Kamber asked.

"Go, sire. You must go in now. I hear breathing, but the breaths grow faint. Be fast."

Kamber tossed rocks from the doorway, careful not to sling any debris in Merk's direction.

263

Genia Avers

"Toss me a couple of those stones." Merk's voice had graveled from his pain.

Kamber stopped moving boulders, confused.

"We need light," Merk said.

"Of course. Fire." To see in the tunnel entrance.

Kamber grabbed two rocks and pitched them toward Merk's feet. He raced to the edge of the woods and grabbed some dried weeds and sticks. While the mercenary worked on starting a fire, Kamber crawled through the open door to resume his excavation.

"Be careful," Merk warned. "You do not want the rocks to...what is word? Cave in."

The man had voiced Kamber's fear, but they didn't have time for caution. Kamber worked, removing rocks to clear a path. He labored for fifteen minutes before he also heard breathing.

Subena. He'd recognize her soft exhalation anywhere.

He hadn't cleared enough debris to get through the tunnel. He dug with more fervor. Not stopping. Desperation kept his muscles strong.

Twenty minutes later, he glimpsed something. "Subena?" Was that a white-blonde curl?

A surge of energy sent rocks and dirt flying through the opening. Minutes seemed like eternity, but finally he cleared enough of the debris to get through.

He rushed into the hole. To her.

"Subena." Thank God.

She didn't reply. Her unconscious body clung to life— barely.

He carried her from the underground and positioned her frail body on the ground. "Breathe, angel."

Merk hobbled over. "She needs healer."

Kamber nodded. He lifted her almost lifeless frame, holding her as if she was made of glass. He placed her on Pollo. "So do you, Merk."

Kamber fought the wetness encircling his eyes. Despair clamped onto his heart like an angry demon. He could not lose her now that he'd come to love her. He couldn't lose his true mate.

"Take her to the palace. Pollo knows the way."

The mercenary's head popped. "But..."

264

"I cannot help her—she needs the healer. I must find my brother. He's in this hole. Otherwise, Subena would never have entered a tunnel." He turned so Merk wouldn't see his pain.

No time to waste. Kamber rushed into the tunnel knowing his heart would burst if he looked at Subena again.

"Please, God. Let her survive."

Genia Avers

Chapter Thirty-Five

Kamber wasn't afraid of death, but fear for Ronan consumed him. He could deal with any adversary, but he wouldn't be able to cope if something had happened to his brother.

Someone knew about the tunnel and that someone had to be Gatslian. He was dealing with a traitor.

He listened for any kind of noise before he lowered himself into the opening. Once he dropped, he'd be exposed. He should wait for reinforcements, but too many things could happen in twenty minutes.

After he pressed the hidden lever that caused the wall to open, he removed the locking mechanism. He wasn't going to let anyone or anything trap him inside.

Cautiously, he maneuvered himself through the narrow opening. "Ahkkk. What the…"

He felt an intense pain in his skull. Someone hit him. *Who*? Why hadn't he sensed anyone?

He tried to turn, to see, but his body wouldn't cooperate. The black tunnel became even blacker.

* * * *

The blackness no longer frightened her—it engulfed Subena like a lover. She welcomed the night. Maybe she acted like a coward, but she succumbed to the hypnotic spell of death.

Wait. She had to find Ronan.

She tried to breathe life back into her lungs. The air wouldn't come. A scream of agony escaped her lips. She jolted upright.

And sat in her bed.

Whose bed?

"Subena?"

She tried to focus. After rubbing her eyes furiously, she recognized Queen Winsome.

"Winsome. How did I..." She blinked again, swallowing hard. The air felt like fire circulating through her ailing body. A bandage covered her forehead and eyebrows. Every bone, tendon, and muscle ached.

"Merciful angels, you're awake." Winsome's smile wobbled. "You've given me such a scare. You seem to have some of the restorative magic of our ancestors. I'm so glad, Subena. Without your ability to heal, you would surely have perished."

Memory flashed through her brain. "How did I get here? I remember...the tunnel."

"Take it slow, dear. You must rest and let your power heal your body. It's a miracle you survived the avalanche. It's beyond miracles that you have no broken bones. The healer said you'd be who's the most powerful of our kind, would not wake this soon after such an ordeal."

Horror grabbed for Subena. "How long have I been here?"

"Only a couple of hours."

Full memory flooded her senses. "Kamber. Is he..."

The queen nodded. "He found you. But he hasn't returned."

Subena touched her face, almost too afraid to ask. "Ronan?"

Winsome's pallor turned deathly white. She shook her head, unable to speak. After swallowing, she tried again, "Remington's searching. Merk said Kamber was still at... Love, why were you in that godforsaken hole?"

"Who's Merk?" Hurt put a chokehold on her heart. Ronan languished in the tunnel. Near death.

"We'll talk later." Winsome's smile looked like she'd rather cry. "You must rest."

Subena couldn't rest. "There's no time. Ronan's in that tunnel. I followed Taslin and heard him talking to someone. That person took Ronan and I don't know who it was."

"You think Ronan's…" Winsome gasped. "I told him to stay away from…"

"Winsome," Subena spoke softly, "If Ronan's down there, Kamber will find him." Her love had found her. He would find Ronan.

Her mother-in-law blinked away a tear. "I don't know whether to applaud your courage or throttle the two of you. You scared me to death. Subena, what if Kamber hadn't found you?"

She tried to smile. "I knew he'd find me. I left the cloak so he'd know where I was."

"I didn't hear about any cloak. Merk heard you breathing. If he hadn't been with Kamber… When you're feeling better, I'll introduce you to the brave mercenary who saved your life. He got hurt during your rescue, but he's doing better."

"Heard me breathing?" Subena's brain hurt. She didn't think even Kamber could hear breathing beneath rocks and dirt. Not a hundred meters below ground. She rubbed her bandaged head. "Who took the cloak?"

The queen shook her head, her expression still grim. "Merk didn't mention any cloak."

She tried to relieve the tension with a joke. "Maybe that silly maid followed me and took it. She's always asking for my clothes."

"Maid? What maid?"

"Kelsie. The maid you assigned me. I've been trying to dismiss her since the first day I arrived, but she just won't leave."

"Subena, I know how you feel about servants. I wouldn't insult you by assigning a maid."

She stared at her mother-in-law. "Bockle help us. I should have placed her accent earlier."

"Let me guess," Winsome snarled. "Northern."

Subena's eyes widened. The gesture hurt. "How did you know?"

Winsome explained about the mercenaries and their search for the renegades. "Rothart sure picked a fine time to be out of the country. Typical."

Subena felt the hurt in her mother-in-law's voice. As much as she wanted to comfort Winsome, she needed all her strength to focus on the immediate crisis. "Kelsie must somehow be connected to the renegades."

Winsome's eyes widened. "What are you thinking?"

"When those thugs tried to kill Kamber in his study, they wanted to make it look like his death was my fault. Someone wants the treaty to disintegrate and I think they wanted me to disappear, too. Kelsie was always roaming the halls—I think she's behind all the trouble. The question is, who is she? And why is she doing this?"

"They tried to kill Kamber?" Winsome screeched. "I thought that horrible thing dangling from the rafters was some kind of morbid joke."

Subena leaned forward, intending to get out of bed. Dizziness overtook her. She gripped the bedpost.

"What are you doing?" the queen asked. "Lie down."

"Can't." Subena repositioned her body, deciding she'd rest her head on the pillow for one more minute. When she gathered enough strength to speak, she told Winsome about the attempt on Kamber's life.

As she talked, an idea formed in her throbbing head. "Whoever's behind this doesn't know I'm still alive. I think Rekita's involved somehow, too. Rather, I know she is. We must question her and Kelsie at once." She stared at Winsome. "Who knows I'm conscious?"

"Just me."

"Good. Spread the word that my injuries are extensive and you don't expect me to regain consciousness."

"Subena, no."

"You must. It's our best shot at getting Ronan back."

"But... We Gatslians believe strongly in self-fulfilling prophecies. I can't say that."

"Someone kidnapped Ronan, Winsome." She didn't add, "And he's dying."

The queen shook her head. "You ask too much. I can't say you won't recover."

"You have to."

Winsome placed her open palms on her cheeks, her breathing shallow. "What makes you think Rekita's working with this so-called maid?"

"My clothes. Rekita knew the gown I wore to the brunch was from Taslin, but only Kelsie could have slipped it into my room. I think they used the gown to identify me. I bet whoever placed that chocolate on my plate didn't even know me. They looked for the dress."

"Slow down. You're going too fast. What does all this mean?"

"It means they wanted to cause discord between Kamber and me. When they couldn't get me to leave Gatsle, they became more desperate."

The queen wrung her shaking hands. "I'll question Rekita, but I don't know if I can say those awful things about your health."

"Please. Rekita will talk more freely if she thinks the plan has worked."

Winsome nodded, not looking convinced. "I'll have to talk to the guard first—he may have heard me talking to you."

Subena nodded. The pain in her head made her wish she'd remained still. "Good idea."

She tried to smile to reassure Winsome. "Be careful when you question Rekita. We don't really know what she's capable of."

After Winsome left, Subena fretted. She needed to be doing something, but every time she stood, dizziness overtook her. Hearing the tap on her door was a welcome distraction.

The queen burst through the double doors before Subena could say "Come in."

"We can't find this Kelsie. Rekita's asking to speak with me. She came forward before I could send for her. What do I do now?"

"We stick to our original plan. Ask the guard to come in."

The young guard entered. Subena addressed him by name. "Kulley, the queen's going to invite Rekita into the outer room. I'm not sure what will happen, but you must not let her leave this room. No matter what. Understood?" The

271

guard nodded. "In the event she becomes hostile, you must also keep her quiet. Can you do that?"

"Yes ma'am." The guard's expression never changed but curiosity lit his eyes.

She turned toward the queen. "Let Rekita do the talking. If she mentions anything about Ronan or me, bring her into this room and I'll finish the interview. Once Rekita enters this room, she can't leave. We don't want her to warn her cohorts. Whoever they are."

Winsome nodded.

"Okay, then. Bring her in." Subena hid behind the door, doing her best to keep from swaying.

"My dearest queen," Rekita said. "I'm so sorry to bother you."

"I'm very distraught, Rekita. I hope this is important." Winsome's distaste echoed in her voice.

"Yes, my lady. I feel there's something I must tell you."

Subena wondered if Winsome's surprise equaled her own.

"Tell me what you want," the queen ordered. "My dear daughter-in-law is so gravely ill…"

"How is the princess?" Rekita asked, actually managing to sound concerned.

Subena wanted to gag. She couldn't hear Winsome's reply because the queen's soft voice didn't resonate loud enough. She just hoped Winsome hadn't lost her nerve.

"My lady, I don't know how to say this." That sounded more like Rekita.

"Just say it," Winsome spoke louder. "Can't you see how difficult conversation is for me?"

"Perhaps it is naught, but one of my servants swears she saw the princess in the woods with Ronan yesterday morn."

"What nonsense is this?"

Subena wanted to hug Winsome. She'd responded brilliantly.

"You're right, perhaps the servant is mistaken, but still she swears…" Rekita let the sentence linger. "Since Ronan's missing, I fear Subena might be involved. The two of them seemed unnaturally close. I mean, Subena's supposed to be married to Kamber."

"We must not speak where the guards can hear!" Winsome snapped. "Come into the inner chamber."

Subena jumped back, not anticipating events would unfurl so rapidly. She leaned against the wall as the two females entered, flanked by Kulley. The guard closed the door, bolted it, and posted himself in front of it.

Rekita stared at the guard before she turned to face Winsome. The Dökkálfar shrieked when she saw Subena. "You!"

Another wave of dizziness attacked. Subena couldn't respond. All her efforts were focused on remaining upright.

The queen assaulted the beautiful facade of a female. "Rekita, what have you done with my son?"

"My lady, I would never..."

"Arrest her." The queen motioned to Kulley, who came forward with shackles.

Where the devil did he get those? Subena stifled a smirk when she realized the chain came from the candelabra.

"No!" Rekita begged. "I swear I don't know where Ronan is."

The queen crossed her arms over her chest. Subena had never seen the gentle Winsome look so formidable. "You have three seconds to tell me where my son is or I will personally see that you never get out of the cell-yard."

Rekita shook her head back and forth in rapid succession. "They told me to come and say Subena had him. They said they would kill Taslin if I didn't."

Time to intercede. "Who are *they*, Rekita?"

"I don't know. Kelsie came to me after the treaty was proposed and told me she'd help me get Kamber back if I did as she said. Once I got involved, she wouldn't let me stop. She threatened to tell everyone what I'd done if I didn't keep helping her."

"Who's she working with?"

"Other than Taslin, I don't know. I swear I don't know." Rekita's tears looked genuine. "I was so jealous at first because I thought Taslin was Kelsie's lover. But he isn't. He can't be, because that creature is threatening to kill him."

"Where is Kelsie?" Subena demanded.

Rekita shook her head, more tears streaming down her face. "I don't know. They don't tell me anything. Other than, 'do this, do that.'"

"When did she tell you to come and lie to the queen?"

Rekita's head popped. Subena glared , although the effort pained her throbbing head.

"This morning," Rekita whispered. "She told me to wait two hours after the evening tea. I was to come here and talk to the queen. I'm sorry."

The little wretch sobbed. Subena suspected Rekita's sobbing was enhanced to save her hide. The wicked elf reached for the queen's hand, but Winsome backed away. "I came because Kelsie said she would kill Taslin. Honest."

Subena continued to glare. Rekita turned to Winsome again. "Queen Winsome, you know I'd never hurt you. You're like the mother I never had."

Subena worked hard to keep from vomiting. Literally.

"Don't play me, Rekita." Winsome glowered at the troublemaker. "No daughter of mine would ever be part of such evil."

Evil. Subena remembered the heated conversation in the tunnel. *How does Kelsie know Taslin?* "Rekita, were you working with Kelsie before you met the duke?"

"Yes." The defiance in her face seemed more like the Rekita she knew. Subena and the queen exchanged a look over the witch's no-longer-sobbing head.

"So when did you meet the duke?" Subena asked.

"Kelsie brought Taslin to Gatsle for a meeting. She introduced us. We…connected. I wanted to go back to Mydrias with him, but they wouldn't let me. The way he waited for you, like a lap dog. It made me sick."

Rekita took a half step toward Subena, an unnatural light in her eyes. She cowered back when Kulley moved toward her.

The queen motioned for the guard to halt. "Don't raise your voice again, Rekita," Winsome warned.

"So what exactly did you do for Kelsie?" Subena asked.

"Nothing big. I just had to listen and tell her anything I heard. She wanted to know everything about the treaty."

"How is Taslin involved?"

"I don't know. He showed up after the treaty had been proposed. Kelsie said I was to follow his orders. He told me to keep sleeping with Kamber. Even after he and I... I hate him for making me act like Kamber's slut."

Rekita glared at Subena. "I heard about you and Taslin, and I hated you, too. Then Tas told me he'd never loved you and..." She started to sob again.

"Rekita," Winsome hissed. "Stop sniffling or I'll have you gagged."

The sobbing stopped.

Subena asked, "Who found the entrance to the tunnel?"

Rekita didn't answer.

The queen barked, "Unless you like shackles, Rekita, I suggest you tell Subena everything you know."

"I found the entrance by accident. I followed Ronan every time he looked for it." Rekita talked so fast, little bits of spittle flew from her mouth. "The day you rode with him, I had to conceal myself behind the big rock. I accidentally sat on the mechanism that opened the door while I was hiding."

"Did you shoot at us?" Subena asked.

"What?" Rekita and Winsome spoke in unison.

"The day I went riding with Ronan, someone shot an arrow at me."

The queen's mouth gaped.

Rekita shrugged. "It wasn't me."

Winsome swallowed hard. "I suspect that much is true, Subena. Rekita thinks a bow is something you wear in your hair." The queen whirled and fixed a stare on the Rekita. "One more thing, missy. Where's my mother's ring?"

Rekita's jaws puffed when she swallowed. "I don't—"

"No more lies. Give me the ring and tell me how you got it."

Subena's jaw dropped when Rekita pulled the ring out of her pocket and handed it to the queen. "Taslin gave it to me. He didn't even know I recognized it."

Winsome handed the ring to Subena. "I believe this belongs to you."

She met the queen's gaze. "How did you know she had it?"

"I have eyes, dear. I saw her flash it under your nose at the luncheon. After that, I made some inquiries and found out my foolish son lost it in the tavern. Apparently Reklaw, or one of his spies, hovered nearby and picked it up." Winsome winked at her. "I have my sources, too, you know."

The queen called for another guard. "Have someone locate Remington immediately. Then send me another guard, I have a warrant to issue."

Rekita looked up. Her eyes magnified her terror.

"Not you, you silly twit. Not unless you open that mouth of yours again."

The queen sprang into action, a bundle of nerves. Subena remained still. She knew what she had to do.

Chapter Thirty-Six

Subena paused, letting her body adjust to the persistent dizziness. Winsome put her hand on her shoulder.

"You must lie down. The healer told you to stay in bed."

"I have to go."

"You can barely walk. I'll send the guard to assist Kamber. Remington will be here soon."

"No, I have to go. Now."

Winsome froze. As if she'd been struck. The look in her eyes hardened into understanding. The queen's intuition was also strong.

"I'm going with you." Winsome looked determined.

"No—no time. I have to hurry. Have someone saddle Pollo—and fast."

The queen opened her mouth but closed it again without attempting to argue. She rushed to the door, barked orders, and returned. "Put your arm on my shoulder. I'll help you down the stairs."

They waited by the palace entrance while a lad ran to the stables to saddle the equestor. The crisp night air cleared some of the fog from Subena's head, but standing upright proved a tricky endeavor.

Ignore the pain. Her body convulsed in protest.

The queen gripped her arm. "This is crazy. You can barely stand. Let me at least send—"

"No time. I may be the only one who can find them. Send someone after me as soon as you can." She refrained from moving but another wave of pain assaulted her body.

The queen fidgeted with the buttons on her gown. "I don't mean to embarrass you, but I know you have visions. Did you have a vision about Ronan? Or Kamber?"

"No vision, just intuition."

* * * *

Kamber saw a blazing flame but felt no warmth. The light disappeared only to be replaced by a bolt of pain. His head hurt like hell.

Being a seasoned fighter, he knew the drill. He regulated his breathing and heart rate so the pain would get less oxygen. When he managed to contain his agony, he remembered. *The tunnel.*

Without raising his chin, he looked around. He felt the bindings restraining his hands behind him. His fingers groped at the constraints. Metal shackles instead of rope. *Frig.* He could've gotten free of rope.

His feet couldn't move and he felt icy steel where leather boots had been. His eyesight was uncertain when he tried to focus. In the torchlight of the tunnel, he could barely make out another figure.

Ronan. His heart leaped.

Irons immobilized his brother, but his stomach methodically sucked in and then out. Thank God, he still breathed.

He smelled a scent he didn't recognize—a strange rosy fragrance. The odor overwhelmed. He kept his chin low and pretended to be unconscious. *Let them think I'm still out.*

He saw dainty feet but made no move to see more; he needed time to plan a counterattack.

An argument raged around him. At first he couldn't make out the voices, but as his consciousness improved, his hearing became more acute. He knew the male. The whiny voice belonged to the Duke of Reklaw. He wondered if the bastard was still naked.

"What do we do now? It's bad enough Rekita hasn't returned, but what do we do with him?"

"We kill him, of course." The female snorted. "No one will find either of them when we blow up this tunnel."

Kamber didn't recognize the female's voice. Nor did he remember the scent.

"We can't be sure no one else knows about this place," the duke pleaded.

"Of course we can. Ronan has no guile for lying. He said no one knew about the underground passageway with the possible exception of his older brother. And, voíla. We have the brother."

"What if he told Subena?"

"Don't talk to me about that bitch. If your aim had been halfway competent, she would have died at the opera."

"My dart landed exactly where I wanted it to go. If I'd meant to kill her, she'd be dead. What happened to your arrow?"

"She moved." The dainty foot stomped. "Not that it matters. You said Kamber doesn't trust her. Why would he tell her anything?"

"I don't know, but I don't like taking chances. I picked up his cloak at the tunnel entrance. Maybe she left it there. For him to see."

"For once, I agree with you. It's better to be certain. Talk to your little girlfriend before we leave. If Subena knows about the tunnel, kill her. And do it right this time."

"I can't talk to Subena again." Taslin's voice echoed with fear. "I'll be arrested the minute she sees my face. Have you forgotten? I pointed a gun at her and the precious prince. Hell, I'll never be able to go back to Mydrias."

"God, you're such a wuss." Kamber heard a sharp intake of breath. The female was clearly in charge.

A boot kicked at the dirt walls. The thud echoed in the passageway and a surge of dust and grit rose up from the tunnel floor. The cloud billowed around Kamber, reached into his nostrils, and made breathing impossible. He coughed.

"So, the brave prince awakens. Daddy's favorite son," the female voice mocked. "So sad you have to perish."

She grabbed Kamber's hair and yanked his head up, forcing him to meet her gaze. She looked so familiar.

The she-wolf tightened her grip. She possessed amazing strength.

"Who are you?" Kamber ventured.

"Look closely," she challenged. "I'm sure you'll figure it out. I think I resemble my father."

Kamber stared, forcing his pupils to open wider. Dark hair, possibly green eyes. The familiarity of the smirking face overwhelmed him, but he couldn't identify the evil beauty.

"I suppose a deal's out of the question?" Any attempt to bargain would be futile, but he needed to keep the female talking. Just long enough for the reinforcements to arrive. Merk would send help.

She laughed, letting go of his hair and shoving his head. "Alas, no. I considered keeping you as a slave. We need more people to clean the sewers in my country. I'd love to see you suffer, pretty boy. Too bad I cannot take the risk."

"I can get you a large sum of money. And free passage to the north."

She sneered. "I don't need your stinking money. All I want is your demise. With you gone, I'll have free passage. For that matter, I'll have large sums of money, too."

Kamber played to her vanity. "You seem like a smart lady. Murder's a tricky thing. Why take the risk?"

"There's no risk, pretty boy. No one will ever connect me to your death. Since your darling wife didn't die like she was supposed to, I'll make sure she's blamed. For the death of two Gatsle princes. Not my original plan, but still perfect."

Subena blamed for my death? He couldn't let the female see her words affected him. "If you're going to kill me, at least tell me what you hope to gain by framing my innocent wife."

"Innocent?" the harpy shrilled. "That bitch depleted centuries of quartz with her technology projects. She squandered our life sustenance in her arrogant pursuit of toys. And what does she have to show for it? Defunct motorcars and a starving country."

Kamber felt the same way once. Now, he resented his captor's accusations. Subena had tried to fix centuries of abuse. She'd had no part in the squander.

But why would a Creshinite care about crystals? "What do you mean life sustenance? Aren't you from the north?"

She laughed, the sound shrill and unnerving. "And here I thought you didn't have one working brain cell. I am Creshinite, but as much as I hate to admit, part of me is like you. My essence needs earth magic."

Kamber's head reeled. A Creshinite would probably assume all elvin people were alike, might assume Gatslians needed crystals. But why did this female need crystals?

"Killing me won't restore the quartz."

"I'm not killing you because of the quartz, you idiot. I'm killing you to end the treaty."

He didn't understand her logic. "Killing me won't kill the treaty either."

"Of course it will. Your dear sweet wife has already been linked to Ronan's disappearance. Once you disappear, she'll be blamed for that, too. Rothart will have someone's head in a noose when his precious sons are gone."

Kamber felt some satisfaction. The Creshinite underestimated his family's trust of Subena. The king would never believe Subena would hurt Ronan. Or him. The treaty would hold.

"I also want you dead for more personal reasons."

He jerked his head in her direction. "What?" He couldn't care less about her personal issues, but the longer she talked, the more his odds improved. He had to keep her talking. "Personal reasons? Why? Who are you?"

"Look at my face again." She pressed her nose an inch away from his. Kamber couldn't see well, but something about her looked too familiar.

Keep her talking. "I'm looking. Not seeing anything." He scrunched his nose, hoping to provoke her into rage. "What am I supposed to see?"

"So many questions, brother. So little time. What you should see is that I intend to destroy Gatsle. In the name of my father, or rather, my stepfather."

"What have you got against Gatsle? Wait. Did you call me brother?"

"That I did." The female sneered. "I suppose I should have said half-brother. Our dear old dad seemed to have dipped his wick in every pot around. While Gatslian females get pregnant only by a tryst with a true mate, my kind, and my mother, weren't so lucky."

Kamber felt as if he'd been buried alive. Her face—it was his father's face. If Rothart's screwing around caused Ronan's death, he'd kill his father. Even if he had to do it from the great beyond.

"Who are you?" he whispered. "Is Rothart really your father?"

The mad lady snorted. "The people who know me here call me Kelsie, but my real name is Vilavettia. You may have heard of me."

Creshin's daughter?

Her laugh sounded like audible evil, like a siren from hell. The warlord's daughter was notorious, having a reputation as the most fierce of mercenaries and even more notorious as a spy. Too bad Dallison and his men hadn't gotten to her.

"If you really are Vilavettia, I'm not your brother. Creshin is your father, not Rothart."

"You're as stupid as your sire. Of course you can be my brother. Don't you listen? Creshin is my stepfather, you dimwit." The female's fists curled into tight balls. "Creshin took pity on my mother after that piece of dung Rothart used her, dumped her, and then refused to acknowledge his bastard daughter. Me." Her voice screeched.

She pounded a fist against her chest. "Our father kisses your ass but he'd never even acknowledge me. That would mean admitting he fornicated with a Creshinite."

She rose off the ground and hovered in the air. "Damn fool."

God of the Mountain. She could fly. That's why Subena had asked him if he could fly.

Brave as his troops were, they were also superstitious. They might bolt when they saw a flying harpy.

"I'm the most powerful person on the planet," she squawked. "I have the skills of your ancients and all the skills of the Creshinites. Despite that, the arrogant fool Rothart still wouldn't acknowledge me."

Kamber felt supreme fear. Kelsie—he supposed he should call her Vilavettia—was a female scorned. *A lunatic scorned.*

It didn't get any scarier. "If you want to go after my father, I'll help you, but my brother's innocent. Let him go."

"Are you insane?" She glared at him. "Don't you get it? I hate you and your asinine brothers. Your father wouldn't acknowledge me, but that didn't keep him from coming back to sniff around my mother. The damn elf never shut up about you. I hate your little bride even more. She's Rothart's newest favorite."

Kelsie, a.k.a. Vilavettia, lowered herself to the ground. The witch slapped him across the cheek, making him see a new round of stars.

"Did you know Rothart insisted on the wedding because he wanted Annika's daughter? That Mydrian bitch was the only female to ever refuse our father. Annika wasn't married at the time, but she was promised to the Mydrian emperor. When the leader learned about our dear-old sire's obsession, he confronted Rothart and tensions between Gatsle and Mydrias reignited. I intend to see that tension intensify and destroy both countries."

Kamber's head reeled. His father had wanted Annika?

No. He couldn't think about his father's love life. For Ronan's sake, he had to keep the crazy witch talking.

"I'm sorry you got a raw deal, Vila. Have your revenge. Kill me if you must, but there's no need to start a war."

"You really are dense." She looked at him as if he was some bloodless vermin. "My objective is to dissolve the treaty. I've tried to convince my stepfather to destroy Mydrias. He wanted the cilosange, but he wouldn't strike because Gatsle and Mydrias became allies. He probably wouldn't have attacked period, but I will." She made a growling noise. "After Mydrias burns, I'll go after Gatsle. I need that quartz."

Holy hell. If the female were half Dökkálfar, she'd need blood, not quartz. No wonder she was psycho. If she'd spent her life drawing on the power of crystals, she'd be completely mad. Crystals destroyed the life essence of Dökkálfar four times faster than the glass affected the Mydrians.

Keep her talking.

"You really think you're a match for Gatsle?"

"My stepfather will help. Unlike Rothart, Creshin loves me."

"But Creshin is de—" Taslin's voice surprised Kamber.

283

He'd forgotten the duke still hovered. And Kamber also had conformation that Creshin was indeed dead.

"Shut up," Kelsie screamed.

"Creshin won't fight against my father," Kamber said, being intentionally deceptive. And keeping his voice soft when he wanted to yell. "They're friends."

"I'll lead the troops to victory myself. Your death is just a little bonus." Kelsie turned toward Taslin. "Kill him."

Kamber didn't react externally, but he envisioned Subena's face. He wanted to be thinking about her in the end, because he no longer harbored any hope of freedom. This psychopath's reputation was ruthless and he sensed her reputation was underrated. If she could hold him hostage, she could certainly kill his essence.

He prayed the end would be swift. "One last question?" He stalled the inevitable. "Reklaw?" He nodded toward the duke, who was fully dressed. "Is he your lover?"

Kelsie spat at him. "You mock me."

"He couldn't get it up for you, huh?" Kamber goaded her. "Of course we can't blame good ole Tas. The bastard gets a hard-on every time he's around my wife. Probably has nothing left for you."

Kelsie gasped. "Taslin's a cousin, you imbecile. I would never have sex with a relative."

Kamber felt like the planet had swallowed him and spit him into the sea. What she suggested was sick. The damn duke could not be his relative. "Reklaw." He gulped. "Tell me she lies."

Taslin looked at his feet.

The unpleasant sound of Kelsie's laughter echoed in the chamber. "He's not related to you, if that's what you're worried about, you arrogant swine. His mother and my mother were sisters."

"She's a step-cousin. We're not related by blood." Taslin hurried his words. "Her mother and my *stepmother* were sisters. My father didn't touch another female until years after my mother died."

"See how ashamed he is," Kelsie mocked. "Doesn't want anyone to know his daddy also dallied with a Creshinite."

The duke's head popped. "My father was never ashamed of his second wife. He took care of her."

"Took care of her?" Kelsie whirled and knocked him to the ground. "He threw money at her. He treated her like a whore. Wouldn't even take her to Reklaw."

"Not true." Apparently the duke did have some balls. "She wanted to stay with her sister. After she died, my father took care of your mother. He visited her as often as he could. He was happy until—"

"Until I threatened to expose him?" Kelsie shot back. "If he loved her so much, why was he so terrified that someone would find out?"

"It doesn't matter," the duke snapped. "You've held this over my head long enough, Vilavettia. The truth is out and I won't do your bidding anymore."

"You'll do as you're told." Kelsie growled. "Your estates are still mortgaged and I hold the papers. Or did you forget?" Her voice had turned sweet. "Enough talking. We must go." She pulled a silver knife from her belt and tossed it to the duke. "Finish them or I'll finish you."

Taslin let the knife fall to the ground. "I won't do it."

Kamber stared at the duke. A combination of surprise and sorrow consumed him. He realized the duke had been a victim. Like him, a victim of his father. And unlike him, the prey of a vicious stepsister.

"Must we go through this again?" Kelsie seemed equally surprised at the duke's resistance.

"You want them dead," Reklaw said, "you kill them."

"Well, perhaps you don't care about your sex kitten either. Do you think I won't break Rekita's pretty little neck before I drive a blade through her unfaithful heart?"

"You can't. She's in a safe place."

"Dear Taslin. You don't think I'd leave a thing like that to chance, do you?" She shook her head, feigning regret. "If my messenger doesn't hear from me tonight, your paramour is dead."

"No."

"Last chance." She picked up the knife and moved toward Kamber.

"Wait." The duke ran toward her. "I'll do it."

Kamber interceded. "Don't do it, Taslin. There's no messenger. In case our remains are discovered, she wants you to be the one tried for murder."

"Shut up!" Taslin shouted. "She speaks the truth. I have to kill you."

The female handed him the knife. "And you will kill the boy as well."

"Thunder help me," the duke said. "I will."

Chapter Thirty-Seven

Subena scarcely remembered the ride to the rock. Adrenaline muted the pain. Love made her strong.

She didn't pause when she reached the tunnel. There was no panic when she rushed into the dark earth, no fear. At least there was no fear of the tunnel.

Her eyes adjusted as she crouched low and scurried through the passageway, dodging the falling debris that covered the tunnel floor. She heard voices.

Subena slowed, but kept moving. Her eyesight hadn't completely recovered after the earlier ordeal, but her nose identified everyone in the tunnel. She found Ronan. And Kamber.

Thank Bockle.

She stayed hidden, formulating a plan. She watched Kelsie hand Taslin a knife. Not good.

The duke said he'd kill Kamber. *Bockle help me.*

Unable to delay any longer, she charged Taslin with every ounce of strength she possessed. His body hit the wall with a thud.

The attack left her disoriented, dizzy. She shook her head, trying to vanquish the stars, and crawled to Kamber. "Are you all right?"

"No, he's not all right. He's on the verge of perishing." The maid, who was not a maid, walked toward her. Kelsie held the knife that had flown from Taslin's hand. "I'm going to end his pathetic life and you get to watch."

"No," Subena screamed. She flattened her back against Kamber, glaring at the evil witch.

Kelsie sneered, "If you press real close, honey, I can push this piece of silver through both your hearts. You can die together. So sweet."

Subena didn't move, she just maintained her glare. For the first time, she understood hatred.

Kelsie tumbled backward.

"Did you do that?" Kamber whispered.

"I'm not sure."

Kelsie lifted herself off the floor and circled. "A little mind combat, huh? You're stronger than I expected. You won't get away with another stunt like that."

From her peripheral vision, Subena saw Taslin slide his body off the wall. "I wasn't going to kill him."

Kelsie twisted slightly. "Shut up, Taslin."

The duke didn't look at the screeching monster. "I promise, Subena. I wasn't going to kill anyone."

An ugly snarl marred Kelsie's perfect complexion. "No, he couldn't do it. You know how it is, princess?" The witch made the word princess sound like dung. "If you want something done right, get a female to do it."

Kelsie lifted the stake. And attacked.

Taslin grabbed one of the boards supporting the underground wall. He yanked the beam out of place and struck Kelsie from behind.

Another roar claimed Subena's attention. Remington rushed through the tunnel, bellowing a battle cry. A bevy of soldiers flanked him.

"Stop!" Kamber cried.

Remington fired. The main rafter cracked.

The tunnel started to collapse. Again.

Epilogue

Kamber didn't see her, but he sensed Subena. He'd hoped she'd join them, but he'd been afraid to ask her. She'd acted strange since the incident in the tunnel. Natural, he supposed, but he didn't like it.

Maybe the stress of the past few days had made her distant. Maybe she was still mad about the Givers. Hell, he'd stop drinking blood and draw essence from the stinking crystals if that would make her happy.

"Kam, you with us?" Ronan asked.

Remington snorted. "The prince is in love, Ronan. Is he ever really with us anymore?"

Kamber grinned at his old pal, finding it impossible to be angry about the truth. "Sorry. Guess I drifted."

During the week since the kidnapping, Kamber thanked the God of the Mountain every single day. Ronan survived, Subena survived. He could ask no more.

Kamber also said a prayer of thanks for Remington. If the big warrior hadn't held the rafter until they'd all sprinted from the tunnel, no one would be sitting around the fire drinking fermented brew.

"I've been wondering," Ronan paused and poked the fire with a stick. "Are we sure Kelsie died in the tunnel? I saw her fly. How could someone that powerful die from a little cave-in?"

"She's dead," Remington declared. "She might have possessed the powers of the ancients, but she was also half Creshinite. Vulnerable."

"What he's trying to say," Kamber added, "is that she had some of our skills, but because she was part Creshinite, she had their weakness. A blow to the head or the lack of air would have destroyed her."

"I didn't really need a translation, brother," Ronan quipped.

Kamber shrugged. He didn't really want to talk about that witch. The night in the tunnel easily ranked as the worst in his life.

He believed his half-sister had perished, but he'd positioned a guard at the tunnel entrance. And several more near the castle. Kelsie hadn't come out. "She's dead."

"Then where's her body?" Ronan persisted.

He shrugged. "Buried." His brother would learn about the disintegration of essence soon enough.

Kamber downed the contents of his mug, hoping to forget, hoping to remember. Everything had happened so fast in the tunnel, he still couldn't be sure he remembered the sequence of events. After Remington fired on Taslin, his wife had removed his shackles. How, Kamber wasn't sure.

Together they'd released his brother while Remington held onto the rafter. Subena helped Ronan get out of the tunnel and he'd followed, dragging Taslin's inert body from the wreckage. He wasn't sure he would have gone back for his half-sister, even if the tunnel hadn't collapsed. The dirt-filled passageway seemed like an appropriate grave.

"I can't believe she was Creshin's daughter," Ronan mused. Kamber hadn't told him the harpy was actually their half-sister. Someday, he'd have to confess all.

"We got a message from Dad," Ronan said. "They still haven't located Lord Creshin. What do you suppose happened to him?"

Kamber shrugged, not really sure why he didn't tell the truth. He supposed he wanted to understand his new power before he tried to explain it to anyone else. Subena knew. That was enough for now.

"What about the Creshinite soldiers?" Ronan asked. "Did we catch all of the renegades?"

Remington patted him on his back. "You can rest easy. We got all of 'em and we got the scoundrels that tried to hang your brother, too. Kamber interrogated the lot of 'em. If there'd been more assassins or spies, we'd know."

"Remington's right," he said. "Our soldiers conducted a thorough search. There are no more renegade Creshinites in Gatsle." Kamber opened his mouth to say more but closed his lips. He sat up straight. *Subena.* She'd come outside to join them.

"And the elf who fired the dart at the opera, did you get him, too?" Subena asked.

Kamber twisted his head and started to stand. She placed a hand on his shoulder.

"Don't get up." Her face radiated life and she was a vision in her new blue gown. He didn't know a lot about fashion, but the dark color seemed to make her long hair shine brighter and emphasize the silver in her eyes. The fabric also clung to her curves. Looking at her was not conducive to normal breathing.

"The guy at the opera?" she reminded him.

Kamber gulped. She wasn't going to like his answer. "I'm afraid that was Taslin."

He felt her good mood dissipate. After everything, she still cared about the scum.

"Taslin said he missed on purpose," Kamber added, scarcely able to believe he'd defended the scoundrel.

His wife nodded. "He's come out of the coma."

She'd checked on the damned duke every single day. Kamber squashed his spurt of jealousy. She'd joined them around the fire. That was a start.

"Four days he was in that coma."

She sat down next to him. Kamber's stomach did a funny little twist.

"The medic thinks he'll recover, but doesn't know when we can question him."

If only she'd stop talking about Taslin. "I can't believe the cur saved my life," he mumbled.

"And how are you doing?" she asked Ronan.

Subena reached over and tousled his brother's hair. Kamber wished she'd do that to him.

"I don't know how you survived in that dark tunnel. When I think... I'll right back."

Subena rushed behind a tree. They heard her retching.

"My poor wife cannot even think about tunnels without being sick. The experience in her youth must have been more harrowing than I imagined."

Remington looked at him. "You, dear friend, are a monumental idiot."

"Hey, I'm really sorry she's sick, but she's so..." He paused to smile, "So damn near perfect, it's good that she has one weakness."

He glanced at Subena when she reemerged, feeling a twinge of concern. Her face seemed a bit pale. "Are you okay?"

She nodded. "So tell me, Ronan, how did you manage to keep your sanity in that hole?"

His brother relished retelling the story. Despite his need to confirm Kelsie's death, he didn't seem to have any permanent scars from his experiences underground.

Kamber ached to touch Subena's hand. He dared not.

When Ronan got to the part of his story where he ran from the tunnel, Subena fled again. This time she ran toward the castle.

"I know she has a phobia, but this is too much," Kamber blurted. "She'll probably want to sleep with the lights on, too."

Ronan and Remington stared at him. Did he have ale foam on his face?

"Hey, you have to admit, my normally brave little wife is being rather wimpy." He grinned. "Radiantly beautiful, but wimpy."

Ronan shook his head and addressed Remington. "I do hope my little nephew takes after his mom. His dad is rather daft."

Kamber felt his dark skin turn ghostly white. He looked first at Ronan and then at Remington. "Bockle."

He heard them laughing at him as he dashed after his wife. He found her in her chambers, rubbing a soft cloth against her face.

He slipped up behind her, nuzzling her neck. "Why didn't you tell me?"

She shrugged, but he could physically feel the happiness radiating from her body. Or maybe it was his skin that pulsed with energy.

"I wanted to be sure," she whispered. "Somehow, a baby seems too wonderful to be true."

He couldn't remember ever feeling so good, as if he weighed nothing. He took the cloth from her hand. Letting it fall to the floor, he turned her around and pulled her into his arms. "You know what this means?"

She leaned back to flash him an *I'm not a moron* expression. "Of course I do, Dökkálfar, but let's hear your iota of wisdom."

He tried to contain his grin, not entirely succeeding. "A baby means we're true mates. You can't pretend you hate me anymore."

She gave a weak punch at his chest. "Of course, I don't hate you, you big lug. Since you're not not smart enough to figure it out on your own, I'll just tell you. I love you."

He'd thought he couldn't feel any happier, but her words changed that. "I love you, too."

Somehow, words weren't enough. He pulled her lips against his, needing contact more than air.

His erection grew. He sensed the moment she became aware of his passion. He lowered his lips to the tender spot where her neck met her beautiful shoulder. Between nibbles, he managed to speak. "Why don't we try to add some more art to the walls?"

"On occasion, your ideas are almost brilliant." She tilted her head to give him better access to her exposed skin.

Suddenly, he felt her muscles tense, but his body refused to let any reality intrude into his desire. "Uh, Kamber."

"Hmm?"

"Kam..."

He lifted his head to stare into her brilliant silver eyes. "You're not feeling sick again, are you?"

She shook her head. "No. And don't look now, but I think we're floating."

Other Titles by Genia Avers

FORBIDDEN FLAME

FORBIDDEN TWICE

www.ingramcontent.com/pod-product-compliance
Lightning Source LLC
Chambersburg PA
CBHW051414170626

46809CB00006B/2158